DEATHSONG

MAX McNABB

Beloved Captive Trilogy Book 2

ISBN: 978-1-7373797-2-0

Interior design by Booknook.biz

Max McNabb is a writer from Lubbock, Texas, and the editor of TexasHillCountry.com. He grew up on the family farm near Ropesville. He's the author of the Beloved Captive Trilogy: *Far Blue Mountains*, *Deathsong*, and *Sky Burial*. Contact him at maxmcnabb.com.

Dedicated to my parents

Scott & Amy

And grandparents

Ronnie & Sandra McNabb

Bill & Gwen West

This novel was inspired by the real events of the Fimbres Apache conflict of the 1920s, a latter-day frontier war between the last free Apaches and a Sonoran rancher. May the spirits of the dead find peace in eternity.

TABLE OF CONTENTS

THE STORY SO FAR

Sonora, Mexico, spring 1927—rancher Jubal McKenna takes in a young Apache girl with an injured ankle. She's a member of the last free Apaches, the band that refused to surrender with Geronimo decades earlier, choosing instead to dwell in the high solitude of the Sierra Madre where they keep the old ways. The McKennas call the dark-eyed girl Dolores. She's welcomed into the family by Jubal's wife Sara, their epileptic son John Russell, and baby Claudia. When her ankle heals, Dolores chooses to return to her people. She finds the Apaches camped in a cave. Gouyen the wise woman is like a grandmother to the girl. She tells Dolores they've been watching and they've seen that she has a home in the valley, far safer than the wild sierras where life is brutal and short. Gouyen tells her she must go back for her own good and if she ever sets foot in the blue mountains again, she'll kill the girl herself. Heartbroken, Dolores returns to live as McKenna's adopted daughter.

An eye for an eye, blood for blood. November 1928— Apaches ambush the McKennas on the trail home from Nácori Chico. Gouyen cuts Sara's throat as warriors carry

John Russell away. Later an Apache named Matzus shows John Russell a scalp covered in fresh blood and tells him it's his father's. In truth the scalp is old and the blood is Sara's. Believing his entire family has been killed, John Russell is carried off into the Sierra Madre with the raiders.

While Jubal readies his vaqueros to chase after the kidnappers, Dolores tells him a hard truth. He must wait until the boy is accepted into the band, until John Russell believes himself an Apache. Otherwise, if Jubal attempts a rescue too soon, they'll simply kill the boy. Only when he's become a beloved captive will it be safe. Jubal can't bear to hear it. He leads out his vaqueros on the chase. They trail the raiders high into the sierras before abandoning pursuit when Jubal discovers a bloody warning left for them to find. He must return to the valley and wait in hope that John Russell's heart will remember.

The Apaches take John Russell to their sanctuary hidden within a labyrinth of peaks and canyons: Pa-Gotzin-Kay, Stronghold Mountain of Paradise. There the boy is stripped of identity, immersed in Apache culture, a world of brutal conflict and strange magic. He meets Ishton, the beautiful older sister of Dolores and favorite wife of Carnoviste the chieftain. Only Ishton shows him kindness and he loves her for it. He meets Nantan the medicine man, Gouyen's twin brother who has a crippled leg, a black star tattooed to his chest, and mystic Bear Power. The boy is forced to work as a slave for the women.

In the U.S. a man called Cain, once a legendary soldier

of fortune, is now middle-aged and reduced to working as a strikebreaker. He works alongside his friend Mosby, a veteran of the negro 10th Cavalry. When a coal company strike turns into a bloody massacre, Cain puts a stop to the killing, but his employers blame him for the negative publicity. He discovers an item in the newspaper—a young boy kidnapped by Apaches in the Sierra Madre. He knows those mountains well. Cain was there with his old mentor, a cavalry officer named Aubrey Eliot, when Geronimo surrendered. He tells Mosby they're done breaking strikes—he wants to be a soldier one last time. In the darkness of Cain's skull a tumor incubates. Headaches and eerie visions plague him. Old ghosts torment him with the dark secret that has followed Cain like a shadow through all the many wars he's fought. First he practices meditation to suppress the visions, then turns to opium. He sees the ghost of Aubrey, he sees a dead Filipino boy. They call to him, biding him remember.

On Pa-Gotzin-Kay Apaches place wagers on a wrestling match between the captive boy and a Mexican slave his age. The boy defeats his treacherous opponent and wins the admiration of the People. No longer is he a White Eye slave. They accept him into the tribe as a beloved captive and Carnoviste adopts him as his son.

In the valley below, Jubal drowns his sorrow with whiskey. On a desperate enterprise Jubal and Dolores travel north of the border and visit the San Carlos Reservation in Arizona. They hope to convince the reservation Apaches to send a message, a ransom offer, to the unsurrendered in the sierras.

Seasons pass. The captive boy receives his Apache name. From this time on, he is Denali. He witnesses the medicine man perform many supernatural acts. The People say Nantan is immortal—no warrior's hand can slay him. He makes a friend—Chatto, the son of Carnoviste's rival Zunde. The boys are tasked with protecting the women while they go out to gather wildberries. Denali and Chatto are standing guard when a grizzly rises up from the brush. A white star on its chest, a crooked left hindpaw. The beast falls upon the women and kills Alopay. Denali looses arrows and Chatto fires his Springfield rifle, but the grizzly escapes through a gully hidden in the tall undergrowth. The boys join Carnoviste's hunting party, tracking the killer bear to its feeding place. The grizzly is nowhere to be seen, his trail vanished, but there sits Nantan as though awaiting them. He'd been gathering herbs, he explains, when his Power told him something was wrong and led him there. Denali and Chatto share a look between them—the medicine man has a black star tattooed where the grizzly had a white mark in the shape of a star. Nantan's left leg is crippled like the bear's. Could Nantan transform himself into the grizzly? Denali and Chatto can tell no one of what they suspect. The People love their medicine man too well, for Nantan's Power ensures the survival of the band. The boys resolve to partner together to follow Nantan's movements and seek proof of their dark suspicion.

CAST OF CHARACTERS

Jubal McKenna: A powerful rancher in the Bavispe Valley, father of John Russell and Claudia, adopted father of Dolores. Widower of Sara.

Dolores/Bui: Apache girl adopted by the McKenna family. At the beginning of *Deathsong*, she is fifteen years old. By the last chapter, she's seventeen.

John Russell/Denali: The young, red-haired son of Jubal and Sara. Kidnapped by Apaches and adopted as the son of Carnoviste. An epileptic. At the beginning of *Deathsong*, he is thirteen years old. By the end of the book, he will soon be sixteen.

Cain: Once a legendary soldier of fortune, now a middle-aged strikebreaker who longs for one last war.

Mosby: Cain's right-hand man, a veteran of the 10th Cavalry.

Carnoviste/Apache Juan: The last chief of the unsurrendered Apaches, husband to Ishton, Tsaltey-koo, and Hanlonah. Father of the young boys Neiflint and Oblite. The adopted father of Denali.

Gouyen: The wise woman is the twin sister of Nantan. She uses her Power of Finding Enemies to sense the presence of nearby hostile forces. Childless, Gouyen treated Bui as her granddaughter.

Nantan: The medicine man, twin brother of Gouyen. His supernatural Power ensures the band's survival and grants him authority that rivals Carnoviste's own.

Ishton: The beautiful older sister of Dolores and favorite wife of Carnoviste.

Sara McKenna: Jubal's wife, mother to John Russell and Claudia. Murdered by Gouyen.

Claudia: Baby daughter of Jubal and Sara.

Wesley: An old ranch hand who works for Jubal.

Hector Cienfuegos: Ten years older than Jubal, Hector is the foreman of the ranch and Jubal's closest advisor.

Angel Ochoa: A young vaquero, later the fiancé of Dolores.

Zunde: Apache warrior, rival to Carnoviste for the chieftainship.

Chatto: The young son of Zunde, he's also Denali's best friend.

Moroni Thayne: Mormon rancher in the Bavispe Valley.

Aubrey Eliot: Cain's old mentor, a daring cavalry officer who convinced Geronimo to surrender peacefully. He died in the Philippines during the war, but Cain is haunted by ghostly visitations.

Estoni: Apache warrior.

Oblite: Son of Carnoviste, much younger than Denali.

Neiflint: Son of Carnoviste, much younger than Denali.

Matzus: The brave John Russell falsely believes is responsible for murdering his father because he showed a bloody scalp to the boy.

Horus Applegate: Elderly investment banker, former client of Cain's.

CHAPTER ONE

Sierra Madre,

Spring, 1929

The Power of their song failed to protect the women from the beast. It had risen from hiding and fallen among the wives and maidens in the woods where they were picking wildberries. Ravenous, tearing. Now Alopay must enter the Other World missing an arm. The boys assigned to watch over the berry-pickers had struck back, but Denali's arrows and Chatto's Springfield rifle weren't enough to kill the grizzly.

Nights following the attack Denali would jolt awake in his wickiup, images haunting all his dreams. Alopay's crushed skull, her lifeless eyes. The white shape like a star on the grizzly's chest, slowly blackening until it was the dark star tattooed above Nantan's heart. The medicine man had a crooked left foot—the grizzly's left hindpaw was twisted inward. Such coincidence was a curious thing.

After the bear escaped down a gully hidden in the

undergrowth, Denali and Chatto joined the hunting party. The blood trail soon dried up, but the warriors happened upon the beast's feeding place, a rock dome overlooking the village below, and there sat Nantan as though awaiting them. The medicine man explained he'd been searching for herbs on the ridgeside when his Power told him something was wrong and led him to that place of bones.

"If the bear is witched," Nantan told them, "only my Power can defeat it."

The warriors felt great comfort to have their trusted medicine man at their side, but Chatto and Denali shared a look between them. The star on Nantan's chest, the crooked left foot—could such a thing be?

They spoke only to each other of their dark suspicion. No one else could know. The People loved their medicine man too well. Nantan was an immortal, it was said—and not without reason to believe it. Denali himself had seen Nantan cut his own chest with a blade, deep and bloody, and he'd seen the wounded flesh quickening, closing. The only wounds he couldn't fully heal were those he'd suffered long ago as a young man when a grizzly lamed his foot and scarred his face. Nantan's Power was great and no one could deny it, but had that Power turned to the witching way? Had the medicine man transformed himself into the beast?

They had to be sure before they told the chief of their suspicions.

Over the following days they kept a close watch. Nantan stayed in the camp, curtailing for a time his usual practice of wandering alone, but Denali and Chatto remained vigilant. Often it seemed half a game with them, the boys playing warriors on a secret mission, then the face of Alopay would rise up and they'd remember their duty for the grave enterprise it was.

After a few days the women were ready for a return to the thicket. They gathered berries without incident, Carnoviste and three other warriors standing by, and there was no further sign of the grizzly.

At last came the morning when Nantan took up his staff and limped out of the village. Denali and Chatto watched him crossing the pasture, heading for the rise of pines, and they gave him a long lead, allowing him to enter the woods before they set out armed with bows and full quivers.

Denali believed himself a decent tracker, but Chatto was a master. They trailed the medicine man up the slope and past the berry thicket. Denali watched his friend's eyes scanning the ground and undergrowth, noting the impression of Nantan's staff, spiderwebs ripped at his passing, and then the ground was rocky, torn lichen alone pointing them on.

They walked side by side. They walked like Child of the Waters and Killer of Enemies together in an older time, gone out to slay the monster.

For a while it appeared the trail was taking them to the overlook, the place of bones. Fear fluttered like a raven in their bellies. There was no way to approach the high bluff without being observed from above. Then Nantan's course swung away, moving instead toward a secluded meadow Denali once visited on his own wanderings, and they followed him through the trees, silent and intent.

They were no more than a stride from the trunk of a great pine when Gouyen stepped out from behind it. She stood before them gripping a long knife.

The boys were as shocked as though the grizzly itself had leapt upon them.

"Where are you little rabbits going?" she demanded.

She stared through cold eyes like the eyes of the dead and her knife dangled from a gnarled hand. In his mind Denali saw the blade dripping with his mother's blood.

They were speechless.

"Why are you following my brother?" she asked. "Don't you know there's a bear in these woods who loves to eat up little rabbits?"

It was Denali who recovered first. "That's why we're following Nantan. To protect him from the bear. It's not safe for him to wander alone."

"The People couldn't survive without our medicine man," Chatto spoke up. "He needs warriors to guard him."

"And you think you're the warriors for the job," Gouyen said.

Chatto stood straight. "I'd die for the People."

She slipped the knife into its sheath under the fold of her moccasin. "Nantan is immortal. Have you forgotten my brother's Power? No two-legs or four-legs can harm him. He doesn't need you to protect him from the bear or anything else. You understand?"

They nodded.

"Now go back," she said. "Hunt something for the stewpot like good boys. You'll have time enough to be warriors later."

They turned to go. Denali hesitated, then looked back.

"Did you hear us coming?" he asked. "If we're to be warriors, we can't make that kind of mistake again."

"I followed you following Nantan," she told him. "I was behind you the whole way until the end when I ran ahead. It was you who didn't hear me coming."

Denali nodded and started back down with Chatto. Neither of them spoke, but they were thinking the same thought—it was impossible. Even if they hadn't sensed her on their backtrail, they'd have heard her moving through the undergrowth to advance on them. Gouyen hadn't followed them.

She'd been waiting in the woods.

Waiting for Nantan.

* * *

Gouyen paused at the edge of the pines. Farther up the slope a slant of bare rock jutted skyward. A shadow passed across its face and she looked into the cobalt blue where a hawk glided in a rising gyre, wheeling under the noon sun. Something long and dark clutched in its talons.

She stood watching the hawk for what it had to tell her.

When its shadow touched the stone again, the hawk let go and a snake came falling like a length of rope. It struck the rock and lay still.

The hawk began a slow descent.

Unbidden, the lost girl rose up in Gouyen's memory. Not a day fled into dark without thought of the girl she'd loved like a daughter.

"Bui," she whispered. Then felt the selfsame trespass as though she'd spoken the name of the dead.

Gouyen had saved the girl's life. In return Bui gave meaning and purpose to the wise woman's old age, a tenderness for which she'd dared not hope.

It was on a night in Bui's tenth winter, camped in the foothills, when the girl had missed her appointment with death. A Yaqui rancher named Torres attacked out of nowhere, storming the camp. His vaqueros fired from the saddle and tossed burning torches on the brush arbors. Bui's mother and father were running with the young girl, trying to get her to safety, when a pair of shotgun blasts dropped them at their daughter's feet.

Gouyen's horse had been picketed in a distant stand of oaks. She'd run into the trees and slashed the picket line with her knife and swung up bareback and gripped the rope hackamore. She gave the mount her heels.

Warriors fired at the vaqueros, holding them off while women and children retreated into the woods. Enemy horsemen trampled the wounded. Gouyen spotted Carnoviste and his new wife Ishton racing past.

"Where's Bui?" Ishton shouted. She glanced over her shoulder, looking for her younger sister.

Gouyen scanned the ravaged camp. She caught sight of the little girl staggering in the glow of flames and muzzle flashes, cut off from the main line of retreat as horsemen swarmed about her.

Gouyen charged into their midst. She leaned from the horse's back and snatched the girl up and then Bui was trembling against her.

Gunshots all around. Gouyen pulled her pistol and snapped off a shot and a vaquero slumped forward in the saddle, a hole in his belly. They raced into the moonless night, hellbent, headed away from the other survivors and they drew a chase. Torres's men thundered after them, but somewhere in the depths of the oaks, Gouyen eluded pursuit.

She turned her horse toward the sierras. Hours riding in silence, tracing a circuitous route, difficult for any tracker to follow. Just after dawn Gouyen looked at the girl's face. It was streaked with the blood of her parents. She stopped and got down and wet her bandana with the dew of the grass and gently cleaned her cheeks. Dark eyes full of sadness, grief's young changeling. The child's gaze in that moment was forever seared in Gouyen's memory.

That afternoon they crossed the tracks of Mexicans. Gouyen grew worried they were being hunted. Once when she thought riders were close on their trail, she hid the girl in a pit so narrow Bui couldn't move. Gouyen spread leaves over her, then mounted up and rode away. Only well after dark did she return for the girl.

Bui wept against the wise woman's breast. "I thought you left me."

Gouyen told her to hush. Then she made a promise. She swore she'd always come back for her, that she'd never leave her for any reason short of death itself.

They rode on and encountered no other soul. Days passed without sign of human presence. Each sunset they kneeled and raised their palms to the sky and spoke not a word. Cold nights in a lonesome grove. Gouyen and the orphan girl camped without a fire to warm them. She sang Bui quietly to sleep, then lay down beside her and in those moments it was like they were the only pair alive in the world after some profound cataclysm. Or else spirits haunting an empty wood.

They were seven days wandering the mountains before they crossed the trail of survivors. They followed them to a tearful reunion at the foot of Pa-Gotzin-Kay.

Over the following years Gouyen cared for Bui, protected and guided her. She'd sewn her a fine buckskin dress. When she presented it to the girl, Bui's eyes lit up. Gouyen began teaching her to read the cards and found in her new ward a burgeoning seer.

Life in the sierras was a promise no one kept for long. The mountains were unforgiving, tolerated few mistakes. Survival meant pain and callused hearts. Perhaps Gouyen saw in the orphan something of her own stolen girlhood, an innocence snuffed out long ago, because she determined to guard Bui's goodness no matter the cost.

Then the White Eye rancher stole her away.

In the days after Bui was taken Gouyen and Carnoviste crept up through the pastures and watched the hacienda from a distance. They watched Bui with the White Eye family and watched her among the vaqueros and they saw how it was between them, the home and peace she'd found.

Even then Carnoviste wanted to ride away with her. His wife Ishton was the girl's older sister and she desired Bui's return as well, regardless of the situation below. It had been Gouyen who told them it was not to be.

She had dreamed a diverging path in the pines. In her dream a blue jay sang along the declining fork, but on the rising trail snow lay in shadow and an owl watched from above. Did they understand her dream? the wise woman asked. Carnoviste and Ishton shook their heads.

"In the valley," Gouyen explained, "her life will be long with days of kindness. But if she returns to the sierras, Bui must die before another winter passes."

Carnoviste and Ishton conceded it was best—Bui would remain in the valley. So Gouyen abandoned the girl in order that she might live, breaking her sacred promise and her own heart with it.

Now the hawk landed on the stone and folded its wings. Gouyen watched it step to the dead snake. It tore the flesh and ate, but the feast was soon interrupted.

A pair of ravens swooped down, diving for the bigger predator, and the hawk rose with outspread wings. It took to the air as the ravens mobbed it. They squawked and dived and kept up a constant harassment.

Gouyen stood taking those strange auspices. Finally the hawk retreated into the west with the ravens giving chase. When at last the birds were out of sight, Gouyen turned and continued on her way through the trees to meet Nantan.

CHAPTER TWO

For Jubal the summer and early autumn of 1929 passed in a whiskey haze. He believed the old Apache scout on the San Carlos Reservation had been true to his word—the message was sent. The reservation Apaches had contacted the wild ones in the Sierra Madre and informed them of Jubal's offered ransom for his son. Gold, guns, whatever they might demand for John Russell's return. Now he could only hope the bronco Apaches would agree to a deal. He hunkered down and waited. He waited till it seemed waiting was all there was, all that would ever be.

The mountains kept their silence.

In mid-September a horseman arrived from Moctezuma, the nearest telegraph station. Jubal had left word that any news from San Carlos was to be carried to him immediately and the messenger would be well compensated. Now Jubal set his bottle down and rose and shook the man's hand. He tore open the envelope the man carried.

Dasoda-hae's telegram was subtle—

> *Sent nephew to horse trade with broncos STOP*
> *He saw your horse in good health but no sale*

STOP Broncos dying out STOP They need him as stallion for their mares

Jubal paid the messenger and told him to stable his horse and stay the night if he would. Then he marched into the hacienda. He found Dolores at the kitchen table reading from a Spanish translation of the New Testament. The Apache girl was fifteen years old now. She glanced up and he tossed the telegram down in front of her.

"They won't make a deal," Jubal said.

She closed the book. "I'm sorry."

"Tell me it's been long enough. Tell me I can go after him now."

She watched him a long moment. Taking measure of the desperation coiled so tightly in his heart like a serpent aching to strike.

"Not yet," she said.

He cursed.

"We've got to be sure he's one of them," she told him. "You have to hold on."

Jubal walked out. He slammed the door shut behind him and crossed the patio and returned to his bottle.

* * *

That night his mind reached out in the dark while he slept. Jubal saw himself on the edge of old age, a beard more gray than brown, and he stood in the doorway watching the orchard road and a wagon approaching the gate. Two men on the box, impossible to recognize in the distance.

When the wagon passed through the gate, he saw John Russell beside the driver. A grown man now, dressed in a fine suit of clothes, but there was no mistaking him—Jubal would know his son anywhere.

He left the door open wide and took the porch steps and started into a run. When he reached the wagon and drew up, gasping for breath, the driver reined in and set the brake. John Russell climbed slowly from the box. His skin was deeply tanned, a long red braid of hair falling over his shoulder. Jubal rushed to take him in his arms.

"My son," he sobbed.

John Russell stood frozen in his embrace.

Then Dolores ran out toward them. Claudia followed at her heels, the young girl now a beautiful woman, the image of her mother.

They stood in the road and shared many smiles and tears and much laughter while John Russell looked on, indifferent. Claudia questioned him about his time with the Apaches, but he only shook his head in confusion. It was apparent he'd lost both his English and Spanish.

"Thank you for bringing my son home," Jubal told the driver. "How did you find him?"

The driver was an old Mormon farmer from Colonia Morelos. He leaned down from his seat to shake Jubal's hand.

"He walked down from the hills one day," the Mormon said. "Strolled into town wearin nothin but a breechclout and moccasins and like to scared my wife about half to death. Come quick, Bridger, she hollered, there's a Indin out in the yard. Well sir, I could see right away he was a white man on account of that red hair. I said, Zina, that ain't no Indin I ever saw."

He slapped his knee and grinned, enjoying the telling. "Well sir, I stepped out with my shotgun and hollered, What do you think you're doin, dressed in that get-up? He stopped dead in his tracks. Jabbed at his chest and kept repeatin, *Mack-inna, mack-inna,* which I couldn't make head or tails of. Then it come to me—he's sayin *McKenna.*"

The vaqueros had joined them. They took from the wagonbed John Russell's bow and quiver of arrows and examined those articles, each man removing an arrow for his own souvenir.

"I yelled, Zina, draw a bath—we got the McKenna boy out here," Bridger went on.

"All this happened today?" Jubal asked.

"Two, three months back, I reckon. We couldn't carry him over to you like he was, stinkin and naked, so we got him cleaned up and dressed presentable. Then Zina give him lessons on table manners. It was like pullin teeth, teachin him to use a fork and spoon, but finally we judged he was half-civilized, so we figured it was time to let you see your boy."

Jubal swore. He reached up to take hold of Bridger's throat and strangle the life out of him there in the road, but then the Mormon was gone and they were standing in the great room of the hacienda, arrived in that curious

14

transportation of dreams. Dolores and Claudia gripped John Russell's arms and led him where the light was strong. They faced an old-fashioned camera on a tripod. The photographer was hunched over, hidden under a black cloak.

Jubal stepped up behind his family and rested his hand on John Russell's shoulder.

"Smile," the unknown photographer said.

Jubal and the girls smiled for the camera, but John Russell stared through a stoic mask. There was a burst of light, then John Russell glanced back at his father, a mixture of rage and fear in his eyes, and he scowled and jerked free of his sisters. He barked at them in Apache. He tore open his shirt in a hail of buttons, then pulled off his shoes and hurled them at Dolores and Claudia, the girls ducking, crying out.

Jubal watched, heartsick. He stepped forward and touched John Russell's arm, thinking to calm him, but his son rammed his elbow backwards and struck Jubal's jaw. He collapsed to the tiles and lay there, a frail old man.

John Russell looked down and snarled.

Dolores dropped down beside Jubal. "Are you all right?" she asked. He ignored her and stared up at his only son, returned home, yet somehow as lost to them as ever.

John Russell stepped to the hearth. He reached into the dead fire and applied the ashes to his cheeks and brow and started chanting what was surely his deathsong. Then a sudden change came over him. His face took on a strange expression and for a moment it was possible to see the face of the child he'd once been. He touched one of the hearthstones. A gentle tug and the stone pulled free.

Little trinkets lay inside the old hiding place. John Russell removed them one by one—a striped top, a silver dollar, the Jew's harp Wesley had given him in that vanished boyhood.

His eyes glistened. Jubal rose to his feet and went to him. John Russell turned and buried his face against his father's shoulder, weeping.

"It's all right," Jubal said. "You're home, everything's all right."

And for a moment it was. The sorrow of the years fell away, those countless days of rage and despair, and Jubal thanked God he'd kept faith in the boy's heart that he would remember.

Then he woke up.

* * *

Jubal lay in the empty bedroom with the dream so close, so far out of reach. A sense of irrevocable loss gripped him and he grieved for what had slipped his grasp in that plunge to the waking world, the faith that was almost his own.

* * *

Finally one morning late in the fall Dolores came and found him. Jubal sat at the empty table in the courtyard, the great table where they'd shared so many meals, a bottle and glass before him and a cigarette burning between his fingers.

"It's time," she said.

"How can you know?"

"I know."

"You're sure it's safe?" he asked.

"If he's not one of them by now, he won't ever be."

Jubal stepped inside. He retrieved a Colt single-action from his study and checked the cylinder and went back out into the courtyard. Dolores gave him a look. He snatched the whiskey bottle from the table, three-quarters full, and kept walking.

Out in the pasture he took one last pull from the bottle. Then he gripped it by the neck and threw it into the air, spinning end over end, sunlight glaring off the glass, and he raised the pistol. His first shot went wide. He thumbed the hammer and fired again and the bottle burst in the air, raining whiskey and glass.

* * *

Jubal began preparations immediately. From the outset he made it clear this was to be a rescue mission, not a revenge quest. They'd hit every Apache camp they could find, every band that might be holding John Russell, but he wasn't out for blood. Vengeance had to wait—all Jubal wanted was his son back home.

The incursion would be launched in early winter. Jubal

organized a small force, dependable men experienced in tracking and hard riding. They'd travel in stealth following whatever trails revealed themselves and they'd take the winter camps by surprise. Friends cautioned against such an undersized group—what if they were outnumbered, slaughtered in the mountains? Jubal told them he welcomed attack. Any risk was acceptable to draw the Apaches out of hiding.

His own vaqueros would comprise the bulk of the squad. Hector chose men who could suffer cold and deprivation, who'd brave the brutal pace of the hunt, and Jubal promised a reward on his son's safe return.

To fill the balance of the hunting party Jubal rode out one morning to the Square and Compass Ranch.

* * *

Moroni Thayne slammed the post-hole diggers into the hard earth. David and Jeremiah, his young boys, stood back down the line, attaching barbed wire to the new cedar posts, repairs to the pasture's south-running fence. Their horses stood picketed in the grass.

"Pa?" David said. "Somebody's comin."

Moroni looked up and saw a lone rider approaching.

The boys stopped their work and stared. "You want your pistol?" Jeremiah, the youngest, asked. Moroni's gunbelt was draped over the finished part of the fence.

"Leave it," he said. "I recognize him."

A cold wind stirred the yellowing grass. The Thaynes

stood watching the rider come.

"Hello, Moroni," Jubal called. "Boys, how are you?"

"Hello, sir," David and Jeremiah spoke in unison.

When the horseman drew up, Moroni nodded. "Jubal, what brings you out this way?"

Jubal swung down and shook Moroni's hand. "We're goin up into the foothills," he said. "After the first snows. We're goin to find the Apaches that come down from the cold and we're goin to bring John Russell home. I'd like you to ride with me."

Moroni raised his hat. He wiped the sweat from his brow on a shirtsleeve and leaned on the post-hole diggers, looking off toward the mountains.

"Nobody back in the states would believe it, how many of em are up there," Moroni said. "I've thought on it some and I reckon there's as many as fifty braves in those mountains. No way to be sure, but that's my estimate. Maybe that ain't a lot of Apaches compared to the old days, but it's a hell of a bunch to run into."

"That estimate strikes me a little high. My daughter tells me it's closer to twenty-five. But even if you're right, all fifty won't be together at once. They'll have split up, scattered in small bands with antique rifles. The odds are on our side."

"Maybe so," Moroni said.

"Is that what's holdin you back?"

"We've lost a steer or two to Apaches, but all this time, they've never got rough with us and we never looked for a reason to make em."

19

"You think I wanted this? I didn't come lookin for a war, but they brought one down to me. Sure as hell I'm goin to carry it back to em."

"Easy, Jubal. I didn't mean it like that."

"You ridin with me or not?"

Moroni hesitated. "Zelda's pregnant, needs me around the place. I got to do what's best for my family."

"That's why I'm askin you," Jubal said. "Because you got a family and you know what it'd mean if it was one of your boys. Help me find John Russell."

Moroni held his gaze, then glanced away. He was silent a long moment. "I reckon if it was the other way around," he said at last, "if I was the one standin here askin you for help, I don't have to wonder what you'd say. All right, Jubal. You got yourself a recruit."

* * *

Winter came at last.

In front of the hacienda Hector went down the line of vaqueros. He made sure each man was well-supplied with ammunition, then he examined the panniers of the packmules once more and pronounced them ready to ride.

Jubal stepped out onto the porch with Claudia in his arms. He kissed the girl goodbye and handed her to Adela. Out of the shadows Wesley stepped toward him, the old man taking a pipe from the corner of his mouth. "Wish I was goin with you," he said.

"Got to stay here and keep an eye on things for me,"

Jubal told him.

They shook hands. "Bring that boy home," Wesley said. "This old place is fallin to pieces without him."

Jubal came down the steps with the Colt 1911 strapped to his hip and walked up to his waiting horse. The buckskin was called Bardo, a new purchase from the Square and Compass, a mount whose mustang blood was no stranger to the high country. He patted Bardo's chest and examined the spade bit in the horse's mouth, worked in beautiful silver, the same one Wesley had given John Russell so long ago. The ornate silver design held no appeal to Jubal, but he wouldn't consider using any other bit, not for this mission, though he couldn't have said why he should insist so. Perhaps he thought it a talisman to lead his horse down the very paths John Russell would've chosen, to draw him toward its rightful owner.

"Let's head out," he told the men. Jubal climbed into the saddle, then Hector and the vaqueros followed suit.

Adela and Claudia waved goodbye while Wesley stood beside them smoking his pipe, everyone present for their departure save Dolores. She'd refused to see them off and Jubal felt her absence like a heavy weight. All week leading up to their departure the girl had grown steadily aloof, a darkened mood coming over her. Earlier that morning Jubal had knocked at her door. Dolores spoke from the other side, telling him goodbye, but she wouldn't open the door or step out. He stood there in the hall asking what was wrong. She wouldn't speak of it, no matter his intreating, and after a while he surrendered in frustration and walked on.

Now Jubal gave Bardo his heels and led them out.

Just before he reached the open gate Jubal heard Dolores calling, shouting for them to stop. When he glanced back, she was running after them through the dust they raised, the girl barefoot, something clutched in her fist. Jubal stretched out his arm and the riders halted in the orchard road. He sat waiting.

Dolores approached Bardo and held up a small leather bag. "You have to wear this," she said.

"What is it?" Jubal asked.

"Sacred pollen, so you'll be protected. Wear it around your neck. Here, let me."

He took his boot from the stirrup. She gripped his offered hand and stepped into the empty stirrup and rose, then Jubal removed his hat and she placed the string around his neck. The bundle of pollen hung against his chest.

Dolores stepped down again. "Come back," she told him.

She turned and walked down the line of riders. When Angel leaned from his horse, the girl stopped beside him and stood on her tiptoes and kissed the vaquero. Jubal saw the bag dangling from Angel's neck.

They rode out.

BILDUNGSROMAN I

Devilchild

1870, Texas

The man called Cain was born at the river crossing of Los Ebanos on the Texas-Mexico border. The twin whose birth preceded his own by seven minutes did enter the world with the umbilical looped about his neck and a true knot in the cord. The stillborn's face was pale blue when the midwife placed him lifeless in the crib. Then she returned to the bedside for the second labor.

Hedda Killcrop died with her son's first sharp cry of life in her ears. Her husband, the big German, wept over her body in the bed. When the midwife offered him the swaddled baby, bright-eyed and perfect of limb, Otto Killcrop refused him. He went to the crib and picked up the stillborn instead, cupping his head in a callused palm, and placed the body at Hedda's breast, then dried his tears.

Again the midwife approached with the baby. "He's healthy and strong, Herr Killcrop. Hold him and you'll—"

Killcrop pushed her aside. He ran a hand through his

long blond hair and stared at the wall in confusion, stunned grief, then a look of sudden determination crossed his face. He stepped to the door and stormed out of the cabin muttering, Teufelkind, Teufelkind, over and over.

Franny, the midwife's fifteen-year-old daughter, stood solemn and quiet, shaken at what she'd just witnessed. Such cruel accounting, the ledger all out of balance. One life arriving as two departed.

The midwife rocked the newborn. "Franny, please cover poor Mrs. Killcrop," she said.

"Yes, ma'am."

Franny stepped to where the dead woman lay. She stared a moment before raising the sheet over her ashen face and jet black hair. "Sure was a pretty lady," Franny whispered.

"This one favors her some," the midwife said, looking at the baby in her arms, his tuft of dark hair.

Outside it was a blustery and overcast day. They could hear the German's shovel striking the rocky hillside and they could hear his curses carried on the wind.

"Can you drive the team?" the midwife asked.

"Yes, ma'am."

"I need you to go into town and fetch Maria. We've got to have a wetnurse out here."

Franny stood at the door tying on her bonnet. "Momma, what did that word mean?"

"What word?"

"That Dutch word Mr. Killcrop kept sayin."

"I don't know, child," she lied. "Now don't dawdle, this little chap's goin to be hungry."

When Franny unlatched the door and pulled it open, a gust of wind howled into the cabin. The baby cried and the sheet blew from Hedda's face. Franny stepped out, struggling to close the door behind her, then finally got it shut and the midwife latched it.

Sometime later after much rocking, the boy quieted down. The midwife was alone in the cabin with the sleeping child and the dead.

Franny's question lingered.

In truth she knew the word. Her grandparents had come over from Prussia and they'd often spoken the old language when she was a girl. She recalled more of it than she'd have thought.

The baby woke and cried his motherless cry. She paced the earthen floor, making soft noises at his ear.

Teufelkind.

It meant devilchild.

* * *

One side called the river Brave, the other called it Grand. Whatever its name, the river flowed on, fourteen years swept away. Cain grew into boyhood under his father's watchful eyes and learned early how quickly a fist could strike, how sudden and sure the man's judgement.

* * *

Cain stood on the flattop ferry. He gripped a pole with a

hook on its end and watched the slow current carry the dead man toward him. When the corpse was passing along the side, Cain reached out and caught him with the hook and the corpse turned face up in the green water.

Turtles had eaten the skin from his eyes. The boy met that lidless gaze, then the stench hit him and he dry heaved.

His father laughed. Killcrop pulled the platform along the rope grip by grip.

"You see, Herr Dixon?" Killcrop called to their passenger. "Mein teufelkind has a stomach weak as a woman's."

Thaddeus Dixon took a handkerchief from his coatpocket. The retired lawyer was making his weekly crossing, going to visit the whores in San Miguel de Camargo. Dixon pressed the handkerchief to his nose and leaned down, looking into the thing's face, the flesh pale and wet. He rushed to the rope railing and vomited over the side.

Killcrop roared until his belly shook. His callused hands worked the thick hemp cable, drawing them toward the Mexican shore.

When they docked at the landing, Cain dragged the corpse up into the reeds, struggling against the weight.

On this side of the river the rope was secured to an iron post sunk deep in the banks. Hanging from the post was a brass bell and painted on the brass a grinning calavera. Those seeking passage to Texas would ring the bell to signal the boatman in his cabin across the water.

Killcrop untied the reins of the ex-lawyer's horse and

led it onto the dock.

Dixon stared at the body lying in the shallow water. Whatever its starting place the dead man's journey downstream had reached its terminus shortly before the river's own. From Los Ebanos the Rio Grande flowed on past Matamoros and emptied into the Gulf.

"You'd like to say some words over him?" Killcrop asked the lawyer.

"Probably a Mexican, isn't he?" Dixon said.

"Hard to tell. Maybe he was Mexican, he's fishy now."

"What's there to say? I'm no preacher. And if he was Mexican, I certainly don't know any papist last rites."

"Ja, me neither."

Cain leaned out and looked into the corpse's mouth. "He's got a gold tooth," the boy said. "You want me to prize it loose?"

Killcrop glared at him. Cain felt instant shame at his father's displeasure and realized his mistake, speaking of such a thing in front of the passenger.

"A Mexican with a gold tooth?" Dixon asked. "Must've been a bandit."

Dixon stepped off the ferry and mounted up. A western wind stirred the reeds and mesquite lining the banks. He reached in the breastpocket of his suit coat and took out the coins for the fare and handed them to Killcrop.

"Danke schön, Herr Dixon," the boatman said. "Be careful, this is no certain country."

"You'll hear the bell in the morning." Dixon put his horse forward up the trail, heading for San Miguel.

When Dixon was out of sight, Killcrop turned and smacked the boy on the mouth with a balled fist. Cain stumbled backwards, almost falling. He caught himself on the rope railing like a boxer in the ring. Blood poured from his split lip and bright red droplets hit the planks.

Killcrop stood over him. The boatman was six foot three and heavyset, the boy like a waif in his outsized shirt and ragged britches.

Cicadas buzzed in the trees. He waited for the next blow.

"Never talk like that again in front of a passenger," Killcrop said. "Or you go into the river and the turtles and the fishes will eat the skin off your eyes. Understand?"

"I understand."

"Swear to me on your poor dead mater."

"I swear on my mater."

"In Deutsch."

He spoke his father's tongue, swearing on the grave of the mother he'd never known.

"Good," Killcrop said. "Now help me drag him out of the water."

They splashed through the reeds and gripped the dead man's arms, the skin all soft and slick, and tugged him farther up the shore, pulling him into mesquite and chaparral, holding their breath against the foulness. In a dense thicket Killcrop let go. He kneeled and shut one eye and peered into that yawning mouth.

"I'll be damned, Teufelkind. He does have a gold tooth. Use your knife."

The boy opened his claspknife.

"Everyone pays the fare," Killcrop said, turning pockets inside out. "No one crosses on mein boat without fare."

Cain hunkered over the corpse. He worked the tip of his blade under the gleaming crown on the man's molar, not his first experience harvesting gold from the mouth of the dead. From time to time they'd see them floating downstream. Drunks who'd tried to ford the river, the murdered prey of outlaws. Killcrop was always quick to scavenge what they could and he told the boy it was the river's gift.

Killcrop's glasses hung from a cord around his neck. He squinted and slipped them on, then he picked up the man's right hand, a ring on his bloated little finger. He held that lifeless hand much in the manner of a gentleman making the introduction of a fine lady. As though he'd press it to his lips. Killcrop examined the ring. When he recognized the insignia, his face drained of color.

Cain stared at him. A look in Killcrop's eyes he'd never seen there before. Many times despair and rage and more often a kind of guilty loathing, but never this. There was fear in his father's gaze.

Killcrop threw down the hand as if it had burned him. He rose and wiped his mouth on his sleeve and looked around, the brush enclosing them, hidden on all sides.

Cain paused in his work on the tooth.

"Leave it," Killcrop barked. "Don't touch him again. Come on, we're going."

They stalked out of the thicket and boarded the ferry.

Cain untied the rope from the bell-post and they gripped the cable and started pulling the flattop.

The cabin stood on the American side, shaded in the grove of black trees that gave the crossing its name. Los Ebanos where Santa Anna's troops had crossed and Texas Rangers crossed and pilgrims to the salt fields near El Sal Del Rey forty miles to the northeast. Blood and salt, twin enterprises.

Cain brooded over the dead man. Something had upset his father deeply and he wondered why they hadn't dragged the body back into the water, let the river carry him out into the gulf. He could no more understand Killcrop's motives than anticipate his moods.

Then the boatman answered his unspoken question.

"Some men may come around," Killcrop said. "If men who wear rings like the dead one's ring come looking for him, you tell them where he is. How we fished him out of the river. Then soon as we saw the ring we left him alone. Don't lie, not to the men with the rings. Ja?"

"All right," he said.

"Ja, all right."

Cain looked down the straight length of rope to the anchor tree rising from the shore. It was tied to a rusted chain looped about the old trunk. Years earlier the tree had begun a slow process of absorbing the chain, taking up within itself the cold bonds man had placed upon it. If the black tree couldn't burst its fetters, it would subsume them in time.

"Good boy." Killcrop patted his shoulder. "Sit down,

rest. Let me pull the ferry."

* * *

That evening while his father lay in drink, Cain slipped out of the cabin. He walked a distance downriver and pulled off his shoes and undressed. The water was cool when he stepped in.

Swimming the river he glanced upstream and there was a hawk perched on the ferry rope. It opened its wings. He saw it go flying over the water, a slight tremble in the rope at its sudden absence.

He splashed onto the Mexican banks, naked save his underwear. Thick brush ahead, sharp mesquite thorns. He wished for his shoes, but he'd left them behind, unwilling to risk Killcrop's suspicion if he saw them wet later.

Hurry—a passenger might come at any moment.

He entered the thicket, thorns scratching his legs and chest, and chose his steps carefully, but by the time he found the body, his feet were bloody nonetheless. He kneeled and studied the ring on the dead man's hand.

A square and compass engraved on white gold, a double-headed eagle below the number 33. It meant nothing to him.

Nothing save the power of the fear he'd seen it inspire.

When he tugged the ring, it wouldn't budge. He pulled with strength earned from a thousand crossings and still no luck. He kneeled thinking what to do. Then he spat on the ring and rubbed it under his thumb and when he tried again, it slipped right off.

For a moment he stared at the dead man as if waiting for him to rise in offense and repossess his rightful property.

Then Cain put on the ring. It proved too big for him to wear on his little finger as the dead man had worn it, loose even on his index finger. He took it off and gripped it in a fist.

Cain made his way back out of the thicket. When he looked across the river where his clothes and shoes lay, there was no one in sight. Sunset, deepening shadows. Once more into the water.

After reaching the Texas shore he dressed and departed up a trail through the black grove.

Cicada skins clung to the trunks. Sun-dried empty husks. The path led up a hill and he walked to the crest where the gravestone stood, a low fence surrounding the place where she lay. Shells were scattered about the marker. Every few days Cain would see his father lumbering up the hillside to kneel pulling weeds.

The tombstone read—

Hedda Killcrop
GEB 1839 DEUTSCHLAND
GEST 1870

From where he stood Cain could see the river flowing past and the ferry cable stretching between shores. Shadows fell around him. So perished another day in the year of our Lord 1884.

He tried to summon a memory, scent or lullaby, but there was nothing. The boy didn't know for certain how old he was, but he thought it surely close to fourteen years. His father spoke of her when he was drunk. Cain asked him once how she died and learned never to ask that question again.

* * *

Seasons turned one to another and the stranger's body decayed without human witness. Buzzards and coyotes had their way with his flesh and left the bones scattered. After a time the skull came to house a family of woodmice.

From the cabin in the dark grove sometimes laughter, sometimes the lament of the German's violin, Wagner long into the night. Still other times the sound of blows and the boy weeping.

There were evenings he'd steal away, leaving his father to drunken slumber, and walk the riverbank alone. He'd venture from the stream and go climbing the nearby hills. On the slope a series of small caves. Black openings out of which clouds of bats poured into the sky each sunset. Like prisoners escaping the earth's hollow core, something unspeakable loosed on mankind.

One night he clambered to the highest of the caves and struck a match and lit the crude torch he'd made. Daring to trespass the void he ducked through the low entrance and went slowly among the chambers of mystery. Tight going at first, then the long gallery opened onto a great room and the ceiling was lost in darkness. He'd expected rank guano, but there was only the smell of wet stone, endless time. The floor was clean. No bats ever dwelled in that place, perhaps the home of some haunt, tutelary spirit of the cave from whose presence all living beings fled. All save the boy.

No eidolon appeared to him, only the paintings when he shone his torch on the wall. His eyes the first in three hundred years to see them. The blue snaking course of the river. Beasts and men and taller men yet, so tall they seemed giants with strangely flattened heads, long bows in hand, and foxlike dogs at their feet.

Ash and bone covered the floor. He found an arrowhead and a number of shell ornaments, the remains of an ancient camp, and he kneeled in the cave with his torch burning down and tried to dream up that lost tribe from sharpened flint and bits of shell.

When he returned to the crossing, he was carrying a handful of artifacts. He went to the anchor tree and found the hollow place in the trunk where he'd cached a few small coins, gratuities from passengers when his father hadn't been looking. He reached inside and deposited his talismans.

* * *

The river flowed on.

Always there were moments of kindness. The gift of a new pocketknife or the little shake of Killcrop's head sometimes when Cain moved to help with the ferry. Never any apparent reason. He puzzled over these things.

His father's temperaments shifted without warning. Day by day the changes grew more rapid. One instant he'd be telling the boy what an angel he was, showing him the tiny woolen socks his mother sewed in anticipation of his birth, then with no provocation he'd commence beating the devil out of him.

By the time spring bloomed Cain had grown. His clothes still hung loosely on his thin frame, but his arms were sinewy from working the ferry, his hands thickly callused. The ring dangled from a length of twine around his neck, hidden under his shirt. He was fifteen years old and all it took was a glance from Killcrop to cower him. It never occurred to the boy that soon his strength would match the man's.

The afternoon everything changed they were signaled by the bell. They stepped out of the cabin and looked across the river at a solitary man on the opposite deck. Killcrop cupped his hands around his mouth. He called to the Mexican.

"You got the fare? It costs to ride."

He was afoot and leading a mule loaded with a heavy burden wrapped in burlap. He wore a palm frond hat, a bright cotton shirt. The knees of his pants were frayed.

He shouted back, "No English. I need cross."

Killcrop frowned. "Let me see your money first," he called in Spanish.

The Mexican reached in his pocket and took out a

handful of coins, impossible in the distance to judge what currency or value.

Killcrop sighed and patted the boy's shoulder. "Ach, back to work," he said. They went to the flattop and began the crossing.

When the passenger stepped aboard, Killcrop stared in disgust.

"How much to go over?" the man asked.

This close, the Indio blood in him was plain to see. Killcrop gave him a hard stare. The man asked again how much.

Killcrop slapped a mosquito on his cheek and left a bloody smear. Then he told him the price and the man paid and led his mule onto the ferry and once more they set out.

The passenger tied his mule's reins to the railing. Then he joined them at the rope, a man who lacked the nature to stand by while others worked. Cain looked over his shoulder and smiled. The passenger smiled back, a few teeth missing, and spoke in Spanish.

"I'm Cayetano. What's your name?"

Killcrop answered for him. "Don't speak to him, Teufel. Stop talking to the boy."

Cayetano noted the boatman's tone and went silent.

When they reached the other side, Killcrop took the coins from his pocket, the passenger's fare, and pitched them into the water. Cain watched in confusion.

"I don't want your money," Killcrop said. "Don't come back this way. If you try to cross here again, I'll kill you."

Cayetano shook his head. "No cross, no cross," he said

in English. Then he turned and started down the road leading his mule.

All the rest of that afternoon and into the evening Killcrop was away from the cabin, alone on the hill. Cain sat on the porchsteps waiting for a passenger to arrive, but the crossing was quiet save the cicadas droning in the trees. He was still sitting there when he saw Killcrop marching down in the twilight. The boy watched him come, his father ruddy-cheeked and breathing hard. Familiar fury in his eyes.

Killcrop stood in front of him.

"Get up."

Cain rose from the steps. Killcrop looked at him, then looked off down the river. He turned and punched Cain in the belly, the boy folding over, dropping to his knees.

Killcrop grabbed a fistful of hair and jerked him to his feet. He pressed a thumb to the corner of Cain's eye.

"You cry, Teufelkind? In hell, tears are better than gold. Someday you'll be rich in hell, so what do you say to me?"

The boy didn't answer.

Killcrop shook him by the hair. "What do you say?"

"Thank you."

"In Deutsch," he screamed and slammed a fist into his face. "What do you say in Deutsch?"

"Danke schön, danke schön," he repeated.

"I don't believe you."

The punch landed hard on his jaw. The boy fell over.

"Up," Killcrop said.

Cain was coughing, trying to crawl away. Killcrop

gripped his shirt and pulled him to his feet. He'd already begun to swing his fist for another blow when he spotted the ring dangling from the boy's neck—impossible, but there it was.

Cain saw the flicker of fear in his eyes, then his own fear was gone instantly. As though it had abandoned the boy for a more suitable host. Cain moved fast. He blocked Killcrop's swing with his left forearm and curled his right hand into a fist, launching a blow with all the raging strength of a man behind it.

He hit his father in the gut.

Killcrop gasped and went to his knees. He struggled for air.

The boy wiped blood from his lip and let out a bitter little laugh, shocked how easy it had been. When Killcrop started to rise, Cain kicked him in the belly, the hum of cicadas silenced in the bloodrush, and then Killcrop lay on his side and Cain was stomping his boot-heel into his face over and over. Blood poured from a broken nose, poured down the German's thick blond moustache. "Please, please," Killcrop groaned.

He tried to roll off the porch, but Cain stopped him with a boot pressed to his throat.

"I want to know," Cain said.

"What?" Killcrop's voice was strangled.

"I want to know what happened to her, my mater. How she died."

"Giving birth to you."

The boy was silent.

"You guessed that already, didn't you?" Killcrop said. "But that's not why I called you after the murderer, that's not why I named you Cain. You had a brother. You choked him in the womb and killed him. Stole his breath. So I called you Cain because you murdered your brother and then killed my Hedda."

"You're crazy," Cain said. "What made you so damn crazy?"

Killcrop chuckled and spat blood. "There's more," he said. "There's a reason why you got a devil in you, Teufelkind. But you're not strong enough for the truth."

Cain hesitated. "Tell me."

"You're scared. I can see it."

Cain pressed down on his throat. "Tell me," he said.

Killcrop told him the secret.

* * *

When he finished the story, the boatman appeared to sink within himself, his breath shallow like the breath of an old man. As though he'd aged in the telling. He wouldn't look the boy in the eye.

Cain stared down at his balding head and beer gut and for the first time he saw Killcrop as he was, a lonely man, often cruel and afraid, who'd never sought to be any of those things.

He stepped away and slipped the ring back under his shirt.

Killcrop spoke without raising his eyes. "Do you know

what that ring means?"

"I don't much care. Get up. You're takin me across."

Full dark when they made the crossing. He stood on the ferry holding the bridle reins of Killcrop's old roan while the boatman worked the cable. The flattop floated between twin infinities, stars shining above the grove and the river, stars rippling on the surface of the water. Radiance rebelled against the river, the image of the heavens contesting the current westward as night wore on.

When they'd docked, he led the horse off the ferry and Killcrop stood watching.

"You owe me, boy," Killcrop said. "Ja, how many times could I have drowned you in the river?"

Cain stepped into the saddle.

"When did you ever go hungry?" Killcrop asked. "There was always food, a warm place to sleep. You should thank me."

The boy from Los Ebanos reached in his pocket. He took out the coins he'd withdrawn from the hollow of the tree and pitched them at the boatman's feet.

"The fare," he said.

Then he booted the horse and rode up the banks of another country and he didn't look back.

* * *

For a year he wandered a land not his own. Sleeping in the open fields and pastures, drifting as far west as Chihuahua. Nights at first warm and humid turned chill and dry. The people of the country took him in, this orphan with hair darker than a raven's wing, eyes that hold the gaze of any man who challenges him, never downcast in shyness or submission. They recognized the quality. Not just confidence. Those were the eyes of one without fear. Families shared their meals with him and asked no question of home or past or destinations to come and in the morning when he departed, the women would offer up to him on the horse bundles of tortillas and machaca.

He made camp one moonless night under a dead oak, the outskirts of an abandoned mining town.

When he woke in the dawn, Cain discovered he'd spent the night in a cemetery. Headstones unsuspected in the dark now stood in plain sight all about him. The horse, tethered to a branch of the oak, stood cropping sparse yellow grass from a grave. Cain rose from his bedding. He walked out to a far corner that housed a potter's field and in that potter's field a great heap of stones. He stood looking it over, what seemed a mass burial, the resting place of perhaps eight men. A lone cross marked the common grave and carved in the wood of the cross were the words *Los Pistoleros Americanos* and the date 1870.

He stared at the marker a long time.

At last he rode down the cemetery hill into the ghost town. The shops and homes that had sprung up during the mine's great booming days stood as empty husks. Handmade curtains fluttering in a shattered window. A rusted ore cart on the steel tracks, the rails themselves vanishing into dunes.

A mule was tied in front of the ramshackle old chapel. Cain unhorsed and tied his own mount, then took the steps up to the ruined church and removed his hat. He hesitated at the open door that hung slanted on broken hinges. "Quién es?" he called.

He walked the length of the nave. A shaft of sunlight shone through a hole in the roof and nameless dust danced in the beam. In the sanctuary he found a half-blind anchorite seated at the foot of the altar. He was eating peaches from an old tin. Cain inquired of him what town he'd entered and the anchorite wiped his mouth on a filthy shirtsleeve and told him this was a place called Soledad. The silver mine had been called La Soledad and such was also the name of the town. The anchorite asked if he were a huérfano. Cain answered that he was indeed an orphan and had been so all his life. The anchorite licked his dry cracked lips and replied that he had suspected as much.

Then Cain posed him the question of the potter's field and the Pistoleros Americanos.

A gang of ex-American soldiers and their Indio scout, the anchorite explained. Death-dealers from across the border. They'd tried to rob the payroll of La Soledad many years earlier and had perished in a great bloody gunbattle with the mine guards and the workers. Most of those in the cemetery had earned their rest on that day. Cain said he wasn't surprised to hear of such an end. The anchorite eyed the boy. He asked if the huérfano had come so late in search of the death-dealers, perhaps to cast his lot with them, but Cain told him it had only been curiosity that drew him there.

When he rose to go, he asked the old man if there were not some more populous settlement where he could escort him.

The anchorite shook his head. "A piece of advice, young man?"

Cain stood with his hat in hand. "Yes, sir?"

"If you ever offend a hermit, best to kill him too. Because how could a hermit forget?"

The anchorite rose unsteadily to his feet. He reached out a stained and reeking hand, Cain tense and hesitating, and placed his palm on the boy's head.

"In Nomine Patris…" the anchorite whispered.

Then he sank back down and returned to his peaches.

Cain stood puzzled a moment, then thanked the old man and turned and departed the ruined chapel. He rode out from the Soledad into the west and left that potter's field and its anonymous occupants far behind.

He sought employment as a vaquero for a sprawling ranch. He was young and thin and had no experience, but when the foreman asked if he'd ever done this kind of work, he told the man yes, many times. His lie was soon discovered. Perhaps it owed to his direct gaze or the foreman simply pitied the boy, but despite his lack of skill he wasn't dismissed. He worked hard and learned fast, always given the worst jobs and never complaining. In time he was a first-rate vaquero and he adopted as his maxim, if you want to become someone, pretend that's already who you are.

He spoke Spanish well enough but with a wretched accent his comrades found endlessly comical. Gradually he excised the accent. At the close of each month the other vaqueros rode into town to blow their pay on whores and cards and dice, the boy always staying behind, aloof for no reason he could name. The following day he'd watch them ride to the bunkhouse, bankrupt with pounding headaches.

He began loaning out his savings when the month was young, charging small interest and restricting his loans to men he both trusted and judged he could beat in a fight. In this way he acquired enough funds to outfit himself with a good bay horse and saddle, a Springfield rifle and .44 revolver. Come the spring of 1886 he gave the foreman his notice.

He rode west passing through villages and colonias he'd see again thirty years later as a scout for the 10th Cavalry, Galeana and Colonia Dublán, the eerie ruins of Casas Grandes. Crossing the desert without companion or clear purpose.

One afternoon he watched a tarantula hawk swoop down on her prey. The blue wasp grappled with the tarantula, her hooked claws against his many legs, and her long stinger reached for the underside of the spider's cephalothorax. She toppled her opponent. The tarantula took her sting, blinding electric pain, and went limp almost at once, his battle lost.

Their lone observer knew all too well what would follow. He'd seen various stages of the process before, always curious about the workings of nature. When paralysis was complete, the mother wasp would drag the spider back to his own burrow. She'd lay a single egg on his body before leaving and covering the burrow entrance. Silken darkness, malignant incubation. The larva would hatch with a terrible appetite. It would rip a small hole in the tarantula's abdomen while he still lived, then plunge into his belly to feed, avoiding vital organs as long as possible, ensuring the meal remained fresh over weeks of metamorphosis.

The boy stared at the wasp dragging her surrogate womb across the hardpan. Then he stepped forward like a killer savior and crushed them both under his boot-heel.

No longer did he wear the ring on the cord about his neck. His frame was thin and boyish, but his hands were hard and strong. He wore the ring on his left hand like a wedding band. Groom to an unknown bride.

It was a perfect fit.

He rode on and he rode where cruel flowers grew, the desert light sharp on the edge of every serrated leaf and pale blossom. Nothing moved in that vast emptiness. Nothing save tempests of sand that swirled across the plain and broke against sunbaked stone. He came to see in his travels through that waste a lack of inherent value in all things and it followed to reason that nothing was denied him. So he began to live for the day.

Bandits confronted him at a pass in the hills, a sorry-looking bedraggled lot, and he drew his pistol and shot their spokesman through the breast. The man's confederates deserted before the boy could fire another round. The solitary outlaw sat his horse. Blood running between his fingers, eyes wide and disbelieving. He started to slump over. The boy put his mount forward and wrapped his arm around the man's shoulders and held him upright while he died there in the pass.

Not three days later he met with another party of bandits. Their leader noted the boy's gaze, his hand on the butt of the .44. This time the encounter ended with Cain numbered among their ranks. They lay in wait for travelers on the road. From a great distance they watched a Mennonite driving a buckboard and they watched him for a long while before he approached their position, then they fell upon him as one and murdered him for what little he possessed.

He continued for a time with the highwaymen, but it became clear to him he had no interest in fortune or adventure. The night came when he left without farewell. He thought perhaps he'd be a vaquero again and drifted north, taking his supper at ranch houses along the way or hunting what wild game there was. On occasion he found offers of employment, but each job he refused. Finally he admitted to himself he'd had no intent other than a desire to wander. With this truth in mind he crossed the plains and found himself in a village called Carretas on July 21, 1886, the day his life slipped its traces and followed an altered destiny.

CHAPTER THREE

In Nácori Jubal met Moroni Thayne and his brothers Ammon and Layton. He shook their hands and thanked each man. Now with the Mormon trio among their rank the dozen riders headed for Bacerac, the last civil outpost in the sierras, and they reached it early the following day.

Cloudbanks descended over the ridges. Soon it would be snowing on the high peaks. The plan was to drive into the hills east of Bacerac where they'd begin an initial scouting foray.

First the squad picked up their guide, an elderly Tarahumara named Escobar. He was reluctant to leave his sickly wife and he cautioned it was unwise to trespass in the land of those he called Isnay Indey, the men of the woods, but Jubal offered more money than he'd see otherwise in years. Against his better judgement Escobar agreed to serve as guide.

Jubal had his own reservations. Escobar wasn't a young man anymore. His age and the questionable depth of his knowledge were cause for worry, but no one in the village had more experience of the sierras. His familiarity with the range was invaluable, limited though it was. Existing maps were all useless. As if drawn from the cartographer's memory of a feverdream. For all his shortcomings the guide remained their best hope in that terra incognita.

Some of the men purchased cobijas or woolen blankets from Escobar's wife and daughter. The heavy blankets took a month to weave and would easily stand twenty years of hard use. It was stark country where they were going and for the next weeks, their only beds would be soogans and pine boughs laid over cold ground.

Escobar mounted saying, "En nombre de Dios."

In a valley some distance from the village they set up base camp. Four men would remain there to guard extra supplies. When the scouting party's provisions ran low, they'd return down to camp and resupply before heading back into the hills.

Snow was falling in the sierras when the nine rode out, Jubal at their head snapping the stumps of his fingers, those phantom digits aching in the cold, yearning for touch. They rode up a deep arroyo. Its sides were lined with trincheras, each low stone wall smaller than the one preceding it as the dry wash narrowed toward the top. Juniper rose on the slopes amid stands of fir and madrone. Vegetation was dense in the valleys, but the mesas and ridges were an open wood of great oaks. Following a faint trail through the trees they came upon a cross and a mound of rocks that marked the place at which some wayfarer discovered eternity. Each man save Jubal and the Mormons crossed himself and climbed down to add another stone to the pile.

All day and into the night Escobar led them through country he knew only dimly and they found no sign of Apaches. A full moon rose with a halo ringing it. Scudding clouds, sweeping shadows. In a deep forest they heard the call of a wolf, or what was made to sound as though it were a wolf, somewhere behind them in the dark. The old man drew up and they all stopped. He sat his mount listening. After a while another wolf answered to their left and not far away. The men looked at each other and kept quiet and each one felt a chill colder than the night. Escobar sat rigid.

Then a third howl rose through the air.

"Umph, lobo," Escobar said, certain now, and they could hear the relief in his voice.

They continued on some distance looking for a suitable place to camp and after a while they spotted the glow of a fire. Jubal could hear men talking, laughing. He told the others to hang back, then he climbed down and gave Hector his reins and walked ahead. He called out hello to the camp.

The laughter and conversation died. A man rose fumbling for his pistol. "Quién es?" he demanded with a faint American accent.

"A friend," Jubal said, switching now to English to put the man at ease. "Mind if I come on up?"

"Go ahead, but come slow."

Jubal stepped alone into the firelight.

* * *

49

The camp belonged to an agent of the Phelps Dodge Company named Ellway. He was leading a mule train in search of the ruins of Tayopa, the fabled Jesuit silver mine, with thirty men in the party, mozos and mule drivers. They sat about the fire with a bottle of lechuguilla making the rounds. Mules stood hobbled in darkness.

"So you're McKenna," Ellway said. "I'll be damned. I read about that business, those Indians taking your boy. Wish you all the luck in the world."

Ellway waved and called for Jubal's men to stake their mounts and come have a drink. "Pass that bottle here," he said. He grabbed the bottle and offered it to Jubal.

Jubal shook his head.

"Suit yourself," the company agent said. He shrugged and took a swig, then they sat down by the fire.

"Have you run across any tracks?" Jubal asked. "Any sign of Apaches?"

"Sorry to disappoint, but we haven't seen a damn thing. This is the end of the line for us."

Ellway admitted their own search was a failure and drawing to a close. He'd been sent into the sierras with a map, in his opinion a forgery like so many others, but his employers had full confidence in its authenticity and so they'd financed the expedition.

"These nights are cold," Jubal said. "This is the wrong time of year for what you're doing. Why winter?"

"Phelps Dodge isn't the only one with the map, unfortunately. A competitor has a copy, but they're waiting till spring to launch their expedition. So in the interest of beating the bastards to it, here we are."

Now Jubal's men came forward, all save the Mormon brothers who'd chosen to stay behind and guard the horses and mules. They greeted the agent and mozos. A vaquero named Eduardo Gutiérrez grinned at a man holding the bottle of lechuguilla. "Hey, let me have a bite," he said.

Before the bottle could change hands Jubal spoke up—"No drinking. I need you alert."

"Just a bite," Gutiérrez said. "That's all, uh?"

Jubal held his eyes and didn't say a word.

"All right, no drinking," the vaquero said. "You're the boss."

They sat about the fire and conversation turned once more to the failed enterprise. "The thing about treasure maps," Ellway said, "you're never buying the map. You're buying a story. I suppose for what it's worth, this one's not bad as stories go."

Dated 1646, Ellway explained, the chart was purportedly drawn by the bellmaker of Tayopa, the campanero who cast the old mission bells. It claimed to lead by way of natural landmarks and Spanish treasure symbols to the Jesuits' secret hoard.

Everyone in that part of Sonora knew the tale of the lost mine. Tayopa was the Order's closely guarded secret, a clandestine mining operation somewhere between Nácori Chico and Guaynopa. In 1621 Philip III enforced an old law banning the priesthood from owning or working mines in New Spain. Though their rich lode yielded many tons of silver bullion the Jesuits were unable to export it—

so they began stockpiling instead. For years Indio slaves labored deep in the tunnels. Accidents occurred. Miners died under fallen rock, others simply worked themselves to death. Meanwhile the priests grew fat and filled their vault with fantastic wealth and nightly had their pick of village women.

Then the Apaches struck.

"There was writing on back of the map," Ellway said. "Almost too faint to make out."

According to the faded message the bellmaker was sole survivor. He'd hidden in a secret place on the slope while down below warriors killed the guards and hacked the priests apart limb by limb. A few of the miners were of Apache blood. These men were set free, the rest shackled to the walls of the central tunnel. The warriors raped the village women, then put them to slaughter with every suckling child and took the older children as captives.

Tayopa lay in smoking ruins. The Order's church was reduced to foundation stones and crumbling walls, but the Apaches weren't satisfied yet. They sawed into the wooden beams above the entrance to the tunnel. After weakening the shoring timbers they placed the outpost's store of blackpowder just within the tunnel entrance and trailed a line of powder outside, then a warrior dropped his burning torch. The line raced hissing and flaring.

The roar of the explosion echoed down the valley. There was a deep rumble and rising cloud of dust. The bellmaker watched from above and when the cloud dissipated, he could see the collapsed entrance, the great pile of debris.

The Apaches mounted up with their captives and drove out the stolen mules. They left the vault of silver untouched and they left the miners in chains and darkness, sealed alive in a common tomb, two dozen souls to guard that cursed place should the priests return seeking their fortune.

After dark the bellmaker came down the slope and staggered through the carnage to stand at the fallen tunnel. He could hear them crying under the earth, begging mercy, but the mound of rubble was too much for one man. He kneeled at a small opening and called out that he was going for help. They cried for him not to forsake them. The bellmaker swore on his soul he would return with men to free them.

He started running. The bellmaker didn't stop until he'd reached the nearest river settlement. In the dark plaza he fell to his knees, his cries waking the villagers, and they gathered around him and heard his desperate story. Come with me, he said. We can still save them.

The men only shook their heads.

There's silver, he confessed. More treasure than you can imagine, enough you'll never work again.

Neither charity nor greed would persuade them. Nothing out-weighed the risk of torture and death at the hands of Apaches. The bellmaker's pleading turned to curses, then night turned to day. The village went about its business, women carrying water from the river, men tending herds and tilling the fields, while the bellmaker lay drunk in the shade, his dreams all of thirst and darkness.

For many months he remained there. Sickened at last

with a fever he lay close to death in the home of the alcalde while a little girl placed cool rags upon his brow. Certain the end was near he gathered his final strength and called for paper, pen, and ink. He drew the map and set down his account, perishing soon after. The document passed through generations of his caregiver's family until finding its way to Arizona and a Phelps Dodge executive.

Centuries of Apache occupation and bloody insurgency had protected the secret mine. Few dared enter those mountains, whatever treasure they might hold. By the bellmaker's map Tayopa lay in a hidden valley within a fork of the Yaqui River, its vast wealth of silver contained in a tunnel beyond an iron door 2,281 varas east and 63 varas south of the entrance to the ruined church. Ellway had conducted an exploration of the mountains east of Nácori. He'd found perhaps three or four of the landmarks mentioned but discovered no treasure symbols, no valley of ruins. Now their supplies were exhausted and the men exhausted and Ellway was ready to give up the search.

"So much for fame and fortune," he said.

"Every few years," Jubal told him, "strangers show up in Nácori. Men with maps and questions. One time a priest rode out to the ranch, a young guy with an Italian accent. His story wasn't much different than yours. Wanted to hire my vaqueros to take him up into the sierras."

"What'd you tell him?"

"I told him to go home. All of these mountains are supposed to be filled with lost treasure. The only thing they've got more of is dead treasure hunters."

"Did he take your warning to heart?"

"The story was too good, I guess. He went up there alone."

Ellway whistled. "Tell me the lunatic returned with his scalp and vows of poverty intact."

"Never came back. Like a lot of others."

"Hey, boss?" Gutiérrez said. "How about a peek at that map? I'm not drinking, got to have something to keep me busy. Maybe we'll run across some landmarks."

Jubal hesitated.

Ellway laughed. "Actually, I was going to suggest something along those lines. If your men could keep an eye out for certain features, Phelps Dodge would be willing to pay a finder's fee."

"We didn't come up here to hunt Tayopa," Jubal said.

"We're here for your boy," Gutiérrez assured him. "I won't forget it, boss. But what can it hurt? Just to keep our eyes open."

"I don't want to sidetrack your expedition," Ellway said. "But while you're riding, if you happen to stumble across something…"

Jubal shook his head. "Fine. Show him the damn map."

"Come on, Miguel," Gutiérrez told a fellow vaquero. The two men rose and stepped to the mining agent.

Ellway removed a paper from his breastpocket and unfolded it on a rock. He clicked on a flashlight and shone the beam on the chart and they huddled around it, staring.

"That's a lot of silver," Miguel Ortiz said. "A man would be a king."

"Se chingo," Gutiérrez whispered.

"Hell, I'll give you a copy," Ellway told them. "Our competition will be here by spring and I'd rather take a chance on you men seeing any of these markings. Any landmark you spot, get word to me in Bisbee and I'll make sure you receive the finder's fee." He looked up at Jubal and nodded. "Much appreciated, sir."

Jubal laughed a bitter laugh. He rose and stepped out into the dark and left them to their map and talk of treasure.

CHAPTER FOUR

Denali stood over the field rat's mound. He held the curved end of a stick just below the mouth of the hole and got ready. At the other entrance Chatto kneeled prodding a yucca stalk into the burrow, their old plan a success every time, the rat guaranteed to panic and go for the only exit not under attack.

Denali waited. His friend kept prodding.

Then the rat stuck his head out, pausing an instant to scan for enemies, and Denali jerked the stick up and snapped the rat's spine. Chatto whooped. He clapped Denali on the shoulder and bent to pick up their prize by the tail. The dead rat did a slow twirl.

"Look at those fat hindlegs," Chatto said.

"Let's go," Denali said. "I'm hungry."

* * *

Crossing the plateau they met with a pair of families heading down the trail, a small band departing the stronghold for the winter. The boys called out their goodbyes and said they'd think of them when the thunder rolled. It wasn't the first such band to leave Pa-Gotzin-Kay that season.

Denali looked back. He watched them turn onto the trail that would take them down from the mountain. The time was coming when the rest of the families must depart as well, a day he dreaded for the sake of his friendship. Denali hoped his family would be in the same band as Chatto's, but how likely was it, when Carnoviste and Zunde were so often at odds?

It was Denali's fourteenth winter. In the year he'd lived among them they'd remained on Pa-Gotzin-Kay, following Carnoviste's counsel and denying their nomadic nature. They'd suffered through one harsh winter, now another was beginning. He knew nothing could hold them back from going down to the foothills.

In the village Ishton sat scraping the hair off a cowhide with the rib of a horse. Other hides lay tied out on racks, curing, smeared with animal brains to make the leather soft, prevent it from drying like tin. Ishton caught him staring and she paused in her work and waved. Denali raised his hand and looked away.

A group of men lounged under the shade of an awning. They drank tiswin and talked of hunts and raids, the heroes of their youth. Out in the pasture boys fought with sticks and slings. Girls sang lullabies to cornhusk dolls.

Denali and Chatto stepped to the camp kettle, steaming over a low fire, and dropped the rat without preparation into the scalding water. They let the rat boil for a time, then Denali reached a long wooden spoon into the pot and lifted the rat out and took it by the tail. He drew his knife and stripped the hide. He gutted the rat with practiced ease.

Denali and Chatto found a place in the shade. They sat together and shared the juicy hindlegs, a fine little meal between friends.

* * *

Denali walked alone in the dark of the woods with his bow in hand. Cold in those shadows, growing colder by the day. A gust whispered through pine-needles high above him, the trunks of the old patriarchs rising a hundred feet to stand like masts in the north wind. His moccasins were silent crossing a stone slab covered in lichen. Green altar amid the undergrowth. Long branches reached out to him as though the trees yearned to be known, yearned so ardently because they themselves were denied knowing.

He crested out on a promontory overlooking the river and the snowcapped citadels in the west and he stood watching the sun descend bloodred upon a jagged peak as if impaled. The rays of that tortured sun reflected on frozen granite. They shone pure and without warmth, the crimson diminishment of him. A chilling wind stung his cheeks. Denali felt himself nearer being resolved into the elements of things than ever before. It surprised him how easily it fell away. Like shedding an illusion.

These days he seldom thought of his old life. Sometimes in dreams it would come back to him, moments with his mother and father, things they'd told him, but more often it returned as stray images. The flowering tree outside his bedroom window when he was nine. His mother singing. A hummingbird observed on a lonely afternoon. Always less and less attachment to those dreams, drifting from him until they seemed a stranger's memories. As if the boy who'd lived them had died with his family down below. He didn't fight the transfiguration. Now when he looked out at the world, he looked with a newness of vision, seeing each object and person as though for the first time. A running dog, Ishton's dimpled knee. The starflung heavens. Like a man waking in a strange place and taking it all in with eagerness, expectancy, the world at once sweet and unbearably sad.

Denali nocked an arrow and held the bow crossways. He raised it high, pulling back the string. When he released his grip, the arrow shot skyward and slowly arced and fell in perfect silence from the heights of paradise.

* * *

That night the earth shook beneath them. Tremors seized the land and everyone rushed from their wickiups and stood by the central fire, children hugging mothers and fathers. The dogs whined and sent up a chorus of howls.

After Nantan prayed the quakes soon subsided. "The mountain spirits make the ground tremble," he told them when it was over. "They rage at what the People have allowed to happen to their home, at the strangers who defile it."

For years Mexicans had invaded the foothills and torn

holes in the sacred earth, digging for their yellow and white metals. They cut entire woods to supply the boilers of the stampmills for their mines. Game was becoming scarce along some stretches of the lower slopes, the companies hunting deer and turkey to feed their workers, driving away the herds and flocks.

This was the People's home. The mountain spirits called for them to defend it. Zunde suggested raids on the logging crews and the braves yelled their approval.

"So it must be," Nantan said.

Zunde looked to the chief. "Will you ride with us?"

Carnoviste gave him a slow nod. "If Nantan says it has to be done, we'll raid the loggers."

The braves grabbed rifles and shook them over their heads and danced an eager dance. Zunde and Nantan sat down to talk of strategy. Carnoviste joined them, committed to the necessity of the raid despite his reluctance. The mountains spirits had spoken—now they must act.

When they'd agreed on a plan of attack, Carnoviste rose from the council.

He called to Denali, Neiflint, and Oblite, then took a thick blanket and led them out into the pasture. They lay in the grass with the blanket warming them and stared up at the stars, the outstretched arm of the galaxy, luminous seeds scattered by the fighting twins. Carnoviste pointed to a constellation burning in its cold blue chains.

"How many stars can you see?"

Neiflint squinted. "Seven."

"Seven," Oblite said.

"And you, my son?" Carnoviste asked.

Denali hesitated. "Six. I see six."

"That's not good. When there are only six, it means the bear is the enemy of the People again. Or that your brothers have better eyes."

Denali smiled. "When will you raid the loggers?" he asked.

"Soon. Nantan says we can't wait long." He started to add something more, then decided against it. He sat up and rubbed his neck. "I don't think we'll be here much longer. They want to go down where it's warm and eat beef all winter, but there are too many of us to stay together in the foothills. Zunde will take a few families and go his own way."

Denali thought of Chatto, his best friend who was Zunde's eldest son. "You're sure Zunde will leave?"

"He wants to show himself what kind of chief he would've made. His Power was always stronger than mine, but Nantan favored me instead. Zunde was my friend just as Chatto is yours, but he can't forgive me for who I am. My son, be happy in this time while we have it."

They fell silent a while. Then Carnoviste asked Denali, "How would you like to go raiding with the warriors?"

"I don't know," Denali said.

Oblite spoke up. "If he gets to go, then so do I."

"Me too," Neiflint said.

"You're both hardly out of baby grass," Denali told them.

At once they assailed him from either side, Neiflint

gripping Denali's ear and twisting while Oblite pounded a fist into his belly. Denali groaned. He kicked at Oblite, jabbed his elbow in Neiflint's ribs.

"Boys," Carnoviste said, breaking them up. "Don't be so quick to turn your spring into summer. I know it feels endless now, like your time will never come. But when it finally does, it goes so fast you don't notice till one morning you're old as gray Taklishim. Patience. Do you kill deer by running them down or waiting till they come close?"

They lay back in the grass and calmed.

Denali rubbed his burning ear. "There's no choice, is there? If you say I have to go on the raid."

"You're ready. Even if you don't know it." Carnoviste took one last glance at the cluster of stars, then rose. "It's too cold for counting stars. Come, the old ones are talking by the fire."

* * *

Often the elders would relate the tale of Gouyen's past, recounting for the children her escape from slavery and her long journey home, but there was much they never knew of her struggles, many secrets unguessed.

Her name meant One Who is Wise. When she was young, Gouyen often raided with the warriors and followed them in battle, proving her bravery countless times. It was a strange thing for the People to allow a maiden to ride among the men, but her Power of Finding Enemies accorded Gouyen special honor. Through a prayer she could sense the presence and direction of enemy forces. The wise woman observed the flights of birds, understood the shape of things to come. Like a blind woman tracing her fingers down the face of time itself. Her Power saved the People from destruction on many occasions and warriors never considered a raid without first consulting the wise woman.

"She's my right hand," Nantan said. "Who is wiser than my sister? Who has shown more courage?"

She'd never married. Some said her only love was killed in a raid and afterward no other man would suit her. A few of the older women whispered it wasn't so, that the true reason she remained unwed lay in the horror she'd endured as a slave to the Mexicans in her youth.

Decades earlier Mexican troops ambushed a party of women at a mescal-cooking camp. Gouyen was among the maidens taken captive. They were marched to the City of Mules and shackled twenty-one days in prison before being shipped by train to Mexico City. Once there Gouyen and two companions, Ih-tedda and Leosanni, were sold to the owner of a maguey plantation, an old gentleman of Castilian blood named Sandoval. On average a captive fetched $150, but in those days Gouyen was young and lithe and firm-breasted. Her master paid $500 to possess her.

Ropes bound their wrists. They ran behind the master's coach on the cobblestone streets where once ancient canals flowed through the great doomed city of Tenochtitlan.

64

Their course turned to the north and onto a rutted dirt track through the countryside. Up a road bisecting fields of century plants, Gouyen kept the pace toward the hacienda rising like a Moorish castle ahead, a high adobe wall about its perimeter.

At last the iron gate groaned shut behind them. In the courtyard an old Mexican woman loosed their hands. She told them to sit on the ground, then she handed out bowls of frijoles and poured cups of pulque made from the fermented sap of the plants outside. Later Gouyen learned the woman's name was Marta. She was the head cook and servant in charge of the Sandoval household.

When they finished the meal, Marta led them into the hacienda and down a hall to a small room with a clawfoot tub. She made all three undress. She gathered their buckskins and told Gouyen to bathe.

"The other girls can wash after you," Marta said, "but only after. Señor Sandoval said the pretty one washes first."

Then Marta stepped out and they heard the key turning in the lock.

The girls spoke enough Spanish to understand what they'd been told and to realize the implication for Gouyen. Her companions wept. Gouyen's eyes were dry while she searched the cramped room, flinging open cabinet drawers, desperate to find a mirror, anything she could break for a jagged edge. She was intent on taking her own life, slitting her veins and bleeding out in the tub before she'd allow her enemies to dishonor her.

There was nothing in the room that could be made a weapon. Perhaps in the hall. Wait until Marta returned, she thought, then shatter a window in the hallway and take a shard to her throat. Blood and fleeting light, the unknown beyond.

A darker thought occurred to her. If she were successful, her master's favor would fall to one of the other girls. Both were younger than herself, both dear as sisters to her.

For their sake she had to endure.

When Gouyen eased herself into the tub, she could smell the faint scent of roses in the perfumed water.

How many nights in all the winters since that moment had she lain sleepless, wondering at her resolve, if it were born of courage or, in truth, utter cowardice?

After a while Marta came back and unlocked the door. She gave Ih-tedda and Leosanni simple cotton dresses and handed Gouyen a silken gown. When they were clothed, she ordered them into the hall. A male servant of Indio blood was waiting to lead the younger girls away. They wept.

"Don't be scared," Gouyen told them. "Stay alive and we'll see the Blue Mountains again."

The old woman escorted her down a shadowed hall. They passed framed tintypes of the Sandoval family and went on past a series of low windows, Gouyen keeping her eyes straight ahead, then they were standing at the door of the master's chamber. Marta knocked, a soft rap. She patted the girl's arm and walked back the way they'd come. Gouyen started to follow. Marta turned and hissed at her to stay.

She stood in the silk gown, the tiles cool under her bare feet. So quiet in the hall she could hear the beating of her heart.

The door swung open.

In the following months she learned a new endurance. When the sun rose, she worked with the others, scrubbing floors and carrying wood or cutting the big thorned leaves in the fields. Her nights were divided between her cot in the female servants' quarters and Sandoval's chamber. No longer did she think of suicide. Revenge and escape occupied her mind entire. On her knees scrubbing tiles she planned a multitude of deaths for her master, a thousand strategies of escape. Always a single thought running below it all, a solitary and constant doubt—were these nothing more than a coward's fantasies designed to soften the revulsion she felt for herself?

She was called by the Mexicans Salome, but Gouyen never forgot her true name. When she became pregnant with the master's child, she did her best to hide that fact from the household, telling only Ih-tedda and Leosanni. Finally when she stood naked before the master one night, he looked at her and knew.

That night when Gouyen stumbled bleeding and dazed to her quarters, Ih-tedda and Leosanni tended her during the birth that came all-too early. When it was done, she lost consciousness and Ih-tedda took the silent little boy, his face so gray and cold, and buried him in the courtyard where he wouldn't be found.

Gouyen was bedridden three days, until Marta ordered her out into the fields once more.

After that, Sandoval became distracted with a new mistress in the city and Gouyen was forgotten at once.

Every day for two years she worked and every day she plotted escape. Not hers alone, for she wouldn't leave without her friends. When the girls asked in despair what was to become of them, Gouyen promised they'd live to see the Blue Mountains once more.

Sandoval's first wife had passed away some years earlier of the consumption. His second wife, several decades his junior, had given him three young children, but now most days, she lay abed with some delicate illness. Her chamber was on the opposite wing of the hacienda from her husband's and rarely did she see him or the children. Only the church's stricture against divorce preserved the shambles of their marriage.

Gouyen was given the task of caring for the Sandoval youths, a girl and two boys, spoiled and ill-behaved. Under Gouyen's hand and watchful eyes they soon acquired a new disposition. The change in them was much celebrated by their parents on those occasions when they deigned to notice their offspring. Gouyen found the work suited her. She enjoyed the presence of children and after a while a restrained fondness grew between the slave and her young charges.

Gouyen also served as Marta's kitchen helper and pupil. In these capacities she worked another year until she was well-trusted and she'd perfected the Mexican dishes the old cook taught her.

They'd require knives for their journey home to the sierras. The machetes the fieldhands used were too large, too difficult to conceal. The kitchen knives were counted every night and locked away and should one go missing, the servants would be searched and their quarters searched and the household placed on alert. Gouyen meditated on the problem of the knives.

Save the trio of captive girls the workers all were peons, at liberty to walk as far beyond the maguey fields as they wished. The fieldhands and servants frequented a small church on the northern edge of the city. The slave girls were granted only one exception to their confinement—the master permitted them to attend Mass with their fellow servants. They were allowed to visit the church. Elsewhere in the city, however, their presence was strictly forbidden.

Marta's duties took her to the mercado daily for the purchasing of fresh meat and fruits and vegetables. As chief house servant she boasted her own quarters. The old woman didn't sleep in the female barracks with the others, but in a one-room jacal behind the hacienda.

Gouyen watched and waited.

The morning came when the master's wife went shopping in the city, brief respite from her demanding schedule of rest. While she was gone, Gouyen stole into her bedroom. In the open closet countless shoes and hats and fine dresses. Gouyen stepped to the chiffonier and started opening drawers. She ignored the array of perfumes and jewels and kept searching until she found what she was looking for.

She hid it under her dress, then turned and left.

That night Gouyen climbed from her cot and crept between the rows of sleepers. She went barefoot across the courtyard and crouched at the door of Marta's jacal. She eased it open.

A long pause. Then a harsh snore from the dark.

Gouyen crawled to the bedside. She gripped the stolen hatpin, long and sharp with an ornate head, and held it over the opening of the sleeper's ear. She steadied herself.

Gouyen thrust deep. Her free hand clamped Marta's mouth while she stabbed again and again. Save a low moan, the old woman never made a sound.

Matches and an unlit candle rested on the nightstand. Gouyen set the candle burning and examined the pillow and sheets for blood, but she found none. She used a handkerchief to clean the hatpin, then carefully poured from an olla of water and wet the kerchief and cleaned the cook's ear. She held the candle close, gazing into the fatal hole, until she nodded once in satisfaction and blew out the flame.

In the morning everyone heard the news—the old cook had died in her sleep. What more peaceful way for the elderly to go?

The Sandoval children were all away at boarding school and everyone knew Gouyen had been the old cook's pupil.

Before noon she was made head cook.

Her new position brought her to the mercado each day. She did her shopping and remained watchful, the patience of a hawk. It was a month until an opportunity presented itself, a merchant arguing the price with an irate customer, and Gouyen took a risk. She slipped the merchant's knife under her skirt and walked away.

The master's youngest son, a curious and shy child of eight, had been sent home from boarding school after a severe bout of an unknown sickness left him frail and needful. Gouyen split her kitchen duties with caring for the boy. Long nights he lay awake, unable to find rest. Only Gouyen's tales soothed him to sleep. She told the boy of White Painted Woman, how her son Child of the Waters was born with a great Power. In those days monsters ruled the earth. Child of the Waters fought many battles to vanquish the beasts of old. In his struggle with Owl Man Giant, a sacred blue stone protected Child of the Waters and when the last blood was spilled, the young hero stood victorious and the land was safe for the People.

From time to time she'd test the boy, changing an aspect of the old tale just to hear him correct her. It pleased her, the enemy's son raised on sagas of the nation his fathers destroyed.

One evening after the boy finally nodded to sleep she heard Sandoval enter the house, returned from inspecting his fields. Gouyen rose and stepped out of the boy's room, shutting the door with care, then hurried down the hall.

When old Sandoval stepped into his chamber, she was waiting naked on the bed. He hadn't touched her in a great while, always more interested in the novelty of new flesh, but to see Gouyen present herself for him unbidden, out of the blue, fired his lust.

Afterward he was quick to fall into a heavy sleep as always. He lay naked on his side, facing her. Gouyen waited a long time. Then she reached down to her clothes on the floor and found the hatpin.

She leaned over her sleeping lover. She eased the pin into his earhole ever so slightly. He stirred. Gouyen froze, her hand absolutely still, and he slept on.

Her first thrust went deep enough to penetrate the brain, but she didn't stop until she was doubtless sure.

Gouyen cleaned his ear. She struggled with his fat body, dressing him in his usual robe, then she smoothed the sheets on her side of the bed and fluffed her pillow and dressed. Slipping on her huaraches she paused a moment. Unsure if she'd heard a sound from beyond the door, a light footstep in the hall like the footstep of a child, or if her mind was playing tricks. She stood listening.

Silence. Whatever she'd heard, it didn't come again.

The hall was empty when she cracked the door. She stepped out and strolled to the boy's room, then hesitated with her hand on the knob. She swung the door open—

And saw the boy in bed much as she'd left him.

She stepped into the room and stood over the boy watching him breathe, studying the rhythm, if it would stay true. She finally bent and kissed his cheek, then turned and departed.

In the servants' latrine she took out the hatpin and the bloodstained rag and committed them to the hole.

That night Gouyen's sleep was long and pleasant.

The following day Dr. Ybarra's examination of the body proved superficial, routine for the times. He suspected a ruptured aneurysm, cerebral hemorrhage in Sandoval's sleep, and he tried to comfort the widow with the knowledge it had been painless.

"Swift in the night," the good doctor said. "Still in his prime. For most of us, it's a slow decline, but the Virgin grants a tranquil passing to the noble of heart."

The widow's elderly father soon arrived to manage the estate. Concurrent with her grief the widow Sandoval appeared to experience a sudden alleviation of her illness. A greater frequency of shopping trips to the city evidenced her reinvigoration. She left it to Gouyen to comfort the tearful young boy.

Gouyen waited.

A full six months crawled by before she'd even consider running. If they made their escape too early, the master's death might be recalled with newfound suspicion and a bounty placed on their heads.

Then one morning crossing the courtyard she glanced up and saw three small dark birds passing overhead. They formed a V cutting through the sky. She noted their number and the northern course of their flight and she knew the time had come.

She found Ih-tedda and Leosanni cleaning the patio and told them to prepare themselves. This was the night.

The church would serve as their ruse.

From the start Gouyen had made it a point for them to keep regular attendance, to learn its ways and rites.

Endlessly strange. A place where old men were called father who were father to none, where they spoke an alien tongue and carried sweetly smoking vessels. They worshipped a God on a tree, but whispered their prayers to the God's mother and the images of many small gods.

Of the three girls only Ih-tedda had taken to the religion. She'd kneel on the stone floor of the nave reciting prayers and worrying the beads of her rosary.

"Get off your knees," Gouyen would whisper to her. "If their God sees everything, He's seen you scrubbing floors all day."

A priest gave Ih-tedda the gift of a crucifix and she hung it over her cot in their quarters. Gouyen stared. "Why is their God nailed to a tree?" she asked. Ih-tedda tried to explain what the priest had told her, the only Son of God a blood ransom for the world, but Gouyen shook her head in puzzlement.

"Who did this?" she demanded. "Who nailed Him to the tree?"

"Everyone," Ih-tedda said. "All the people everywhere."

"Not me," Gouyen told her. "I never did such a thing, not our People. If their God has so much Power, why didn't He just kill them all?"

Ih-tedda had no more answers for her.

That night as vespers approached they fell in with the peons and passed through the open gate. They kept an unhurried pace down the road. Soon they left the fields behind and entered the city, the great belltower rising ahead, worshippers streaming into the church.

Gouyen stopped at the stone steps to fasten the thong of her huarache. The girls paused as though waiting for her. When the last of their fellow workers entered the narthex, the captives walked on and left the church behind.

Vesper bells tolled as they began their long walk.

All night they trekked. At dawn they hid beneath a bridge and slept in shifts till darkfall. Then it was time to continue on, cold with only their rebozos to warm them, walking beside the road and hiding in the tall weeds at the sound of approaching horsemen. Gouyen stole a gourd jug from a sleeping jacal and they carried water in it.

It was winter and the tunas of the prickly pear were ripe in that country. Far to the north they ripened in the summer, food to be had all along their journey. As though the seasons themselves conspired with the runaways.

Gouyen used her butcher knife to prepare the tunas. They huddled in the day's hiding place and ate, then all three slept without a guard, dead tired.

Ih-tedda carried her rosary and crucifix. Each night she propped the crucifix against a stone and kneeled before it praying for safety on their journey. Finally Gouyen had enough. While Ih-tedda slept she took the articles and walked out and buried them.

"We don't need to pretend anymore," Gouyen told the maiden when she woke. "We're not their prisoners now."

Ih-tedda wept. Afterward to Gouyen's irritation she kneeled and made the sign of the cross.

Two weeks out they killed a calf at a lonely waterhole and skinned and butchered it and made of the stomach a

75

waterbag. They cut the meat and wrapped it in the skin and left the rest for vultures. Gouyen obscured their tracks should a vaquero arrive at the spring. When she judged they'd gone a safe distance, they found a place to hole up and Gouyen sliced the meat in strips and hung them on a bush to dry.

They avoided villages, kept a close watch on their backtrail. When a clear landmark rose in the north, they'd split up, each woman following a different route before uniting once again at the rendezvous.

By the time they arrived in the sierras three months later their dresses hung in tatters. They'd abandoned their worn-down huaraches in favor of crude footgear fashioned from calfskin. Ashamed to greet their families, naked as they were, they walked first to a cave well-known to them, where the People had cached ammunition and bolts of calico many years before. Mice had damaged the cloth. They used what they could to make new dresses. Only then did they set out on the final distance to Pa-Gotzin-Kay, clothed in their new raiment.

When the People embraced their lost ones, every eye brimmed with tears and wonder. Six winters had elapsed since they were carried away. "I've seen no greater courage," Taklishim said, "than what these daughters have shown today."

Nantan stepped out of the welcoming crowd.

Gouyen ran forward and hugged him. "Our father and mother?" she asked.

He shook his head and she felt the strength go out of

her legs, then he was holding her up, bearing his twin sister in his arms.

That evening the People held a feast for their daughters returned from the dead. Nantan sprinkled each woman with sacred pollen. They wore fine deerskin dresses and moccasins and Nantan presented Gouyen with his long knife. The drummers played and the dance began. Ih-tedda and Leosanni rose, basking in the attention of suitors.

Gouyen also caught a warrior's eye. Though no longer a young maiden, her features still were pleasing. She danced with the warrior in the firelight, but when he gave her a look of desire, she flashed to her master's ravenous gaze. The warrior touched her arm and she felt a cold hand reaching from the grave.

Gouyen broke away, leaving the wheel of dancers. She stepped out into the night. A full moon hung over the spring, its light shining on the surface of the water, and Gouyen kneeled and wept.

After a while she dried her eyes and stared at her reflection in the pool. From this night on, she determined, she'd see to it that no man would want her.

She pulled the long knife. She touched the tip to her cheek, just below her right eye, and a prick of blood appeared and ran like a solitary tear. She took a breath—

A hand gripped her wrist, stopping her from drawing the blade downward.

"Why scar so dear a face?" Nantan asked. He stood behind her, manifested as though by magic.

"So no man will hurt me," she told him. "So they won't

want to touch me again."

"You fear a man's touch?"

Gouyen nodded.

"Mine as well?" Nantan asked.

Her tears joined the line of blood down her cheek. "I know my brother would never hurt me."

Slowly he brought his hand to her face and wiped away the blood and tears with a thumb. Gouyen shut her eyes.

"I've made myself a great man of Power," he said. "No warrior is my equal. My Power is strong, but with all that my sister has to give me, it can grow stronger."

"I know your strength," she told him. "But what can I give you? I have nothing a man of Power wants."

"You have more than you know. My Power can heal your fear, but only if you wish it. My Power can make the dead winter earth green again with sweet fruits."

She looked into his eyes, darkly gleaming, and she was hesitant.

Then she made her decision.

"I wish it," Gouyen said.

CHAPTER FIVE

For a week after meeting the mule train Jubal and his men wandered the sierras without sighting a trail or recent camp. They began running low on supplies. Jubal cursed the luck of the last days—soon they'd have to return to base camp. He decided that once down below he'd dismiss Escobar. The old man knew the country little better than himself. The sierras were vast and unknown. With no trail to follow, only blind luck could lead them to the Apaches.

Darkness in the heavens. A snow storm hung over the highlands, those peaks rising to vanish out of sight in gray clouds, veiled pinnacles a thousand feet above their position. The Apaches would soon descend, if they hadn't already, and Jubal intended to be waiting for them. Escobar led the way through stone passes where the wind moaned like a purgatory of celestial spirits and they rode down empty valleys, the trunks of pines standing sentinel in midmorning fog. Then came clear nights when the stars arrayed in undiminished brilliance shone like an impossible fresco on the ceiling of the world.

They camped one evening on an upland vega. They made no fire and sat wrapped in their coats and blankets, the tips of cigarettes flaring. Only the Tarahumara seemed exempt from the cold. Escobar wore a thin coat, his own cobija spread on the ground beneath him, always uncomplaining, his face expressionless. Inscrutable and patient as one of those stone visages abandoned on some tropical beach.

They ate a supper of pinole, toasted corn pounded to a fine meal, and sat talking in the dark. Gutiérrez unbuttoned his breastpocket and took out the rattle he'd cut from the tail of a serpent that morning. When he'd woke at dawn, the rattlesnake was lying outside his soogan at his feet, drawn to the warmth, and he unsheathed his machete and lobbed its head off.

He shook the souvenir and laughed.

"Do you have to do that?" Angel asked. He lay on his bedroll. "I hate that damn sound."

"Scared of snakes?" Gutiérrez asked. "This is the wrong country for you. Never know when one will crawl in bed with you and snuggle up for a kiss." He kept shaking the rattle.

Moroni Thayne kneeled, unrolling his soogan. "Ammon had a ten-inch centipede in his blanket this morning. I found a tarantula in mine. All we're missing is a vinegarroon and a Gila monster."

"I wonder what a Gila monster tastes like," Gutiérrez said.

"Hell," Moroni said. "If we could roast it over a fire, I'd try a bite. Anything warm for a change. This is one too many cold camps for me. I'll be glad when we run into some Apaches so we can quit this sneaking around."

"Me too, my friend. You think the gut-eaters know where Tayopa is?"

"Why don't you ask them? They'd probably take you straight to it, help you tote all that silver back home."

"No thank you."

"Come on, snake killer," Angel teased. "Don't tell me you're scared of a few gut-eaters. I thought you had balls."

"I'm not afraid of anything above ground," Gutiérrez told him. "But they say sometimes at night you can hear them digging."

"Who?" Angel asked.

Gutiérrez looked at the young vaquero. "Ghosts of the miners, the poor bastards left to die in the tunnels. They beg for water."

Angel stared in silence.

Moroni burst out laughing. "Careful, you'll give the boy bad dreams."

"It's true," Gutiérrez insisted. "I knew a man who heard them. He said they'd grunt and curse each time they swung their picks. They cry out for food and water."

"Must be halfway to hell by now," Moroni said. "You wouldn't let a few ghosts stop you from making your fortune, would you?"

"I'd kiss a rattlesnake for Tayopa." He nodded at Angel. "How about you, boy? How much silver would it take for you to rob the old ghosts?"

Angel shook his head. "I don't want anything to do with spirits."

"Don't let his talk scare you," Jubal spoke up. "Fear is only useful when it can keep you alive, so you'd better be afraid of something real. Flesh and blood. There's another kind of ghost up here. Worry yourself about them."

"Apaches," Angel said.

"Yes. Apaches."

Gutiérrez chuckled and rose. "I got to piss."

He walked off in the dark where the horses and mules stood cropping grass. The men could hear his stream hitting the ground, then a high-pitched drone, calling for agua, drawing out the syllables, pleading for relief.

The vaqueros and Mormon brothers laughed.

"Cover your ears, boy," Gutiérrez shouted. "They're calling for you."

* * *

On their return to base camp Jubal paid Escobar what they'd agreed and told the man to go back to his family. They resupplied the packmules and abandoned camp, joined now by the men who'd stayed behind on the previous foray, and with Jubal riding point they set out once more into the hills.

The squad was restless, bored. They smoked as they rode and their talk turned to women they'd known or claimed to have known. Angel sang verses of corridos, ballads immortalizing some tragedy from older times, his voice soft, almost a whisper among the stones and stands of juniper.

They climbed higher into the foothills and after several days reached a trapper's cabin. He told them of witnessing smoke rising from a valley of caves the evening before. It lay some six hours ride east, a likely Apache camp. Jubal glanced up at the sun. A race against the dark, but if they strained the horses they could make it.

The trapper urged them to stay the night instead. "Start out in the morning," he advised. "There's a storm on its way. Floods in this country kill quicker than Apaches."

"I'm done waiting," Jubal said and turned his horse.

Raincurtains overtook them before the afternoon was out. They entered the valley in a drizzle. Raindrops beaded on their slickers and clung to the manes of the horses. A little stream began trickling through the valley floor and the men looked worried, flooding a deadly possibility. They spoke in favor of heading for high ground and waiting it out, but Jubal kept riding.

"The caves can't be far," he told them. "Just a little farther."

Moroni spat. "A wall of water could come sweeping through here and kill us all."

"That's not going to happen."

"How can you know for sure?"

"I know," Jubal said.

Whether his confidence was born of desperation or blind faith, nonetheless the men chose to follow him. They skirted a huge oak uprooted in an earlier flood. The eroded valley walls stood naked and slashed and they passed more fallen trees with tangled roots and rotting trunks. The horses' hooves were splashing now every step they took as the rain fell harder.

Jubal spied a faint flickering on the wall high above. He came to a halt. "They're up there," he said, pointing to the cave.

"We need to start climbing," Hector said. "It's flowing faster."

"We can camp inside the cave, it's high enough up the wall."

"But Apaches are inside."

"So let's get them out."

They dismounted and led the horses and packmules up the slope, hard progress in the downpour. Midway to the top Jubal gave Bardo's reins to Hector. "Wait here," he whispered. He went on afoot.

From where they stood on the valley wall they could smell smoke in the air. Through blowing rain Hector studied the cave entrance, the glow of firelight reflected on stone.

After a while Jubal returned with his pistol drawn. "I could hear them talking, speaking Apache."

"How many inside?" Moroni asked.

"I couldn't get a look, the cave curves around just past the entrance. There's only one way in, one way out. We got them." He turned to Hector. "The smoke's coming through a narrow hole farther up the slope. Take Fuentes and some blankets and cover the opening."

They hobbled the horses and mules on the slope. Three vaqueros remained behind to guard them while the others resumed the climb.

The men drew their weapons. Jubal gave a final order. "Don't fire on anyone you can't see clearly," he said. "I'll kill the man who shoots John Russell by mistake."

They went up the slope and crossed at an angle toward the mouth of the cave. Hector and Fuentes split off to circle around. Down below on the dark valley floor an unseen deluge rumbled and growled, carrying away everything that stood in its path.

* * *

Jubal positioned his men to the side of the entrance. Moroni offered him a double-barreled 12-gauge. Jubal took the weapon and broke it open to check the loads, then snapped it shut and cocked both hammers back. They stood waiting in the rain and the dark.

Angel cradled a .30-30, eyes wide, his world washed in a strange clarity. Each second seemed building toward profound release.

Smoke drifted out the entrance. Muted voices, tones of panic. Then coughing and shouting over the cries of a child.

Jubal shouldered the 12-gauge and called out in Spanish. "Leave your guns and step outside if you want to live. We're here for the red-headed boy."

They waited.

A rifleshot cracked inside the cave.

There was a long pause, then a muzzle flash in the

smoky opening, another rifleshot, and a bullet whined past Jubal's ear. A warrior charged out of the smoke. He wore buckskins and he raised a pair of big revolvers over his head and ran screaming toward them. Behind him a young girl burst out of the cave, gripping the hands of two smaller children. They ran in the opposite direction of the warrior, away from the line of gunmen.

The warrior leveled his pistol-barrels at Jubal. He never got off a shot. The vaqueros opened up on him all at once—bullets riddled the Apache, a dozen hits, then Jubal emptied the shotgun into his chest. For a moment the warrior remained on his feet, his momentum and the impact of the barrage contorting his body in a danse macabre that seemed to go on forever, but a split second later he lay motionless in the rain.

A squaw stepped into view. She raised an ancient-looking rifle and stood firing half-blind from the smoke, working the lever as fast as she could, trying to lay down a covering fire for the running children. When Angel shot her through the heart, the rifle spilled from her hands.

Jubal's ears were ringing. He shouted for them to go after the escaping Apache children. Moroni and his brothers raced down the slope. They started running full tilt when they realized the girl was leading her charges directly to the floodwaters. The children were determined to fling themselves into that raging torrent before they'd suffer capture.

The boy slipped and fell in the grass. The girls went rushing back for him and jerked him to his feet, then they ran on. It gave the Mormons the time they needed to catch up. They stopped the children at the water's edge.

* * *

Jubal yelled into his cupped hands. "Hector, open it up."

Waiting for the smoke to clear they smelled a horrendous stench emanating from the cave. They swore and covered their faces with bandanas.

Angel stood staring at the squaw. He took his hat off and rain soaked his hair.

"I never killed a person before," he said, looking as though he were going to be sick.

"Put it away," Jubal told him. "She'd have torn your throat out like a mountain lion. You didn't do anything wrong here."

Ortiz pulled the pair of old single-action Colts from the warrior's hands. He released the cylinders. "Not a round or even an empty shell in either one. The crazy bastard rushed us with empty pistols."

"Why did he do it?" Gutiérrez wanted to know.

"To give the little ones a chance," Jubal said. "So we'd fire on him while they made their run."

They stared down at the dead man. Raindrops clung to his eyelashes.

"Hell," Gutiérrez said, "that was almost human of him."

Moroni returned carrying a girl perhaps four years-old. Ammon trailed after him with a thrashing little boy in a bear-hug. The other girl was older by about three years or so and she walked calmly up the slope, Layton's hand clamped around her wrist. When she reached her companions, she jerked free of his grip and went to the weeping boy and took him from Ammon. She stood before the killers of their family.

Ammon Thayne rubbed his palm and scowled. "Little wolf cub bit my hand," he said.

"Should've let him jump in and drown," Ortiz said.

When the smoke dissipated, Jubal entered the mouth of the cave. He held a bandana against his nose and mouth, the stench still rising from the fire, and his shadow played huge and distorted on the wall. He stepped farther inside and saw the gray-haired woman lying in the flames.

A poultice was tied about her right ankle and there was a staff, cut from an ocotillo stalk, resting nearby. Most of her head was missing. He remembered the first rifleshot they'd heard—the crippled old woman had killed herself, unable to run with the others or stand and fight, and her body had fallen half in the firepit. The air reeked of burnt flesh. Pale smoke rose through a gap in the ceiling like ascending spirits.

A stock of dry wood rested in the corner. Iron shoes and mule bones on the floor amid the ash. Their possessions were meager indeed. At his feet a fallen cornhusk doll. A bow and quiver of cane arrows, knives fashioned from scrap iron, leather purses, gourd bowls, and a braided horse-hair rope.

He turned and stepped back toward the entrance. "Lead the kids away," he called. "There's another dead one in here and I don't want them to see."

Even though they'd already seen the worst of it. Even though he knew they'd be seeing it in their dreams for years to come.

Jubal bent and gripped the dead woman by the ankles. He dragged her from the fire, her dress still burning, and he was weeping as he pulled her out into the rainy night.

"We'd better keep that fire going," Gutiérrez said. "How's hot coffee sound in the morning?"

* * *

They led the horses and mules to an oak grove above the valley and cross-sidelined them. Jubal chose two men for the first watch over the caballada and they reloaded their weapons and settled in.

The others returned to the cave. The interior still reeked, but it was all the shelter there was. Jubal added wood to the fire and they sat warming cans of beans. The Apache children huddled against the far wall, whispering to each other, strips of rawhide around their hands and feet. When Angel offered them jerky and beans from his plate, they fell silent and cast terrified glances at him.

Moroni stood guard at the entrance, cradling a Winchester. The men lay down to sleep. Those few who managed to nod off were troubled with black dreams that night.

* * *

Gutiérrez and Ortiz had last watch over the caballada before dawn. When the rain abated, they stood in the oaks, the horses cropping grass nearby, and Gutierrez took a leather purse from his pack and shone a flashlight on it.

"Look at this."

"What is it?" Ortiz asked.

"Our fortune. I found it in the cave."

He opened the bag. It was full of rocks and he picked one up and turned it in the beam for Ortiz to see the veins of silver. "That's not all," he said. He set the rock down and took something from his pocket. He handed it to Ortiz—an old Spanish coin bearing the date 1621.

"You know what this means?" Gutiérrez questioned him. "The coin and the ore?"

"Tayopa is real."

Gutiérrez hefted the rock. "This doesn't feel like a myth to me. I've been keeping my eyes open, looking for the markers on that map. I saw a likely place three days ago."

"Why didn't you speak up?"

"You think McKenna would've let me go search? All he ever thinks about is that lost boy of his. Let him chase ghosts. Tonight proved we don't have to be afraid of Apaches. Are you with me?"

"What do you want to do?"

His eyes flashed with a crazed intensity. "We go back, start searching from the place I saw, and claim our fortunes. Tayopa is waiting for us, my friend."

* * *

When the others rose at dawn, the glutted river on the valley floor had reduced to a shallow stream and Gutiérrez and Ortiz were missing. A pair of horses and packmules were gone as well, the tracks leading northwest back into the foothills. They'd taken ammunition and much of the remaining food and left the caballada unguarded. Hector stood in the oak grove and cursed them for deserters and thieves.

"I hope they ride straight into a rancheria full of gut-eaters," he said.

"You may get your wish," Jubal said.

"Where the hell do they think they're going?" Hector asked.

"Gutiérrez has Tayopa fever. He's gone treasure hunting and convinced Ortiz to join him."

"I say we run them down and shoot their horses. They can walk to Tayopa."

"Let them go," Jubal said. He was sipping hot coffee, his first cup since they'd arrived in the foothills. "We're headed home anyway. No choice. We've got to take the little ones down to the valley."

"And then?"

"Then we resupply and do it again."

"Before we ride out," Hector said, "do you want to bury the Apaches we killed?"

Jubal pitched out the remainder of his coffee on the ground. "Leave them for the coyotes," he said.

91

BILDUNGSROMAN II

Is There No Help for the Widow's Son?

July 21, 1886, Sonora

Someone had crossed out *Carretas* on the hand-painted sign at the edge of the village and the prankster had written *Chingada* above it in bright red letters. Cain rode down the empty street, a dirt track running between adobe hovels. He drew up in front of the cantina and unhorsed. Bullet-pocked walls. A thatched roof plastered with mud. Four horses tied at the rail next to a mule outfitted with a U.S. Cavalry-issue McClellan saddle.

Cain tied his horse's reins. He stepped through the open door of the cantina and stood there a moment letting his eyes adjust to the dimness. The fat man behind the bar glanced up. He offered no greeting, returning instead to his game of solitaire and fanning himself with a flyswatter. The bald circle on his head shone with sweat. At the far end of the bar an old man sat drinking alone.

Only one table was occupied—four Mexicans sitting with a gringo in a blue uniform. Cain figured him for an

93

army scout. The news had spread all over the countryside: U.S. troops were crossing the border, chasing after Geronimo's renegade Apaches.

The American was silent. His companions laughed and cracked jokes and poured shots from a bottle of clear liquid. All of them were armed with pistols in plain sight.

When Cain walked past the table, the American's eyes flashed to the ring on his finger, then up to the boy's face. Something like recognition in his gaze. Puzzlement as well.

Cain ignored him and stepped to the bar.

"Pulque," he said.

The bartender set down his flyswatter. He poured the drink without a word and took Cain's money and went back to his cards. Cain sipped his mug. He stared at the cracked and filthy mirror behind the bar. At the table it was the American's turn to drink and the Mexicans urged him on with curses and laughter.

A Mexican with a sly grin draped his arm around the American's shoulders. He gestured toward the others. "You see these bad mens?" he said in broken English. "They make me a bet. My amigos, they bet me you can't drink more than them. You win them for me, uh? Then I take you there, my good amigo, where you're wanting to go to. Simple, uh? Win them for me and I show you where Geronimo hide. You ask anybody here, they tell you Raul know the Apache places."

"Afraid I'm not much of a gambler," the American said. He glanced toward the mirror. "More of a traveling man, east to west."

Raul poured another shot from the bottle. "Everybody gamble sometime. You already take a big one, soon as you crossed that border." He clapped him on the back and advised, "Despacio se va lejos."

The American ignored the glass and reached for the bottle instead. He raised it to his lips and rocked his head back and seemed to take a long swig before slamming the bottle down and coughing. Cain guessed he'd used his tongue to hold back most of the tequila. He could see the look of suspicion on Raul's face in the mirror, then the American rose and dropped a coin on the table and put on his cavalry Stetson.

"Gentlemen, I believe that's enough for me." He squared his hat and started for the door. "As I mentioned, the U.S. Government is prepared to reward you for information aiding in the capture of Geronimo. General Miles appreciates your courtesy."

"Set down," Raul told him. He drew his pistol and placed it on the table. "Mucho bad mens around here. You ride alone without your amigos for to protect you, maybe something bad happen. Stay and drink, jes? Then Raul take you where you going."

The American stared into the mirror. "No help for a widow's son, is there?" he asked.

Cain sipped pulque.

Raul laughed as though the American had made a joke. He shook his head. "No, there sure ain't. Very much funny, you. Now set the hell down."

He sank back into his chair, a bleak expression on his face. The next man to drink cursed and drained the glass and slid it across the table for Raul to fill again.

Cain emptied his mug. He understood the situation could turn deadly at any moment, but he remained at the bar, curiosity rooting him. He'd glimpsed the look of impossible recognition in the American's eyes, a stranger who seemed to know him. He had to find out what it meant. How such a thing could be so.

The man who'd just finished his shot rose and stepped carefully to the bar and ordered pulque. He glanced at the boy and told the bartender another for his hermano as well.

Cain shook his head. "No more for me, thanks," he said in Spanish.

"Drink with me, brother. I'm Diego Cortez and I have a secret talent. You know what it is? I can tell when a man's thirsty just by looking at him."

The bartender poured the pulque, filling his mug. Cain kept his eyes on the mirror and didn't take a drink.

It was the American's turn again and this time after Raul filled the glass he set the bottle aside out of the American's reach. The American hesitated. Then he took the shot glass and knocked it back and cursed. Raul laughed his approval and poured again.

Cortez turned from watching them and saw Cain's mug still untouched. "Hey, I know you're thirsty, but you're not drinking. You got some kind of problem with me?"

"I don't have any problem with you."

"Good. Then come on and drink, brother."

It was coming whether he played along or not. Better now than later, he decided, and shifted to face Cortez.

"I'm not your brother, you son of a bitch."

The cantina went silent, everyone staring at the bar.

Cortez smiled. "You know something? I just remembered my knife's dirty." He reached slowly in his pocket and withdrew a claspknife and opened the rusted blade.

"Don't be nervous," he said. "I'm just going to clean it."

Cortez reached over and sank the blade in the boy's mug and stirred the pulque around. He looked him in the eye. "All clean, brother."

He wiped the side of the blade down Cain's shirt and turned the blade and wiped the other side. He stood staring, grinning.

No one said a word. At the table Raul chuckled.

Cain drew his pistol, cocking it in the same blur of motion, and shot Cortez between the eyes. Then he was turning to face the table even as the dead man dropped to the floor. Raul already had his gun in hand. He was bringing up the barrel when Cain shot him twice in the chest and he reared back in his chair and fell over. Still seated, the American fired under the table. He pumped three rounds into the belly of the Mexican opposite him.

Cain swung to deal with the last man. The Mexican was rising up, pistol in hand, firing drunk and desperate, and he sent a bullet thumping into the bar. Splinters stung Cain's cheek. Cain hit him centermass, a pair of shots to the chest, enough to bring him down, then the .44 was empty.

The American jumped up and swung his pistol in Cain's

direction. For an instant the barrel's black void stared across at him, then it spoke with a flaming tongue. The mirror shattered behind Cain. He dove as the American pulled the trigger again.

Cain rolled and came up glimpsing the American's true target, the bartender raising a sawed-off 12-gauge. The pistol barked. A hole appeared in the bartender's forehead like the opening of a mystic third eye. Then the shotgun discharged into the thatched ceiling.

Cain snatched up the gun from Cortez's holster.

The gutshot Mexican was slumped over the table, clutching his belly, three bullets from the American's gun in his bulging stomach. He murmured pleas for forgiveness. Cain shot him midprayer, then stepped to Raul who lay breathing shallow breaths. He cocked the hammer back. Raul looked up and grinned, blood on an eyetooth, and Cain finished him with a coup de grâce.

The old man at the bar stared down at the dead. He cut his eyes to the gringos. They stood working the ejector rods of their pistols, turning cylinders and spitting out empty shells. He crossed himself, leaned over to take a bottle from the stock on the wall, then turned and hurried out.

When they'd finished reloading, the American nodded at Cain.

"Let's go," he said.

* * *

They left Carretas riding hard, the American on the mule, Cain following on his bay, and they kept the mounts to a fast clip. Some distance outside the village the trail led beside an arroyo. A pair of Apaches rode up the banks on mules. They were wearing breechclouts and blue uniform jackets, red headbands holding back their long hair, and they gripped rifles.

The American reined in and glanced back to make sure Cain wasn't alarmed. "It's all right," he said. "They're cavalry scouts."

Cain drew up behind him.

"We heard shots," one of the Apaches said. "You told us there wouldn't be no trouble if we waited for you out here."

"I was mistaken," the American said. "Keep watch on our trail. I've got to have a talk with this young man."

He motioned Cain forward. When Cain stepped his horse up beside him, the American offered his hand and introduced himself.

"Second Lieutenant Aubrey Eliot," he said as they shook. "6th Cavalry."

"My name's—"

"I know who you are."

"You do?"

"You're the little shit who owes me an explanation."

Aubrey swung a left hook. It landed against Cain's chin and his head snapped to the side, then Aubrey jerked him from the saddle and he hit the ground.

The cavalry officer dismounted and stepped toward him.

Cain spat. He rose cursing and charged. They fell and rolled in the dust, their mounts standing by, watching, while the Apache scouts made a bet how long the boy would last.

Aubrey and Cain were both armed and they'd killed five men between them only minutes earlier, but now neither man went for his pistol. They scrambled to their feet, traded punches. Cain slammed a fist in Aubrey's stomach. He moved fast and struck hard, but his reach was short and he was taking three blows for each one he gave. Aubrey was tall, long-limbed. Getting in close was Cain's only chance. He rushed Aubrey and knocked him off balance and they went tumbling down the side of the arroyo.

When Aubrey hit the bottom, he grunted. At once Cain was on him, raining punches, pressed close to defeat Aubrey's superior reach, so close it seemed almost an embrace. Aubrey struggled for distance. He managed to scramble away, then Cain dove after him, but Aubrey was ready. He landed a blow so hard the boy's vision swam. By the time Cain shook himself out of the daze, he was pinned facedown in the dirt.

"Get the hell off," he yelled.

Aubrey spat blood. He wiped his busted lip on the sleeve of his uniform and dug his knee into Cain's back. He twisted the boy's arm. "What did you do to him, you son of a bitch?"

"I don't know who the hell you're talkin about."

"The man who wore that ring. The one you're wearing now, the one you stole." Aubrey made a fist and held it close to Cain's eye. "Look there. You see something familiar?"

Aubrey wore a ring on his little finger. When Cain recognized the square and compass design, a sick feeling came over him.

"Did you kill him?" Aubrey demanded. "Don't lie to me. I hear one word out of your mouth that's not gospel, it'll be your last."

"I didn't kill him. I found it."

"You think I'm bloodsimple?"

"It's the truth."

Aubrey looked at the boy's ill-fitting shirt, too big for him. "You're a road agent. You killed him and stole the ring."

"I swear I didn't. I swear on my mater's grave."

Aubrey gripped the ring around the boy's finger and tried to tug it free, but it wouldn't come loose. He drew his pistol. "One last question. You have a preference whether I cut your finger off before or after I kill you?"

Cain didn't make a sound.

"You know what it means, that ring you're wearing?" Aubrey asked.

"I know what it means to me. I reckon that's all I need to know. You can go to hell."

"Boy, you're flashing the ring of a 33rd degree Freemason. We don't appreciate our brothers coming down here to get murdered by dumb little shits like you. I'll ask you again and if I don't like what I hear, I'm going to put a slug in your brainpan."

He thumbed the hammer back and touched the cold barrel to the boy's temple. "Did you murder the man who wore that ring?"

Cain told him everything. The corpse in the river, his father's shocked reaction to the ring, how the boy used that fear to survive. He told Aubrey of his wanderings in Mexico, his occupation of the previous months. Travelers he'd robbed and killed. He held nothing back save Killcrop's confession.

When Cain finished his account, Aubrey eased the hammer down. He holstered his pistol and rose and offered the boy his hand. Cain took it and got to his feet.

"You believe me?" Cain asked.

"Yeah, kid. I believe you."

Cain slipped the ring free of his finger without difficulty and held it out. "Take it. You say it don't belong to me."

Aubrey stared. "Maybe I was wrong. Hang on to it, you might need it someday. But you can't wear it on your finger—keep it on a string around your neck, all right?"

Cain nodded. He placed the ring in his breastpocket for the time being.

"That hellhole we rode out of?" Aubrey said. "That was Carretas, end of the line. The mountains to the west are Apache country and Mexicans won't set foot in them. You handled yourself back there, saved my hide, but don't expect to go into the sierras alone and ride out again. Not without getting your scalp trimmed. You've been running a long time, but you just ran out of road."

Aubrey explained he was the officer in command of

a company of White Mountain Apache scouts. General Nelson Miles had dispatched him to seek out Geronimo and his band of renegades for a parley. Aubrey chose to venture into Mexico with only two trusted scouts to aide him. Their pursuit had taken them east from Sonora, cutting through the Guadalupe Mountains and into Chihuahua. Already in the sierras was the 4th Calvary on a mission to find and kill Geronimo. Aubrey and his men had been following the trail left by a company of the 4th when they'd reached Carretas and he'd ordered the scouts to wait outside the village while he made inquiries. The locals were understandably skittish around Apaches, whether in the employ of the U.S. military or otherwise.

"You helped me out of a jackpot," he told Cain. "Now you're free to go back to what you were doing, or you can come with us."

"Why would I do that?"

"There's the fact you'd be doing your country a service, if that's any appeal to you. I can't promise you'll live to be old, fat, and happy, but the cavalry will give you something to go against and when you sit at our table, you'll belong there, same as the man beside you. Count on that. What do you think?"

Cain spat. "I reckon I'm goin with you then."

* * *

After two weeks and over a hundred and fifty miles of hard traveling they found the main column of the 4th Cavalry in the Sierra Madre. It was the third of August, 1886. Captain Henry Lawton wasn't pleased to see them. He allowed Aubrey to join his command only after making it clear Geronimo's death remained the goal of his mission.

"If I find Geronimo, I'll attack him," the captain said. "I refuse to have anything to do with this plan to treat with him."

Lawton's men were weary of the fruitless search. The trail of the Apaches had washed away in the rain weeks earlier and no one had any idea where their camp lay hidden.

Aubrey arranged a job for the boy helping with the packmules. When he presented Cain to the chief packer, the man looked him up and down and spat. "Kindly scrawny. You sure he's able?"

"He's not Abel—he's Cain," Aubrey said. "And he'll do just fine."

* * *

Aubrey's family were Boston Brahman. His father Elihu Eliot had been a bank president, his uncle a senator. He grew up on Beacon Hill where his childhood summers were spent running down those narrow cobblestone streets with friends, the red brick homes and high colonial buildings throwing shadows over them.

Aubrey was the youngest of the Eliots, his mother's last pregnancy a surprise, coming long after she'd believed the Eliot brood complete. Her sixth and final child would prove the most stubborn. Even when he was only a toddler the force of Aubrey's will had exhausted his mother's patience.

Edmund, Aubrey's eldest sibling by fourteen years and the family's favorite son, fell at the Second Battle of Cold Harbor in mid-June, 1864, months after graduating West Point. The Eliots were attending a Fourth of July picnic in the Common when a house servant crossed Beacon Street and into the park. The manservant's walk was slow, his face grim. In his hand a copy of the War Department's newly published casualty list.

Six-year-old Aubrey stood with his parents under the Great Elm. His father remained stoic when the servant informed him of the news. His mother's reaction was unthinking, a shocked outburst, Cynthia Eliot crying, "Why couldn't it have been Aubrey?" At once she dropped to her knees and offered a profusion of apologies, but neither mother nor son would ever forget the moment.

Aubrey went on to attend Williams College with plans to study for the bar. The unexpected death of his father and his own growing dissatisfaction set him on a wholly different course. After his second year he arranged a transfer to West Point and against his mother's wishes matriculated there in 1876. Rumors of a scandal involving a married woman, several years his senior and highly prominent in society, caused a severance of family ties. Even his sisters refused to speak with him. His uncle suspended Aubrey's monthly stipend. Perhaps it was hoped these actions would persuade him to choose a career in banking or law. If so, the tactic failed. In addition to providing free education the Point paid a salary and Aubrey's needs were simple and few. In the disciplined environment of the academy he felt more at liberty than ever in his life, pulling pranks, making new friends, all while his studies went exceptionally well. It was also at the Point that Aubrey was initiated into the brotherhood of Freemasonry.

Commissioned a Second Lieutenant in the 6th Cavalry he was assigned to Fort Wingate, New Mexico, where he led patrols of Apache and Navajo scouts. They fought skirmishes with Victorio's band of renegades in the Devil's Mountains. Aubrey earned the respect and loyalty of his men. He found the Indian scouts to be formidable soldiers. For his part he sought to make full use of their talents without too rigid an application of military regulation.

Mindful of Aubrey's esteem among the Apaches, General Crook made him Commandant of the White Mountain Indian Reservation. When Aubrey arrested a territorial judge for defrauding reservation subjects, a clash with the general was the immediate result. Crook insisted he drop the charges. Aubrey refused. His stubborn position on the matter alienated him from his superiors and led to a transfer in 1885 to Commander of Navajo scouts.

Crook lost his own command when Geronimo and Naiche, chief of the Chiricahua, escaped into Mexico with thirty-four warriors, women, and children. General Nelson Miles replaced Crook in April, 1886. Miles dispatched 5,000 troops to patrol the border and guard waterholes. On the general's orders the 4th Cavalry rode into the sierras to hunt down Geronimo and end the renegade problem for good. Months of futile searching followed. Miles hedged his bet, unwilling to see his career—like Crook's—destroyed over a handful of Apaches. He formed a desperate plan to bring in Geronimo peacefully. He needed a man Geronimo would trust, but Britton Davis was a civilian now, Emmet Crawford assassinated by Mexican militia, and all of his own officers were unfamiliar with the Chiricahua.

His only option was the outcast. Aubrey Eliot knew every member of the hostile band, knew their families and the suffering they'd endured on the reservation. Miles summoned the lieutenant to his office and issued an order—find Geronimo and negotiate a peaceful surrender.

By that summer of 1886 Aubrey was twenty-eight years-old and he wanted nothing more than adventure in whatever way it came. He accepted the impossible task.

* * *

Word reached Lawton's camp that Geronimo had sent a pair of women into Fronteras. They'd bartered food and mescal and inquired if the Mexicans were open to peace talks.

"Get the mules ready," Aubrey told Cain.

In the middle of the night Aubrey set out for the pueblo, seventy miles to the northwest. His squad consisted of the Apache scouts Martine and Kayitah, interpreter George Wratten, Cain the packer, and half a dozen of Lawton's soldiers.

By the time Aubrey arrived in Fronteras the Apache women had departed with coffee, sugar, and mescal. Aubrey spoke to the prefecto of the district, a man named Aguirre. When the lieutenant told him why he'd come, Aguirre laughed and said, "There is no war without blood. It's never been done, my friend. You want the killing to stop? Let me show you how." Then the prefecto shared his plan. Feigning a desire for peace negotiations he'd lure the Apaches in, get them drunk, and massacre the entire band.

Lawton and Aguirre both wanted Geronimo dead. Aubrey's mission appeared hopeless.

For the following two days Aubrey refrained from any attempt to contact the Chiricahua. Hearing this news Lawton himself rode out to question him, but by the time he spoke with Aubrey, Lawton was thoroughly intoxicated. Second in command Leonard Wood relieved the captain of his duties and ordered Aubrey to complete his assignment.

Meeting once again with Aguirre, Aubrey lied to the prefecto. His mission had been terminated, he said, and they must rejoin the main column.

At dusk on August 22nd Aubrey led out his small party under the watching eyes of Aguirre. He'd persuaded two additional interpreters to join him, a man from Fronteras named Jesus Maria Yestes and chief of scouts Tom Horn. They headed south as though their search had ended. Six miles out of the pueblo, darkness gave them cover. They rode down an arroyo and turned east into the sierras and soon after midnight Aubrey led them north toward Geronimo's camp.

The next morning Martine and Kayitah picked up the trail of the Apache women's mules.

* * *

Two days later they stood waiting along the shaded bend of the Bavispe. Aubrey faced the boy he'd taken to calling Abel Cain. "If they smell a threat," he cautioned, "we're all graveyard dead before you can blink. This isn't the cantina, Abel Cain. No matter what happens, don't touch your weapon. That's an order."

Cain nodded. "Yessir."

The previous day Aubrey sent the Apache scouts ahead into the Chiricahua camp, a rocky peak overlooking the valley. At sunset Martine had returned alone. Kayitah was being held in the stronghold, a hostage to fortune—Geronimo had agreed to talk with Aubrey.

Martine led them out at dawn.

The bulk of their force had remained behind in a cane brake, too distant to be of any aid. For the final approach only Aubrey, Horn, Martine, Cain, and the interpreters would be present. They watched the mountain and waited.

At eight o'clock the warriors appeared high on the mountain, making their descent with rifles in hand. Cain glanced at Martine. The scout was usually stone-faced, but now he looked nervous as Judas on Judgement Day. A shiver of fear went up Cain's spine. What if Geronimo had lied, luring them in for the kill? There could be no escape from the trap.

Cain looked over at Aubrey and saw him not just composed but excited, looking forward to whatever came, a fight to the death or a friendly chat with the old butcher himself.

When the Apaches reached the base of the mountain, they disappeared.

George Wratten swore. "What the hell are they up to?"

"Stay calm," Aubrey said. He tossed Cain a grin, letting him know they were about to have some entertainment.

Chiricahua Apaches burst out of the brush all about them. Twenty-one warriors surrounded the little group, gripping rifles and pistols. When Cain spotted Kayitah, alive and unharmed, he breathed a sigh of relief.

Geronimo was nowhere to be seen.

Aubrey greeted them in Spanish and unhitched his gunbelt and placed his sidearm on the ground. The Apaches demanded booze and tobacco.

"I'm sorry," Aubrey said. "I don't have any alcohol." Then he directed Cain to dispense tobacco, rolling paper, and matches. The boy went down the line of renegade killers and handed out the makings.

The first warriors were lighting up when an Apache with a polka dot bandana over his hair emerged from the brush. He set his rifle down and stepped forward, offering Aubrey his hand.

"How are you?" Geronimo asked.

For an instant Cain met Geronimo's eyes. He gazed into the coldest thousand-yard stare he'd ever seen in his life, then glanced quickly away. A quality in those eyes beyond the concepts of fear or courage. Absolute resolve, indifference to fortune. Amor fati.

It would be many years until at a mirror one morning Cain recognized the selfsame look in his own eyes.

CHAPTER SIX

Though it was Zunde who'd proposed the strike against the logging crew he wouldn't be joining the raiders. The day after the earthquake he surprised everyone, announcing that he would be joining Matzus and Taza in taking their families and leaving Pa-Gotzin-Kay for the winter. He wished the chief strong Power and fine spoils.

Carnoviste did his best to conceal his anger at what Zunde had done—forcing Carnoviste into accepting the necessity of a raid, then withdrawing from participation. It meant Zunde risked no blame if the raid was a failure and cost them the life of a warrior. Full responsibility for the outcome would lie on Carnoviste's shoulders alone. By leaving with Matzus and Taza, now Zunde no longer operated under the chief's gaze. He'd be free to organize a separate raiding party made up of braves who's already departed to winter down below.

It was a cunning move. Zunde desired the chieftainship or else to go his own way.

The next morning the village gathered at the trailhead to say their goodbyes. Nantan sang a blessing over the families, protection on their journey below. The women all were weeping. Those who would remain behind cautioned their departing friends to stay safe until spring. Denali was doubly saddened—at his friend Chatto's leaving and the departure of Matzus. He hated the brave who'd killed his father and tossed the bloody scalp at his feet. Every day when he saw Matzus in the village Denali was overcome with thoughts of how he might kill him, but now he was filled with sorrow that the warrior was traveling beyond his grasp, vengeance impossible to fulfill until their return to Pa-Gotzin-Kay in the spring.

Denali and Chatto stood apart from the rest.

"I'm sorry you have to finish our duty alone," Chatto said. "It's no easy thing. Be careful, if we're right about Nantan…"

"You'll back again soon," Denali told him. "Then we'll face the bear together. Winter won't last so long."

He shook his head. "Longer than you know. I heard my father talking with Taza. They want to steal cattle all year. We won't be coming back after winter."

The news stunned Denali. Like himself, Chatto was fourteen winters old and they had become the best of friends. He tried to conceal the sudden sense of loss.

"Don't let the bear hurt our People," Chatto said. "Goodbye, my brother."

The friends embraced and broke away.

"I'll think of you when the thunder rolls," Denali said.

The families started down the trail, each of their mules dragging a travois loaded with dried meat and cowhides and a few scant possessions. Denali stood watching. He wondered if he'd ever see Chatto again. Ishton stepped up behind him and placed a hand on his shoulder.

* * *

"To be a good leader," Carnoviste said, "first you must serve."

Denali began preparations to join the raiding party. He would act as attendant to the warriors, seeing to their horses and meals in camp. As a novice he wouldn't take part in the raid itself, but his role nonetheless required much training.

A raider must learn the sacred language of war. On the war path men refrained from the use of common words for weapons and tools, calling each thing instead by its secret name, vouchsafed through the generations. War and raiding were separate duties, each with their own code, and the novice must be schooled in both. For this education Carnoviste sent him to the medicine man.

Denali was uneasy beginning his studies with Nantan, but the instruction was vital. They sat together in the wickiup. "Raiding has always been a way of life for the People," Nantan said. "War is another matter, never to be entered lightly or out of greed." War rose only from the necessity for revenge. Always it was to be treated with honor, its language heeded. Denali memorized the secret words for horses and mules, grass and water, women and enemies.

Raiders must take care not to break any taboo. Even a single mistake could spell disaster. In the four days leading up to their departure Nantan tutored him regarding a surfeit of taboos. More than the success of the raid, their very lives depended on perfect obedience.

Denali must sleep with his head pointed to the rising sun.

He must not eat the organs of any beast.

He must not allow his lips to touch water—instead he'd drink from a watertube.

He must not scratch himself with his fingernails but use a scratching stick.

He must not handle the remains of coyote or owl or snake.

"And most of all," Nantan said, "never a bear."

Denali tensed at the talk of bears. In the wickiup the medicine man stared across at him.

"Do you know why this is so?" Nantan asked.

"Carnoviste says when the wicked die their spirits come back sometimes. They live in wild things."

"Your father speaks the truth." Nantan explained that on death, the People journeyed to Chindin Kungua, the House of Ghosts, but from time to time a few returned to this world, inhabiting animals that the People were forbidden to eat or touch.

Finally when the lessons were complete, Nantan placed a novice cap, plumed with feathers, on Denali's head.

* * *

They were to be a small party, Carnoviste and the warriors

Pericho, Bihido, and young Estoni—with Denali as their orderly. The evening before they set out Nantan danced a circle around each raider four times and sang prayers of protection.

Afterward the warriors retired to their wickiups, one last night of sleep at home before the long trail. They were careful not to allow any pregnant woman to touch their weapons, for if such a thing occurred, their aim would be untrue.

At dawn the People once again lined the path to the switchbacks. The raiders led their horses forward. Only four of them now—during the night Bihido had changed his mind, deciding to stay in the village. "What a lazy one," Carnoviste said when he heard the news. Neither the chief nor any other would accuse a warrior of cowardice for declining to join a raid, but they had a right to judge such men lazy.

They paused for Nantan to touch their foreheads with sacred pollen. "My medicine goes with you," he said. "No bullet can find you. Go make the invaders sorry they entered the Blue Mountains."

Denali stepped down the line and stood before Ishton. "I know you'll make your father proud," she said.

"I hope so," he told her.

Then they were heading down the steep trail. He glanced back at the watchers on the rim and saw Ishton raise her hand. He raised his own and lingered a moment before turning to follow Carnoviste.

* * *

Rifles and ammunition were the prized spoils of a raid, far above livestock, clothes, or tools. In earlier times they'd treasured alcohol and tobacco. These days were more and more a matter of survival. Warriors took only what they needed, what they could get without too great a risk of life.

This raid was different, for it also served as an act of war. Nantan advised they take no spoils. Blood alone was their objective. Strike fear into the enemy—inflict brutal losses and disappear, leave the loggers reluctant to proceed farther. It would halt the line of trespass, if only for a time.

The raiders descended into the foothills. On the lower slopes they camped in the day and traveled by night. Denali tried to anticipate the needs of the warriors and he spoke only when spoken to.

They came upon a rancho's empty line camp and searched the weathered shack and found a cigar box with a few loose rounds of old .44 cartridges and took them. Denali led the mounts to water at a muddy stocktank while the warriors ate a meal of deer jerky. The horses refreshed, they went on a ways, then camped before dawn under an overhang of rock. Denali staked the horses in the grass and took first watch.

The following night they skirted a ravaged woods, low stumps everywhere on the hillside. Carnoviste slowed his horse and motioned to the novice. Denali rode up beside him.

"This is what they make of the People's estate," Carnoviste whispered. "They'll leave nothing to us, no place on the earth where the People can live in the old ways—unless we stop them now. Nantan was right. It has to be done."

They staked the horses in the woods that still remained. The warriors left Denali standing guard. He watched them go afoot to spy out the logging camp, gripping rifles, their long hair worn loose on the war path.

He waited in the dark. They were a long time scouting the camp, but when at last the warriors returned, it was agreed they'd strike early the next morning as the loggers began work. They settled in to sleep.

After Estoni relieved him on watch, Denali lay down with the others and tried to sleep, but sleep wouldn't come. Thoughts of tomorrow raced through his mind, a thousand fatal possibilities. He couldn't believe how soundly the others slept. As though the outcome were preordained, whatever shape it took, and their hearts at peace with providence. Finally the novice drifted to sleep at last.

In the dawn Denali stood holding the horses, listening. He heard the first rifleshot, then the others spaced close together. There was the bark of a pistol, one of the loggers returning fire, followed by three more shots and it was over.

He was startled to find a part of himself wishing he was with them. Darkly curious, how he'd conduct himself in the moment, what it meant to kill or be killed.

When the warriors came back at a run, Denali saw they were uninjured. Each man took his horse's reins from the novice and swung astride the saddle. "Mount up," Carnoviste told him. Denali climbed on his bay and they rode out beneath the shadowed canopy of the boughs.

He was eager to question them how it had gone, but he knew better than to ask. They kept riding all morning, stealth abandoned now for speed and distance. It was noon when they stopped to water at a spring and the horses crowded about the small pool and lowered their heads drinking. Denali stared at Carnoviste, who was examining a newly acquired revolver, a .45 that looked in good condition. The chief looked up.

"You want to know how it was, my son," Carnoviste said. "I can see the eagerness on your face."

"Yes, my chief," Denali said.

"A fine day, three good kills. We waited in the trees and shot them when they came up through the stumps. It was too late for them to run back, all open ground. The man with the pistol did his best to hold us off while his friends dragged one of the wounded behind a big stump. He died well, the man with the pistol. It was my honor to take his life. Not like the wounded one we could hear crying, begging for his mother."

"It's important to die well."

"Even more than how you live. What does a man of courage like him have to fear in the House of Ghosts?"

"A fine day then," Denali said.

"Three good kills. Now let the ones who come to replace their dead wonder who waits for them in the trees."

* * *

Late that afternoon higher in the foothills they came upon the trail of the riders. Two horsemen leading packmules, the tracks still fresh. Carnoviste led them after the trespassers.

* * *

Four days since Gutiérrez and Ortiz abandoned their post. Four days of riding and searching, Tayopa always just over the next rise. They'd found only a shelf of rock marked with a series of strange glyphs, a sunburst and coiled snake, but neither man could interpret the signs and so they wandered on in search of other landmarks. Ortiz soon lost faith in the hopeless pursuit, but all his doubts and begging couldn't persuade Gutiérrez to turn back. They pressed on, Ortiz the prisoner of a mad man's dream, yearning for the bunkhouse and safety more than silver, but too afraid to strike out on his own. "One more day," Gutiérrez told him each night. "Tayopa calls to me in my sleep. Tomorrow, she says, tomorrow I'm yours."

And now she lay before them.

The pair had ascended a timbered ridge, another in what seemed an endless series, and abruptly they found themselves looking down on the secret valley. They sat their horses and stared in disbelief. Just as the map promised, it was located in a fork of the Yaqui River and surrounded by high ridges. Even a skilled mountaineer wouldn't have suspected the valley's existence before almost stepping into it. Everything was exactly as described—at the center of the oval valley they spotted what was surely the ruins of the old church.

"You see her too?" Gutiérrez asked. "Am I dreaming?"

"If you are, then we're dreaming the same dream."

"We did what no one else could. We found her."

"I can't believe it," Ortiz said.

"Believe, my friend. Tayopa knew she couldn't hide from us. Destiny is on our side."

The treasure hunters rode down into the valley of their dreams. No breeze stirred the pines, no birds sang in the branches. Nothing broke that stillness. Ortiz crossed himself and Gutiérrez rested his palm on the grip of his pistol. The ground was strangely devoid of tracks or scat, without sign of any living presence save their own, as if birds and coyotes avoided that place.

They studied the fallen church. Foundation stones and collapsed concrete walls, the lignum vitae cross still standing. All corresponding to the map in perfect fidelity.

Pines with trunks three feet in diameter rose from the rubble of adobe houses. Water lay pooled in open shafts. A pair of nearby tunnels into the hillside looked ready to cave in at any moment. There was no slag heap visible nor the remains of a smelter and this puzzled them until Ortiz took a shovel from the packmule and dug into a mound of earth. He discovered the mound was a great pile of slag covered with an overburden of rock and dirt fallen from the slope above.

They hobbled the horses and mules. Gutiérrez stood in what had been the narthex of the church. Holding the map and a compass he began pacing off an approximation of the varas. Each vara measured thirty-three and a third inches. He judged his steps carefully. His course took them to the southeast toward the supposed location of the old Jesuit vault and they left the ruined church.

When they reached the end of the varas, they found no tunnel or iron door. Only a rocky slope, a steep rise of what appeared to be natural stone.

Gutiérrez cursed. "The door should be right here. I don't understand it."

"Maybe the map was right about everything except the door."

"There's nothing wrong with the map. This map has been good to us. I must have counted wrong, or the door's hidden somehow."

"We should wait till dark," Ortiz said.

"What good is the dark going to do? We won't be able to see a damn thing."

"The ghostlights will show us. They shine blue for silver, white for bones and they rise up at night."

"You believe that shit?" Gutiérrez asked.

"My cousin saw them once. He watched a ball of light rise up in the yard behind an old man's house. Everybody knew this old man was a miser. After the old miser died, my cousin snuck into the yard one night and started digging where he'd seen the blue light. You know what he found? A jar of silver coins."

"Your cousin drinks too much tequila. There's no such thing as ghostlights."

"The Jesuits used them to find minerals," Ortiz told

him. "Everybody knows they're real. It even says so in *De Re Metallica.*"

"You read *De Re Metallica*?"

"Do I look like a priest? You know I can't read Latin."

"Then how the hell do you know what it says?" Gutiérrez demanded.

"Everybody knows. Tonight, all we got to do is watch."

They returned to the church. Ortiz busied himself setting up camp. Gutiérrez paced off the varas once again and met with the same results. He put the map away, cursing.

When the sun sank behind the ridgeline and darkness fell over Tayopa, Gutiérrez joined Ortiz. For all his skepticism he stood watching the dusk, awaiting strange lights to rise from the earth. He even said a silent little prayer to the lights. After twenty minutes and still no orbs, Gutiérrez threw his hat on the ground and stomped it. "I knew it— your stupid ghostlights. There's no such thing." Then he stood cursing the non-existent lights for a full minute.

"No, please, Lalo," Ortiz said. "Don't say such things— you'll make them angry."

Gutiérrez called him a fool and cursed the lights all the harder.

"He doesn't mean it," Ortiz whispered.

After a while Gutiérrez calmed down and they spread their bedrolls in the ruins. The men had caution enough not to make a fire even in that valley. Their rifles and pistols lay close beside them.

"Plenty of time to find the door," Gutiérrez said. "We're wealthy men now and wealthy men can afford all the time in the world. Our supplies are holding up and the fight at the cave showed us the Apaches are nothing. Who's afraid of a few gut-eaters?"

"What will we do after we find it, Lalo?"

"Mark the trail on our way back home, so there's no chance of losing it. We'll carry enough silver to hire a crew and guards. Phelps Dodge can go to hell—Tayopa belongs to the man with the balls to take her."

They listened to the horses cropping the sparse winter grass. Gutiérrez produced a bottle of tequila from his saddlebag and opened it and they each took a swig in celebration.

"You were right," Ortiz said. "We did the smart thing. Think of McKenna and that Hector when they hear. Just picture their faces."

Gutiérrez laughed. "When they're old, they'll brag to their grandchildren they once knew the heroes who found Tayopa."

Ortiz drifted to sleep. Gutiérrez stayed up, sipping from the bottle, knowing he drank more than was wise and not caring. Then after a while he slept as well.

In his dream Gutiérrez woke in a ruins not unlike the ruins in which he slept and the ground trembled beneath him. He looked and saw a fissure open in the earth. Yawning wide as if hell itself would vomit forth a legion of the damned, sinners too wicked even for its climes. He crawled forward and peered over the edge. An iron door was set in the opposite wall some twenty feet below. He looked about for a reata, something to lower himself with, but there was nothing. He was thinking what to do, then the rusted hinges groaned and the ancient door slowly swung open.

Gutiérrez woke to a scream—cut off almost as soon as it began. He glanced toward his comrade.

A bloody smile across Ortiz's throat. Dark figures knelt over him, stabbing again and again, and his chest made sucking sounds as they pulled their blades free.

Gutiérrez reached out, grabbing for his pistol. He cursed—it wasn't there. Then he looked up and the Apache slammed the rifle-butt against his forehead.

* * *

The raiding party returned to Pa-Gotzin-Kay with their prisoner tied across the back of his own pack mule. Boys met them at the top of the trail. They cheered and ran forward to take the horses and mules.

When the raiders entered the village, wives and maidens broke out in eager cries at the sight of the Mexican captive. Widows stooped to pick up rocks. They pelted him, Gutiérrez grunting in pain. He was bent over the packsaddle, arms and legs tied under the mule's belly, no way to shield himself. A girl pulled a log from the fire and walked up and swung it hard against his rump in a shower of sparks. Gutiérrez let out a yelp. The warriors laughed.

Denali thanked those who congratulated him on his first raid. He realized several families were missing, departed for the winter—how much longer till they'd all be leaving?

126

He moved through the small crowd looking for Ishton.

Nantan appeared in front of him. "You performed well, novice?"

Denali nodded. "I did my duty. It was a good raid."

"And you broke no taboo?"

He saw Ishton step out of the wickiup. She wore her beaded buckskin robe and scanned the faces of the raiders.

"I broke none," Denali answered. He stepped past the medicine man and waved at Ishton.

She smiled and came forward. He was walking out to meet her when she veered off and went to Carnoviste and embraced him.

Denali froze in his footsteps. If a look of disappointment crossed his face, he was quick to hide it. He turned and walked away.

The raiders sat around the fire and divided their spoils. Carnoviste and Estoni gave up their share of the Mexicans' horses and mules in exchange for the Winchester rifles and 30-30 ammo. Pericho was content with the livestock. They allotted the supply of canned goods evenly among the women. Carnoviste made a gift of his bolt-action Springfield to Denali, while Estoni's old Krag-Jorgenson went to a brave whose own rifle was unreliable.

Carnoviste cut the Mexican loose. Gutiérrez dropped to his knees before the fire and begged their mercy in Spanish. His forehead sported a swollen purple bruise.

"My name is Eduardo Gutiérrez," he said jabbing at his chest. "I'm a peaceful man, my friends. You can call me Lalo." It wasn't his first introduction. Earlier along the trail he'd repeated his name over and over, hoping they'd be less inclined to kill him than if he was a stranger.

"We're all friends," he said. "We all want peace. No reason we can't get along."

Nantan reached his staff toward Gutiérrez and prodded his beer belly. "He looks like a fat sucking tick ready to pop," he said.

Everyone but Gutiérrez laughed. He rocked back and forth, murmuring endless Hail Marys. The warriors ignored him for the time being, but Denali knew it wouldn't be long before the man would envy his partner's fate.

Back in the hidden valley they'd searched the Mexicans' saddlebags and discovered the silver ore. "Rock-scratchers," Carnoviste had said, hatred plain in his voice. The People despised prospectors and the miners who followed after them, those who invaded their homeland and tore the earth.

Carnoviste had taken a shovel from the Mexicans' packs and dug a small hole near the church ruins. He placed the rocks inside and covered them over. "The white and yellow metals belong to the Mountain Spirits," he told Denali. "They forbid us to dig them. Some of the young braves deny it—they want to trade the white metal to the Mexicans for rifles and whiskey, but no good can come from it."

"Why not?"

"The Mountain Spirits don't forgive. It's bad medicine for any brave who shows the rock-scratchers where to find the metal. If you ever find any, give it back to the spirits."

There was a splash in the dark, the warriors pitching the dead man into a mine shaft. Otherwise the valley was silent. The usual sounds of the forest were missing there, no chirping crickets or songs of nightbirds. Denali studied the ruins and a feeling came over him as though he were being watched.

"What is this place?" he asked.

"Generations ago, our People were slaves here," Carnoviste said. "The priests forced us to dig the white metal. A band of warriors killed the priests and set our grandfathers free. Then a medicine man cursed the valley and they left the other miners, the ones not of our blood, chained in their tunnel. So their spirits would watch over the white metal and guard it forever."

"Only a fool would camp here. It's a ghost place."

Carnoviste nodded, proud he understood. "Come with me. I want to show you something."

The pair set out to the southeast. A waning moon shone on a high slope, everything washed in faint silver light, and they drew up at the foot of the steep incline.

"What do you see?" Carnoviste asked.

Denali shook his head, confused. "Nothing."

"Even in daylight you still couldn't spot it. This is where it's hidden."

"What's hidden?"

"The treasure of the dead."

Carnoviste said the warriors in that long ago had ground up limestone and blended it with water and animal blood, forming a mortar mix. They'd constructed a wall in front of the iron door in the hillside. When their handiwork was finished and dry, the wall appeared as natural stone.

"And behind the door?" Denali asked. He placed a palm on the cool stone wall.

"The skeletons of the priests and the white metal they died for."

* * *

That night at Pa-Gotzin-Kay Gutiérrez drank mescal and danced with them about the fire, a drunken smile on his face, and he clapped his fellow dancers on the back, the same warriors who'd abducted him. He called them his amigos and swore they threw the finest fiesta he'd ever attended. He howled at the moon like a wolf. Carnoviste draped an arm around the man's shoulders and told him in Apache that he danced very well for a dead dog.

When morning came, they gave him to the women. He was spread-eagled in the grass, still in a drunken slumber, his wrists and ankles lashed with rawhide to stakes driven into the ground. The women took the warrior's bows and gathered along one side of him.

Gutiérrez woke to an arrow sticking out of his thigh. He raised his head and stared at the feathered shaft a moment, utterly baffled, then a second arrow stabbed his hip and he let out a ragged scream.

Gutiérrez called to the friends he'd danced with the night before and begged for deliverance. The men watched from a distance, amused at the scene. Some of the women couldn't pull the bowstrings back far enough and these arrows whacked into him and bounced off. Others went deep and struck bone. The men answered his screams, shouting back in mock agony. Denali looked away, trying to put it out of his mind, but the tortured sobs were impossible to evade and at last he couldn't stand it anymore.

He stepped toward Nantan. "Isn't it true that Child of the Waters commanded if an enemy lay down his arms, his life must be spared?"

"So the grandfathers told it," Nantan said. "But this coyote didn't surrender in battle, boy. He was taken while he slept in our mountains."

They were standing apart from the rest of the men. Denali saw Carnoviste staring across at them, curious about their discussion. None of the other warriors paid them any mind.

"I don't mean to let him live," Denali said. "He decided that when he came into the Blue Mountains. But Child of the Waters would make it fast."

"Let him suffer as our own have suffered because of his kind."

"Why does it have to be this way?"

"When you're older and the Mexicans kill one of your brothers and cut him to pieces, then you'll understand. Then you'll cry for blood."

"There's too much blood already."

Nantan watched the grisly display. "Even your mother knows how to treat an enemy better than you, boy."

Denali turned and saw Ishton standing over Gutiérrez, spitting in his face. She handed a bow to a woman who'd lost her son in a raid two winters past. The old woman nocked a cane arrow and stood over Gutiérrez and pulled the string back with all the force she could muster. She smiled down at him and let go. The arrow impaled his stomach. The rest of the women joined in, letting arrows fly, and by the time they finished with him, the dead man looked like an enormous pincushion.

The body lay there all morning. Hawks circling above. After a while Carnoviste cut the cords and got a reata and tied the corpse's feet to a mule and dragged Gutiérrez to the edge of the cliff. He untied the reata and kicked him over the rim.

CHAPTER SEVEN

Dolores rose early while little Claudia still slept. She retrieved a tobacco pouch and matchbook from Jubal's study and took her pocketknife and slipped out of the house. Dew was heavy on the grass and the long blades wet the hem of her skirt. She'd anticipated the morning dew, gathering a bundle of twigs and dry grass the night before and placing it on a shelf in the barn, and now she carried the bundle out into the orchard.

A flat stone lay in a space between the trees. She kneeled beside it and set the kindling on its surface in two separate piles. She lit a match. When both piles were burning, she dropped a handful of tobacco into each flame and watched the smoke rise.

One sacrifice for Jubal and Angel's safe return, the other for the fault she perceived in her spirit.

The isolation of the ranch afforded a surplus of solitude. There were long moments of brooding self-reflection throughout her day. The danger of a mirrored pool. She'd begun to disparage herself with a black judgement that swept past anything she'd ever done or failed to do, swept past all motive and intention, and condemned her at the heart of who she was. A misshapen thing, this heart of hers. Out of true. A subtle voice gave constant accusation, calling her an imposter in her father's house. It demanded penance.

Dolores opened the knife. She touched the blade to her palm and drew it back. Then she turned her wrist and held her hand out over the fires, smoke passing through her splayed fingers, and droplets of blood fell into the flames with a faint hiss.

* * *

That evening Dolores and Claudia sat out on the porch. Dolores held a stereoscope to her eyes and looked on the world's faraway places while at her feet Claudia played with wooden horses on the tiles.

She lowered the viewer and removed the stereo-card, then fitted another into the stand. The card bore a pair of photographs side by side, each an image of the same scene, taken from slightly different angles. She raised the scope by its wooden grip and held it to her face as though she were a guest at a masquerade ball. The image came into focus through the dual lenses—Paris, the Avenue des Champs-Elysees. Dolores peered into another world.

When Dolores lowered the viewer again, she saw riders coming up the orchard road in the dusk. She rose and stared at the lead horseman.

"Papa's home," she told the girl.

"I see him," Claudia shouted, excited. She waved her

arm, toys forgotten. "Wave, Lola. Does he see us?"

As she spoke Jubal raised his hand and put his horse to a gallop.

"Did they find my brother?" Claudia asked. "Can Papa stay home with us now?"

Dolores strained to recognize the other riders, but they were little more than shadows in the dying light. "I hope so," she said. "But Papa might have to go again."

"Because he has to keep looking."

"Yes. Because he has to keep looking."

When Jubal passed through the gate, they saw that a child rode with him, a dark-skinned little boy.

"Look," Claudia shouted. "Look, it's my brother—Papa found him."

"That's not him," Dolores said.

The girl stared, confused. "He's not my brother?"

Jubal came up through the yard and stopped in front of the porch and he climbed down holding the boy and set him on the grass. Then he held his arms out to Claudia, a weary smile on his unshaven face.

"Hello, darlin."

Claudia stared. She backed away from him. He was bearded and covered in the dust of hard travel. The little girl took Dolores's hand and started to cry.

"It's okay," Dolores said. "It's Papa. He just has a beard again, that's all. You remember when he had a beard before, don't you?"

The Apache boy looked from Jubal to the crying girl and back again.

Vaqueros came from the bunkhouse to take the mounts. The searchers climbed down and surrendered their reins. Hector and Angel walked toward the porch, gripping the hands of two young Apache girls.

"See to the kids," Jubal told Dolores. He stepped onto the porch and moved past her and Claudia to the screendoor and disappeared inside.

* * *

Dolores spoke to each of the children in turn, the old words in the People's tongue sounding alien to her now. "Call me Dolores. Don't be afraid—everything's going to be all right. We're safe in the home of a good man."

She asked what they were called. They hung their heads and refused to answer her questions. Finally after much coaxing, the children told her their names very softly like defeated soldiers surrendering at last. Still they wouldn't look at her and no matter how she tried to comfort them they seemed more scared of her than anything else. This dark woman who dressed like a valley person but spoke their language.

When Jubal stepped out of the house, he was freshly shaven and smiling. For the first time in weeks he wore no gunbelt. Claudia jumped up and ran to him. Jubal caught her in his arms and raised her high.

Nestor rushed to make a quick supper for the men. When it was served, the cook apologized there hadn't been time to prepare the feast they'd earned. The vaqueros dined around the courtyard table, all of them ravenous after weeks of strict rations, all save Jubal who was too tired to eat. He only picked at his food.

Afterward the vaqueros retired to the bunkhouse, to bottles and cards. Angel stayed behind on the patio, content to watch Dolores's black hair shine in the glow of the cressetlamps. Hector sat beside his wife on the bench swing. They sipped from cups of coffee spiced with cinnamon and watched the Apache children playing with Claudia's dolls on the tiles.

Claudia didn't join them. Instead she sat in the chair beside her father and affected an unfamiliar haughtiness, from time to time condescending to give the newcomers a look of irritation. As if their easy amusement at common playthings taxed her patience.

Millers circled the lamps. Wesley nodded off in his wicker chair and issued snores so loud they caused the Apache boy to stare in apprehension. As though the sleeper were a rumbling monster. Jubal reached and took the pipe from the old man's hand and placed it on the side table.

The older of the two girls sat rocking a doll in her arms. Her little sister took bites from a tortilla and walked across the tiles spraddle-legged like a buzzard.

Dolores reached for her coffee mug on the table.

"What happened to your hand?" Jubal asked.

The question took her by surprise. She lowered her bandaged hand down to her lap and glanced away. "It's fine," she said.

"What happened?"

"I was washing dishes and cut it on a broken glass."

"Does it hurt?"

She shook her head, changed the subject. "If I went and got your guitar would you play it?"

He hadn't touched the instrument since Sara had been gone. For a while he didn't answer. Then he said, "Go get it."

She rose and ran to the door, bare feet slapping the tiles.

When Dolores returned, she was holding the guitar and a turtle-shell pick. The index and middle fingers of Jubal's right hand were missing at the second knuckle—he could no longer pluck the strings as he once had.

Jubal rested the guitar across his lap. He strummed the open strings with the pick and winced and sat tuning the guitar.

It was a cedar top, mahogany back and sides. If he held the rosette to his face and inhaled, he could smell the fragrance of the living wood. The guitar was of his own craftsmanship, made when he was a young man and entertained dreams of working as a luthier. He'd obsessed over the shaping of the wood, voicing the instrument carefully, countless hours in pursuit of that perfect acoustic balance he'd never quite managed to reach. In the end he believed it was a flawed construction, but it had shown a young man's potential.

Finished tuning, he played harmonics at the seventh and twelfth frets and let them ring. The Apache children stopped what they were doing and gave him full attention.

"What do you want to hear?" Jubal asked Dolores.

"Whatever you feel like playing."

"Give me more help than that."

"*Shenandoah*," she said.

"You know the words better than me."

"I can't sing."

"Of course you can."

He strummed the simple chord progression and raised his eyebrows at her. She shook her head, smiling. Jubal sang alone, getting the melody across successfully but just off-pitch, not beautiful by any means, honest instead, a quality in his voice that made you want to trust him somehow. It was easy to believe in his song.

The children moved closer and listened, transfixed by the music. Angel stepped up to the youngest Apache girl. He gripped her hands in his and directed her to rest her moccasined feet on the toes of his boots. Angel went dancing her about the patio.

When Jubal finished, Adela and Hector applauded.

"That was so good," Dolores told him. "Now do *Streets of Laredo*."

"Let's hear someone who can really play," Jubal said. He held out the guitar. "Angel, you still have all your fingers?"

"I'd rather hear you," Angel said.

"I'm done. Maybe you can get her to sing, I can't."

Angel took the guitar. Laughter drifted up from the bunkhouse on a cool breeze.

"Sing the one you always do at the round-up," Dolores

said.

"Aw, you don't want to hear that."

"Yes, I do. I love your voice."

The vaquero gave her a shy grin.

Jubal rose. "Goodnight," he told them.

"It's still early," Dolores said.

"Not for me." He started to the door, then paused and stood looking back at the Apache children. Orphans of war. Like so many others in that bloody country. "We'll need to find families to take them in," he said. "It should be done as soon as possible."

"You have to be sure of the families," Dolores said. "That they're kind people. I won't let them go with anyone cruel."

"Of course."

"Tomorrow we should take the little ones to Nácori," Angel said. "So the priest can baptize them."

"Why tomorrow?" Dolores demanded. "Let them rest a few days at least."

"We shouldn't wait," Angel said.

"Why not?"

"Because…"

"Because why?"

"They're unbaptized."

"So?"

Her tone was fierce, a current of rage running below the surface of her words. Angel looked at Jubal for help, but he only shook his head and raised his hands—the boy had pulled the mountain lion's tail, now he was on his own.

"Something bad might happen," Angel said finally.

"They might all die in their sleep," Dolores said. "What then?"

"It wouldn't be good because—"

"Because they're unbaptized, I know. But they're little ones who don't know anything about right and wrong. How could they have sinned?"

"They were born in it," he said.

"Born in sin. You believe that?"

The children had returned to their toys and games, unconcerned with the argument. Angel watched them at play.

"I don't know," he said. "I guess I do."

"Then you'd better take them to your priest right now." Dolores bolted up from her chair and stepped past Angel and Jubal. "Goodnight. I'm too tired for this."

"Wait," Angel called. "I thought you wanted to hear a song."

The door swung shut behind her.

Angel groaned. "What's wrong with me? I should never have opened my mouth." He set the guitar down and rose to start after her.

Jubal stopped him, gripping his arm. "Don't make it worse."

"I have to tell her I'm sorry."

"Let her cool off first. Right now, time is all you can give her."

Angel shook his head. "She must hate me now."

"I don't think you could make her so mad if she didn't care for you very much. She's just angry at the way things are."

CHAPTER EIGHT

All the clovenhoofed on Pa-Gotzin-Kay were stricken with a terrible fever. It came upon them of a sudden. One day Carnoviste spotted a buck with a pair of great branching antlers and the buck saw him as well but didn't try to run. Carnoviste brought him down with a single arrow. When he approached the carcass, he saw the foamy drool about the buck's mouth and the ruptured blisters on the skin about its hooves. He left the buck untouched in the grass and warned the other hunters of the sickness. There was no use. Soon the fever spread to the People's small herd of cattle, then the handful of goats they kept. Within a moon all the deer and bighorn sheep had wasted to skin and bones, lame and ravaged with fever. Newborn fawns perished when their hearts burned out. The People killed their sick herds and pushed the carcasses off the cliff. They turned to hunting rabbits and turkeys and trapping moles, but the winter was a hard one and what game they caught was shared in common among them so that there was often little to eat. The People were thin and gaunt. They ached in the cold nights by the fire, the mother mountains become their devourer. They knew then the truth of it—the world held no love for its inhabitants and one stone knife was better by far than all of nature's beauty. Nantan counseled that the plague wouldn't spread wide, for the clovenhoofed didn't cross the Bavispe Canyon. The council decided they would depart that familiar stronghold and go where the fever couldn't follow and the game was fat. Thereafter they'd split into two or three smaller bands with the majority remaining under Carnoviste's leadership and Nantan's protection.

* * *

They left Pa-Gotzin-Kay in the first snowfall since Taklishim died in his sleep four nights earlier. Some of the children were perplexed. They hadn't known death came to their People save through violence.

For several days before he gave up the ghost, the old warrior complained of shortness of breath. Finally he'd taken to staying abed all morning and afternoon with the fire warming his bones and thoughts of his mother and father and his own sons in the Other World heavy on his mind. How they'd soon be together. What welcome he might receive.

Nantan entered the wickiup and inquired if he wished for prayers of healing.

Taklishim thanked the medicine man and told him no. He wasn't sick—he was old and the frayed cords that bound his spirit to this body were fast unraveling.

Ishton visited him the evening before he died. She

kneeled at his bed of skins and leaned close to his ear and whispered her secret. He struggled to raise his hand. He placed his palm on her belly, his lips forming a silent prayer. When Taklishim was done, he called her his daughter and told her not to worry, it was assured. The child would be strong and she'd live to hold him in her arms.

Taklishim had been an elder long before Ishton's birth. She remembered the stories he'd repeated all her life, the running fights alongside Goyathlay, how he'd chosen not to surrender to the White Eye army, retreating up into the stronghold instead and joining the last free bands. Once in his youth he'd traveled with his brothers across Sonora to the western sea. The smell of salt in the air. Roaring waves, conch shells on the sand. They'd stood looking to the far horizon where the water swallowed up the sun and each prayed in his heart for a sign of safe return to their mountains. They'd carried back shells with them, sacred talismans still used in ceremonies to that day.

"Grandfather," Ishton told him, "I wish you'd live forever."

"What?" he asked. "Would you wish that all the old trees in the forest full of dead branches never fell? Only let me go in freedom as I came."

That night closed the last eyes among them that had looked on the ocean.

They crossed the plain in a long line of horses and mules, children as young as five riding by themselves, women carrying babies in tsochs on their backs, and they took the trail down the mountain. The hide coverings of wickiups had been rolled and brought along on the mules. Lodge poles were easily found, so they left behind the skeletal arbors and they left behind cold ashes in firepits. The packmules were stocked with dried meat and acorn meal for them to draw from the common supply and many days to come, the children would sleep with food pouches tied to their chests.

At the base of the trail Ishton stepped aside and let her kinsmen pass. She stood looking up at the high wall of their home where Carnoviste's child within her was conceived, where the old man lay upon his scaffold. She lingered a moment, then turned and caught up Denali.

BILDUNGSROMAN III

The Etiquette of Self-Immolation

1886, Arizona—1901, Philippines

General Miles repaid the faithfulness of the Apache scouts with treachery. Disarmed and declared prisoners of war, they were forced to join Geronimo's band in exile. The Chiricahua were shipped by boxcar to Florida.

In the wet heart of that fever-ridden fort the Chiricahuas would perish in great numbers, struck down by malaria and heartbreak. Geronimo lived to regret not having chosen freedom and death.

Following the Apaches' peaceful surrender Cain enlisted with the 4th Cavalry. For the first time in his life he found himself welcomed at a table where he truly belonged.

The city of Tucson held a gala in celebration of the Apache surrender and Aubrey was invited as the guest of honor. When word reached General Miles, he refused to let Aubrey attend. Miles still viewed the lieutenant as a Crook man and his successful mission only lent validity to the ex-commander's old strategies.

Instead of accommodation Aubrey received harsh reprimand. He'd disobeyed orders in his final approach, meeting Geronimo with a party of six rather than Miles' instructed escort of twenty-five. He'd drawn the general's ire—Miles dismissed Aubrey from his position as commander of Apache scouts and, in what seemed a personal insult, assigned him instead to the 4th Cavalry. Aubrey would be serving under the drunken Captain Lawton. Friends expected to find him full of rage or else despondent. Aubrey decided it suited him fine. Life behind a desk, another gray-haired fixture of bureaucracy, held no appeal to his nature. He was a leader of fighting men.

The only thing he needed was a war.

* * *

Four years of uneventful service in Arizona followed. Aubrey waited like a soul in purgatory. During this time he kept watch on Private Cain, noting the boy's progress as a soldier, how he applied himself to military life with a vigor that first surprised, then pleased Aubrey. The cavalry had imposed order on the boy's inner chaos. His easy adaptation to that new world startled Aubrey almost as much as the acts of lawlessness Cain had confessed before. Now he seemed a perfect soldier.

They passed the days as master and apprentice. Aubrey would describe to him the classic strategies of Clausewitz and Sun Tzu, or brutal tactics perfected by such guerilla fighters as William Clarke Quantrill. He expected Cain to not only remember what he was told but repeat it back for him later. The teacher discovered in his pupil a keen mind for the principles of war. Other times Aubrey would quote passages of his own translation from Homer's *Iliad*, a work he'd studied in the original Greek during his time at the Point. Cain absorbed it all like a sponge. More than anything else Aubrey delighted in sharing his knowledge and deep admiration of the Japanese samurai, their bushido code of martial honor and unyielding loyalty. Aubrey schooled his heart in the etiquette of self-immolation. He was well-versed in the way of the warrior, in the tenets of the samurai and their devotion to their master and calling. In every respect he held himself to a standard of honor other men would've found an impossible burden.

In 1890 the 4th Cavalry received orders they were to be moved to Fort Walla Walla, Washington. The 4th split apart with half the regiment going to the Department of the Columbia, half to the Department of California. Aubrey's hopes were dashed. The prospect of seeing action, already remote, became even more unlikely.

Letters from Boston arrived on occasion. Aubrey's mother and siblings wrote of reconciliation, proposed a visit back east on his next leave. His mother was getting old and craving absolution. There was also the matter of her testament, Aubrey's portion in the sizable estate, the home on Beacon Hill and enough money to fund a comfortable existence for the remainder of his days. You won't ever have to work again, she wrote him.

Aubrey's minimalist reply was a brief list of suggested

charities. He made it clear he'd chosen another kind of life.

Through the next eight long years of garrison duty no one was closer to him than Cain. He acted as sounding board to all Aubrey's frustrations, the conclusion of the Indian wars, the grudge Miles held against him which effectively killed any chance for a transfer. Cain listened without comment while Aubrey weighed the option of mustering out, seeking adventure in the gold fields of the Yukon, but in the end he could never commit to leaving the only place where he too always belonged at the table.

One afternoon he found Cain in the barracks and led him outside away from the others. "It's time you joined the Brotherhood," he told Private Cain. And so Aubrey began teaching him the Masonic catechisms pertaining to the degree of Entered Apprentice. When at last came the night of initiation, it was Aubrey himself who led a hoodwinked Cain by the cabletow.

Often as they stood for inspection in their crisp blue uniforms or marched about the garrison, boots thumping, shaking the ground, Cain would feel the power that comes of disciplined men acting in unison. It thrilled him to his core simply to be among them. He couldn't imagine any life for himself but the life of a soldier.

Nonetheless, had Aubrey departed that table, Cain would've risen as well and followed wherever he led.

* * *

On the evening of February 15th, 1898, the USS *Maine*

exploded in Havana Harbor—and Aubrey's hopes for a war rose up once more.

Hearst and Pulitzer declared Spain guilty of sinking the vessel. Their dailies urged war. Aubrey was champing at the bit, desperate for the 4th to be mobilized. Soon he got his wish, but fortune failed him again. The Spanish-American lasted a scant ten weeks, coming to a close while the regiment was still at sea, bound for the Spanish colony of the Philippines. Aubrey's last chance for glory appeared to have passed him by. Yet in short order, the consequences of the Cuban intervention would cross oceans and gift Cain and Aubrey with a war of their own.

* * *

The 4th Cavalry arrived in the Philippines a week after Manila fell and armistice with Spain was declared. When the transport ship *Peru* entered the harbor, Cain stood on the deck and belted out, "Under the starry flag, civilize em with a Krag." He was now an untested sergeant responsible for boys who'd never fired a weapon in combat. They'd come to liberate the islands from a cruel empire. If you'd placed a globe before him, Cain couldn't have found that archipelago to save his life.

They were put to work defending the city from dissident elements of the Philippine army. An uneasy peace held for a time. Aubrey and Cain went out drinking and whoring in Manila's redlight district. It wasn't Cain's first experience with a whore, but the act was shorter than intended, impatience as usual spoiling it for him. He lay abed smoking while she spoke to him in rapid-fire Tagalog, of what he couldn't have guessed, and he waited for Aubrey to finish with his girl.

Cain's brief rut earned him a visit to the infirmary with the clap. By the time February arrived and war again broke out he was recovered and game to see what he was truly made of.

The Spanish had been cast out after three hundred and thirty-three years of colonial rule. Now Filipino nationalists rejected a simple change in masters, prepared to die for the cause of independence. The rebels were led by Emilio Aguinaldo, only a handful of months earlier the closest of American allies, instrumental in defeating the Spanish army and Guardia Civil. U.S. forces would've been hard-pressed to secure Luzon without the aid of Aguinaldo's Philippine Revolutionary Army.

Three years earlier Aguinaldo had conducted a failed rebellion against Spain. In Singapore the exiled rebel met with the U.S. Consul, who passed along word from Commodore Dewey—the United States was willing to recognize the independence of the Philippines. After the sinking of the *Maine* Dewey again dispatched an emissary to approach Aguinaldo. The Americans persuaded him to join forces. Dewey transported Aguinaldo aboard the cutter *McCulloch* back to his homeland and there he rallied the people once more against the colonial government. Filipino patriots cast their lot with the Americans. After all, they reasoned, the land of the free wasn't infected with the imperial ambitions of Europe's monarchies. Military occupation of the islands would fly in the face of the Americans' own constitution. And so the alliance was formed.

Dewey's ships blockaded Manila Bay. Revolutionaries besieged the capital city and cut off its water supply, complete victory only a matter of time. The Spanish governor feared vengeance at the hands of the Filipinos. He reached out to Dewey. The governor and the commodore made secret arrangements for a mock battle and subsequent surrender to U.S. forces.

When the Spanish hoisted a white flag, control of the Walled City at the heart of Manila fell to the Americans alone. Betrayed Filipinos were denied entry into their own capital.

From the American point of view the problem was the Filipinos themselves. Under the friars and colonial government the bulk of the population had remained illiterate. U.S. officials deemed those they called their little brown brothers incapable of self-governance. They'd have to be educated in the values of democracy. Meanwhile the Germans and Japanese waited for an American withdrawal, predators ready to pounce, so it was decided that the U.S. would take the islands for themselves before another nation could do the same.

The Philippine Revolutionary Army began a desperate war against their new masters. Rifles were in short supply and the Filipinos often had to produce their own ammunition with homemade blackpowder and brass curtain rods. The majority of soldiers were armed only with bolo knives, spears, or bows and arrows. Nonetheless General Macabulos hoped to inflict casualties severe enough the American public would grow disheartened, causing President McKinley's defeat in the upcoming 1900 election. William Jennings Bryan was a staunch anti-imperialist. It was hoped that a Bryan presidency would result in the withdrawal of U.S. troops from the islands. The primitive army had to steel themselves and keep fighting until the election.

The 4th Cavalry's mounts had been off-loaded by mistake in Hawaii. Cain cursed the navy, the endless sea, and idiot horse handlers to the full measure. There was nothing for it but to ride Filipino ponies instead. Cain and Aubrey found them no match for the swiftness of American horses, but their endurance was much to be admired.

They fought the insurrectos in constant rain and mist. Their patrols took them through high grass and dense jungle, potential ambush waiting along every constricted winding trail. In cramped pup tents they fell asleep to the calls of tuckbo lizards and chattering monkeys. Whiskey and quinine kept the dreaded fever at bay. "Damn mosquitos are the size of turkey buzzards," Cain grumbled. "And thicker than horse thieves in hell." He was by Aubrey's side through it all, the stands against charging suicidal bolomen, mud up to their horses' bellies, vile leeches and wretched food. Diarrhea, parasites. Unseen snipers in the bamboo. And hardest to take of it all—the long periods without combat which they both hated more than the heat and torrents and the insurrectos themselves. Cain wasn't surprised when Aubrey confided he'd sampled the islanders' opium and found it much to his liking.

They'd been issued double-action .38 revolvers whose stopping power was dismal. A charging insurrecto could take round after round without slowing until you stood face to face with the mad boloman in all his zeal. Eventually old single-action Colt .45s would be brought out of storage in the States and shipped to the troops, but Aubrey had anticipated the problem. He'd smuggled a pair of frontier Peacemakers and a cache of ammunition on the troop carrier. He gave Cain one of the pistols and told him to keep it on him at all times. If an officer reprimanded him for the non-issue handgun, they'd see to it that man failed to return from patrol.

They raided backwater hamlets. They conducted knockdown body searches and administered the water cure to villagers suspected of rebel sympathy. "Water detail," Captain Potter would bark. Those assigned torture duty stepped forward. Three soldiers held the subject down, one of them shoving a carbine barrel into his mouth, thrusting his jaw back, then the torturer began pouring from his jar. Gallon after gallon onto the subject's face and down his throat and nose, a drowning man who can never drown.

Time to time a soldier would stray into the jungle with a Filipino girl and never be seen again. When the Americans figured out what was happening, women thought too flirtatious were dragged under huts and raped. The first to complain to Captain Potter was a sixty-five year-old grandmother. Potter didn't believe her and she had to mortify him by lifting her skirt and showing the bruises. The captain was more incensed over this display than he was with the enlisted men.

Commanding the 4th was Henry Lawton, Aubrey's old adversary from the Geronimo campaign. Lawton had been a captain and drunkard in those days. Now he was a general employing tactics acquired during the Indian Wars.

In the fall of 1899 General Lawton led troops north in the push to capture Aguinaldo. At San Mateo with the Filipino trench some three hundred yards distant, Lawton paced up and down the firing line, a six-foot three figure in a yellow raincoat and white pith helmet. Godlike, unconcerned. He shouted encouragement to his men, laughing as bullets clipped the grass. The 7mm Mauser that struck him in the chest elicited an incredulous, "I am shot," then Lawton fell dead in the arms of a staff officer.

It gave Aubrey pause, the strange fact of Lawton's death—killed by one of the sharpshooters under the command of a General Licerio Gerónimo.

* * *

One rainy night the patrol camped with the other platoons in Captain Potter's troop in a half-deserted hamlet. They strung a picketline and tethered the horses and packmules. Sergeant Cain posted sentries, then the cavalrymen slept in abandoned bamboo shacks facing a small square. Thick jungle to the west, an open rice field to the east.

Just after dawn they woke to gunfire. Cain rushed out of the shack, Aubrey right behind him, their rifles at the ready. One sentry lay clutching the shaft of an arrow protruding from his throat, the other was blazing away with his Krag, firing into the darkness of the jungle.

"Man down," Cain shouted.

Cavalrymen poured out of the shacks. They gripped rifles and glanced all around, scanning the shadowed trees and undergrowth, stark fear at the jungle's creeping death.

Cain sat down his rifle. He kneeled over the wounded Private Hannah and cradled the boy's head. He hesitated, then gripped the arrow and strained and snapped the shaft below the point, but then he was afraid to pull it out. Hannah's eyes were full of terror. His face a shocking pale. There was a gurgling sound in his throat, desperate for air and receiving none, slowly choking.

Private Terry, the unwounded sentry, lowered his rifle and cursed. The assassin had long since slipped away through the trees.

Aubrey dropped to his knees beside Cain. "He's not going to make it unless he gets air," Aubrey said.

"I know it," Cain said. "But he ain't likely to make it if I pull it free."

"At least that way he's got a chance."

"He sure as hell don't have one now, I reckon."

Cain pulled the shaft out of the private's throat.

Blood spurted across the grass, then Cain pressed his hands around the wound, but nothing could stop the blood and it was soaking his hands, the blood staining his uniform, a metallic scent in the air, and then it was finished and the private from Iowa lay dead.

Cain was silent. Private Terry cursed the insurrectos.

In the outlying rice field a farmer had been plowing through the deep mud with a lone white carabao. He'd paused in his work when the shooting began and now he stood gripping the reins, staring toward the hamlet.

Cain picked up his rifle and rose from the dead man. He tried to wipe the blood from his face with a shirtsleeve and succeeded only in smearing it.

Private Terry stared down at his fellow sentry. He swore again. Terry raised his Krag and worked the bolt and sighted down the barrel.

"Fuckin goo-goo," he screamed.

When Terry fired the first shot, the rice farmer dropped his reins and went running across the paddy, faltering in the mud, then they were all shooting, every man save Aubrey. "Cease fire, dammit," Aubrey shouted. He jerked Cain's rifle barrel down before he could get off another shot.

By the time the shooting stopped they'd pumped dozens of bullets into the field. The farmer lay where he'd fallen a few yards from the edge of the trees. Aubrey stood watching the carabao rocking in the mud, struggling to rise, its wide heavy body pierced with multiple bullets.

There was a scream. They turned and saw an old woman running from the doorway of a shack. She passed Captain Potter and ran barefoot into the mud, stumbling toward the dead plowman.

Aubrey stepped up to Private Terry and punched him so hard in the stomach the private doubled over. Terry dropped to his knees gasping.

Aubrey stared at the men in disgust. "You pack of cowards."

"Watch your mouth, Lieutenant," Captain Potter said. "It had to be done. The snipers need to learn there's a price to be paid."

"That was an innocent man."

"No one's innocent on this island. Maybe you need to decide if you came here to teach Sunday school or fight for your country."

"Go to hell," Aubrey told him.

"Who do you think you are, Lieutenant? Some kind of holy saint sitting in judgement over the rest of us? You're no better than any man here, you self-righteous son of a bitch."

In the field the carabao was floundering, fighting to stand. The water buffalo was the most valuable asset any family in the hamlet could aspire to own. It meant survival. The farmers depended on it to cultivate the fields, then transport the sheaves come harvest.

The carabao let out a deep groan.

"At least our boys had the courage to act," Potter said. "Right or wrong. You just stood back and let them do the dirty work."

Aubrey turned away from Potter and stepped out into the field, his boots sinking in the mud, and made his way out to the carabao. When the wounded beast saw him, it dipped its head, lowering the sickle-shaped horns, dying but prepared to fight to the last in the mud and blood. Its breathing was heavy, strained.

Across the field the woman wept over her husband. She buried her face against his neck and prayed to the Holy Mother in Tagalog.

Aubrey pulled his Krag's bolt back and rammed it forward. He shot the carabao in the head and watched its eyes roll up so that only the whites were visible. It went limp. At the crack of the rifleshot the woman looked up and saw Aubrey standing over the carabao. The widow hurled Spanish curses at him, her face twisted in grief, calling down every form of retribution upon his head for the evil he'd done.

* * *

The re-election of William McKinley was a sharp blow to the insurgents, coming after a number of losing battles against U.S. troops. Faced with brutal defeats Aguinaldo changed tactics. He disbanded the regular army and authorized the use of guerilla warfare and so it was that the conflict dragged on.

In early 1901 the 4th was assigned pacification duty in the southern region of Luzon. By now Aubrey was becoming increasingly cynical of the war. His insolence toward commanding officers recognized no limit and Cain worried it would lead to a court martial.

Their horses stood eating from nosebags of rice. Cain removed the quart bottle of Cyrus Noble from his saddlebag and sat beside Aubrey under the mango tree. He took a pull from the bottle.

Aubrey read from a battered newspaper and let out a bark of a laugh. "Have a look at this," he said. He tossed Cain the paper, folded open to a story about Vice President Roosevelt's exploits in Cuba some three years earlier. In the photograph below the headline Roosevelt stood with his Rough Riders atop Kettle Hill.

"What am I supposed to be seein?" Cain asked.

"Look at that fat bastard's holster, where he's got the barrel pointed."

"Appears to be aimed at his balls," Cain said. Roosevelt's holster was hitched around so that the barrel of his sidearm pointed directly at his testicles.

"Would you carry a pistol like that?" Aubrey questioned him.

"Can't say it strikes me as a good idea."

"I wish he'd blown his balls off," Aubrey said. "What an ass. He must be the biggest phony in the world. I have it on good authority he got his uniform custom tailored from Brooks Brothers in Manhattan."

"Looks mighty sharp in it too," Cain said, goading his friend. "Downright commanding. Yessir, I'd be proud to follow old Teddy to hell and back."

"It's sons of bitches like him that are the reasons we're in this godforsaken country."

"What do you want to do? All of us just turn around and

head back home, leave the place for the goo-goos to run?"

"Why the hell not? It's their country. What business do we have here anyway?"

"The damned Kaiser would take over inside of a week."

"If the Germans want to bloody their hands, let them. What did these people ever do to us?"

"The goo-goos been killin our friends for two years now."

"Let's say you and I plotted to loot a man's house," Aubrey told him. "If in the course of the burglary, the owner wakes up and grabs his gun and kills one of us, who's in the wrong? The homeowner? Or the man killed in the process of robbing him?"

"That ain't how it is, dammit. We're doin the brainless monkeys a favor. They can't look after themselves—which you've damn well seen for yourself. They got to be taught."

Aubrey laughed. "The whole bloody thing's a racket. We never should've come here."

"How's it any different than with the Apaches? I didn't hear you belly achin then."

"Geronimo strung up a little girl by meat hooks. The Chiricahua were killing Americans. But the Filipinos were an ocean away—when did they ever harm a U.S. citizen?"

"You figure they'd rather have the Spaniards back in here? Them fat friars lordin it over em?"

"I imagine they'd rather be free."

"That's what we come here to make em," Cain said, exasperated.

Aubrey shook his head. "We're not liberating anyone.

This war is the abandonment of all human decency. Murder, rape, torture—you call that freedom? You and I are mercenary killers. Looting for the benefit of Washington and New York, doing the bidding of fat usurers with soft hands. The Apaches had more honor than us. At least a Chiricahua warrior killed and stole for the betterment of his own family. Our boys do it for $13 a month and patriotic sentiments."

Aubrey pulled the bottle of Cyrus Noble from Cain's hand and had a long swig. He set the bottle down and rose and went to his horse. From the saddlebag he got a thick book with a golden double-headed eagle on its blue cover. He started toward the brush.

"Where you goin?" Cain asked.

"To take a dump."

"What's that book?"

"Paper," Aubrey said. "To get the job done."

"But what is it?"

"You know what it is."

Cain sat up. "That's *Morals and Dogma,* ain't it? You're fixin to wipe your ass with it."

"And you have a problem with that?" Aubrey said.

Cain rose to his feet. "You're damn right I got a problem with it. That book's sacred to the Brotherhood."

"Have you ever read it, cover to cover?"

Cain stared at him. "No," he admitted.

"I have," Aubrey said, "and now I'm going to wipe my ass with it."

"You hadn't ought to do that." Cain flung the rolled up

newspaper at his feet. "Use the paper instead."

"I couldn't do a thing like that to poor old Teddy."

"What's wrong with you? What the hell happened to get you like this?"

Aubrey shook his head. "I've been led around in the dark long enough. Now the blindfold's off. I'm seeing things as they are."

* * *

A summer rain fell on the barrio and turned the streets to mud. An hour after mail call Cain stood under a palm frond awning, smoking a cigarette, doing his best to ignore one of the little Filipinos who attached themselves to the soldiers. Whenever the amigo spotted Cain, his face stretched into a broad smile under his upturned hat brim. He was perhaps fourteen years old and he wore a crucifix around his neck. A cigarette out of Cain's last pack of tailor-mades hung from the corner of his mouth. The amigo kept up a constant stream of Spanish mixed with Tagalog.

They stood in the marketplace opposite the old church. Merchants bartered and sold food and healing herbs, the popular anting-antings, those talismans said to possess the power of stopping live bullets or making the wearer invisible. The rain had driven away all but a handful of customers. Now it ceased of a sudden, a few last drops falling.

The amigo let out a rapid babble, something about John

Phillip Sousa and his Marine Band. He hummed *Stars and Stripes Forever.*

Aubrey came walking toward them, crossing the muddy street.

"Shut the hell up," Cain told the amigo.

"Sure, Mike," he said and commenced chattering away again.

Aubrey stepped under the awning. He held a letter in one hand and a flask in the other and Cain noticed he wasn't wearing his hat.

"You all right?" Cain asked.

Aubrey shrugged. "News from home."

"Not good?"

"When is it ever good?"

"I wouldn't know," Cain said.

The amigo hadn't so much as paused in his monologue while Cain and Aubrey spoke.

Cain turned to the amigo. "Vamoose," he said.

"Sure, Mike," he said and stood rooted.

Cain reared back and kicked him in the buttocks with his boot-heel. The amigo went sprawling in the mud.

"Vamoose, you damn goo-goo," Cain said. "Don't you know what vamoose means?"

The Filipino picked himself up, his ragged britches and out-sized shirt covered in mud. His cigarette floated in a puddle. He walked off down the street a distance, staring at his bare feet, then paused and looked back with a pained expression on his face.

Cain shook his head. "You believe these little

blabbermouths?"

Aubrey handed him the flask. "He wouldn't pester you so bad if you didn't keep giving him cigarettes."

"I know it. That was the last time. I swear he sounded just like a skeeter in my ear."

Aubrey laughed.

Cain took a swig and returned the flask. "What happened to your hat?"

He raised his eyes. "I thought I was wearing it. You ever do that? Feel like you're wearing your hat, but turns out you left it someplace instead?"

"Done it a time or two."

Aubrey folded the letter and placed it in his pocket. "My uncle died," he said. "Father's brother Herman. My mother sent me the news. Apparently the old man did far more than I knew to replenish the family fortune. The estate is considerable. His marriage to my late aunt was, as they say, without issue. I'm sole heir. Not my brothers, not my sisters. Only me."

"I reckon she wants you to come home. Your momma."

"You reckon right. Herman should've left it all to her—they were close as man and wife at the end. But I suspect she insisted."

"Bait, huh?"

"One last chance to put a hook in my mouth."

"Maybe it ain't such a bad idea," Cain said. "The way you feel about the war and all."

"A man can only listen to so many apologies before it drives him mad and he prefers the offense instead. I forgave her everything a long time ago, but she can't let go of it."

"Well. What are you goin to do?"

"I don't care about the money. What the hell would I do all day? Swill cognac with the Brahmins? Talk about how Richard Harding Davis really gives you a sense of actually being there, doesn't he though?"

Aubrey grinned and sipped from the flask. "I know where I belong," he said. "Now let me have one of those cigarettes and I'll quit buzzing in your ear."

They stood smoking under the awning and it began to rain again and neither of them noticed the barefoot amigo until he stepped up to them.

The amigo shouted, "Noli me tangere!" Aubrey started to turn as the amigo raised a .22 revolver. At the first shot Aubrey fell, then the amigo swung the barrel toward Cain and got off four crazy fast shots, Cain standing there in front of him and every bullet missing. Cain drew his Peacemaker and cocked the hammer.

For all his haste the amigo had been careful to count his shots—one round left. Before Cain could pull the trigger, the amigo shoved the barrel of the .22 into his open mouth and fired.

Faint mist of blood. He crumpled.

A pair of infantrymen came running across the market. Cain screamed for a medic and kneeled beside Aubrey.

"Where'd he get you, bud? Don't you worry about it, we're goin to get you fixed up. Did you see his little pop gun? Hell, I've had worse skeeter bites than what that thing'll do."

Aubrey's eyes were open, but he was silent, motionless. Cain cradled his head. "It's all right. I ain't goin to let you get away. It's all right."

The amigo was still alive. Cain looked at him crawling in the mud, choked-off sounds coming out of him that were supposed to be screams. The bullet had passed out the back of his neck just below the skull. One of the infantrymen kicked him in the belly and he dropped back down and groaned.

"Never figured Little Mike for an insurrecto," the private said.

"They all got it in em," his fellow told him.

When the medic arrived with a group of soldiers, the amigo was trying to crawl through the muck again. The pair of infantrymen had removed the knife bayonets from their Krags and tossed the rifles under the awning. They kneeled and plunged the bayonets into the amigo's back and sides and rectum as he cried shrill little cries and the blades came out dripping red. Aubrey lay still. The medic checked his pulse and examined the wound in his back, then applied a bandage.

"Get him on the stretcher," he said.

Cain and another man eased Aubrey onto the canvas. The soldiers bent over and rose with the stretcher and they began running back toward camp, the medic following behind, clutching his black bag.

Cain couldn't move, rooted to the ground. His hands trembled.

"Shit, the monkey croaked," a private said. "Just when he was startin to get civilized."

The amigo lay dead. A small crowd of soldiers had gathered to watch the two infantrymen work. Now they spat and gave the ravaged body a few parting kicks, then turned and drifted away. Cain stood weeping in the rain and the mud.

CHAPTER NINE

February, 1930,

Bavispe Valley, Sonora

In the winter Jubal learned that the Douglas, Arizona Chamber of Commerce was forming its own self-described Apache Expedition. They intended to capitalize on the publicity of John Russell's kidnapping and bring in tourism. The promoters placed ads in newspapers and pulp magazines calling for volunteers: *ENLIST NOW—Last Chance for True Wild West Adventure. Save the Kidnapped Epileptic Boy from SAVAGE CAPTORS!* Membership was available to anyone who filled out a short questionnaire and posted $50 bond with the committee. Though the expedition's stated goal was the rescue of John Russell McKenna, the members were assured ample time for hunting and fishing. Applications poured in. The *New York American* lampooned the expedition, but caustic editorials couldn't stop the promoters acquiring arms and mounts.

Jubal was furious enough, then word reached him that

Colonel Sanchez had offered the Chamber his assistance, becoming an outspoken supporter of the venture. Now Jubal's rage ran hot. He traveled to Douglas alone and attended a committee meeting at the VFW Hall where he wore his pistol openly. A clerk stepped up to the mayor and whispered in his ear, informing him of Jubal's presence. They cast nervous glances his way, then the mayor approached Jubal and made his offer—50% of the net profits. Jubal smiled and told him to go to hell. He called them a pack of sackless bastards and informed the committee that if they set foot in the mountains, Apaches would be the least of their worries.

He returned to the ranch, still angry but unconcerned. He didn't believe for an instant the Mexican Government would grant permission for a gringo militia to cross its borders. Another week proved him right. The committee's ranks included an ex-gunrunner who'd been involved in the late Topete rebellion. Mexico City found the presence of such a radical more than sufficient reason to forbid them entry. The expedition died before it ever set out and they returned to their day jobs, the gentlemen adventurers whose only wish had been to shoot a live Apache.

* * *

"Sometimes I'll catch myself," Dolores said. "Just an ordinary day, feeding the chickens or walking with Claudia, and I'll catch myself… happy. And then I feel bad."

"Why?" Jubal asked.

172

"You know."

"Tell me."

"It's wrong to be happy when he's still up there."

"It's not your job to feel bad."

"I don't know," she said.

"I know. Don't do that to yourself."

She was silent.

"I want that for you every day," he told her. "To be happy. All right?"

"All right," she said.

* * *

Jubal and two vaqueros staked out an arroyo near the eastern limits of the ranch. It cut down into a pasture where a small herd of cattle were feeding. If the Apaches wanted beef, they'd make their approach through the cover of the arroyo—and Jubal would be ready.

They waited all night hidden in brush on a slight rise overlooking the arroyo—no whispers, no cigarettes. The first two nights passed without incident. Then late the third night Jubal thought he heard something. Faint in the darkness. He gripped his rifle and watched for movement, but not so much as a breeze stirred the grass and whatever he'd heard didn't come again.

In the morning he found the tracks directly below their position. One Apache had crawled along the bottom of the arroyo until he'd sensed the watchers, then turned back the way he'd come.

"It had to be a ghost," Angel said. "No man or animal could've got so close."

"How did he know?" Lopez asked. "We didn't make a sound. How did the gut-eater figure it out?"

Jubal spat.

* * *

All winter they rode chasing ghosts. Jubal led them through the mountains, seeking out the scattered camps and trailing small bands. They passed under jutting outcrops of rock and struggled up tree-lined gorges. The first stars after sunset crowned the black silhouettes of the sierras. In the upper foothills the winter grass was gray and poor and offered the horses little nourishment. They rationed grain.

Days of riding watched by animal eyes. The stares of unseen owls and ocelots. Stalkers of prey, fellow hunters. They crossed a region ravaged by wild fire, the land a desolation of ash and burned trees. Birds flew past that wasteland altogether. Ashclouds rose in Jubal's wake, then they reached where the fire had stopped, the forest a charred ruins on one side, on the other tall pines and grassy slopes.

In the following days they would come upon tracks of unshod ponies and trail them through a wooded valley and over broken ridges, only to lose them on open ground. As if the Apaches had stepped into another world.

A long and bitter search. They discovered old camps,

empty seasonal caves. The canyons were vast and overgrown, capable of hiding a multitude.

One evening on their last foray of the winter Jubal stood on a ridge staring west. A moonless night, dark ranges along the horizon blotting stars and otherwise unreckonable, betraying their existence solely by the light they occulted. He watched a star flickering redly just above that line of termination like a pyre on a mountaintop, beacon to the lost, and he watched it slip behind the phantom mountains.

They wandered the emptiness like children of the bondwoman.

Early of a morning Jubal found the hoofprints in the snow. They trailed them once more, then afternoon melted the pale blankets and the tracks were destroyed. That night it snowed again. Heavy flakes, relentless flurries. They sheltered under pup-tents and took turns pulling sentry. When they woke at dawn it was still falling and they set out in the cold and the wind and they stumbled across the abandoned camp, not a mile from where they'd slept.

A sunken ring in the snow. Jubal got down and squatted on his boot-heels. He dug with his hands, then took off a glove and pressed his palm to the faint warmth of the coals. They'd quit the camp sometime in the night. He rose and turned looking about them, the conquering whiteness, every sign erased. The world gleamed pale and pure, made anew without any path to follow.

"Jubal," Hector called. He kneeled holding something.

"What is it?" Jubal stepped forward.

Hector passed him a hairbrush made of mescal leaves. Jubal looked close and saw the tufts of long red hair clinging to it. The cold wind stung.

CHAPTER TEN

Even though she was pregnant with a child of her own, Ishton never ceased to be very good to Denali. She cared for him when he was sick, giving him strange and bitter medicines, and she was always picking up and putting away the things he scattered about. She washed and mended his clothes and sewed him a pair of fine new moccasins.

Carnoviste included Denali in a group of young warriors who would accompany him on a pilgrimage to the sacred barranca. They'd be gone only a few days, but Denali was hesitant to go. He'd kept a watchful eye over Ishton since learning of her pregnancy, careful to escort her wherever she ventured outside of camp. The danger of the bear was everpresent on his mind. Nantan and Gouyen would be joining the pilgrimage as well, however, and this news made Denali more inclined to go—since it meant the medicine man would also be away from camp. In truth he'd come to doubt the suspicions he and Chatto once harbored against Nantan. How could something so fantastic be true? Surely they'd given too much weight to coincidence.

In the predawn blue they departed the band's temporary camp in the foothills and set out for the barranca to the south.

Gouyen would make them pause from time to time while she used her Power of Finding Enemies. She'd stand alone on a hilltop with her arms outstretched, chanting a prayer and turning a slow circle until her hands would tingle and her palms change color. The intensity told her how close their enemies lurked.

They reached the edge of the barranca late one night and gathered near the rim overlooking the gorge. It was a place sacred to Ussen. In older times they'd have built a ceremonial fire, but they wouldn't suffer such a risk anymore.

They sat down and Nantan led them in prayers for guidance, rebirth of energy.

Denali raised his arms and sang with the others. When the last prayer ended, Nantan placed his medicine bundle in the grass and left it unopened. He rose and danced around the leather bundle.

They looked out across the wide chasm to the opposite wall. At first Denali could see nothing. Then a black circle appeared in the side of the barranca, midway down a sheer drop, and seemed to open like a flower, drawing closer. It was the mouth of a cave, impossible to reach from the rim or the canyon bottom. Only birds could enter there.

He watched a thin white cloud descend into the barranca and linger just below the cave. Onto the cloud stepped forth the souls of previous times. Out of that darkness came Mangas Coloradas, a giant of a man in a red shirt, and following him Cochise and Victorio and The One Who Yawns.

The spirits didn't speak. They walked circles about the cloud and coughed up burning coals and where the coals fell the cloud became mirrored glass. He saw Taklishim in the mute multitude, his youth restored, and all his sons and wives with him.

"The fathers watch over us," Nantan whispered.

It was no longer in Denali to be amazed. He accepted what he saw. The spirits walked. He didn't understand why such a thing should be so, but it was so.

After a time the cloud vanished and the spirits with it, then the barranca lay dark once more.

* * *

They rejoined the others in the foothills.

In the following weeks reports reached them of a gang of armed vaqueros wandering the sierras. They met a small band, one warrior and his women, who told of discovering a massacre at a seasonal cave, bodies picked apart by coyotes and vultures. Shell casings littered the ground. Only the children were missing from those grisly remains and so they knew the Mexicans had taken the People's young.

Then came the night of heavy snowfall when Gouyen approached the chief and Ishton at the fire. She gripped her rifle and wore a grim expression. "We're being tracked," she said. "They're on our backtrail."

"Are you sure?" Carnoviste asked.

"My Power knows," she said.

"How close?"

"Not far. They stopped moving—I don't think they realize how close we are."

He didn't bother sending scouts to confirm it. The wise woman had never been mistaken.

"Put out the fire," he ordered the boys. The flames were hidden in a natural alcove, a crook of the canyon wall. There was no chance of it being seen, but should the wind change direction, the killers might catch scent of the smoke.

They gathered their few possessions and retreated well before first light. It was long after dark when they finally stopped moving.

"Why do they hunt us?" Neiflint asked.

Carnoviste hesitated. Denali looked on, waiting for his answer.

"Because they want what's ours," he said at last.

"The Blue Mountains?"

"Yes. The Blue Mountains."

* * *

The band council decided against a full retreat back to Pa-Gotzin-Kay where the fever still raged and game was hard to come by. Instead they withdrew to the main cordillera but kept west of the river at a favorite campsite, easily guarded, and Carnoviste posted lookouts on the hilltop. Shifts of young boys rubbed clay on their skin and tied bunches of grass about their heads. They kept a close watch over the trails. It was a good camp with warm springs where they bathed, the wooded hill offering protection at their back, and an open view of the country ahead. The game was fair and sometimes the braves went down to the valleys and returned with a steer or mule to be butchered.

They remained there the rest of the winter without any trouble and the following spring found them still encamped at that place.

* * *

Flowers woke in sudden green and blue and the woods were alive.

The great mescal hearts had been roasting a full four days when Denali decided to go hunting in the pines above camp. Tonight the mescal would be ready. His stomach was impatient at the thought of the sweet and juicy meal. He wanted to bring back a deer, venison to complete the feast, and it was a fine morning to walk the woods alone.

Dust floated between the trees in augmenting shafts of light. He went up the hill with the bow around his shoulder and when he reached the meadow where he knew they liked to feed, he got down and lay in the undergrowth and waited. After a while they came. A pair of does, good-sized and healthy. He pulled the string back and slowly rose to his knees, eyes on the grazing target.

He let go.

The arrow struck her in the chest but missed the heart.

Both deer took off through the trees. Denali got to his feet and raced after her, bow in hand, running through the pines. He tracked her by the droplets of blood on the leaves. It surprised him how far she fled, the ridgeside becoming steep and broken, where he risked a bad fall or broken leg. He ducked low branches, the undergrowth slapping his legs, and glimpsed her dash into a brambles. He forced his way through the tangled branches, then burst out onto a high rocky slope.

The doe wasn't in sight. Denali continued down the incline, then stood in the open a moment, scanning for sign. He glanced below and saw the pool of warm springs, saw Gouyen and the medicine man naked in the water.

Denali dropped down on his belly.

Had they seen him?

They were bathing together, talking, laughing. He was too far away to hear what they said, but he didn't think they'd spotted him. The pool was empty save for brother and sister.

The water seeped from the foot of the ridge on which he lay. It collected in a natural basin surrounded on three sides by the high walls of the enclosing ridge, a pool where Denali and his brothers often swam. When a woman wished to bathe there, no man or boy could approach on penalty of death.

He wondered what to do, afraid they'd catch sight of

him if he moved.

Gouyen and Nantan had washed their buckskins and placed them on the rocks to dry under the sun. Their long hair was wet and unbound. They went to each other across the little pool and Denali watched them embrace.

Nantan pressed his lips to Gouyen's, kissed her deep and hard as no brother should.

Denali felt a knot of repulsion and horror in his gut. He wished he'd never gone hunting.

Incest. Such a trespass was known to attract wicked forces. Nantan himself had taught the People that incest and witchcraft were bound together, born of the same evil. Now Denali understood the dark truth—the medicine man was a witch.

Desperation to run overwhelmed his fear. There was a stand of rocks above his position on the slope—if he could reach it, he'd have cover all the way back to the tree line. He started slowly moving.

Gouyen's soft moan rose from the pool and burned in his ears. He didn't want to listen to this. Denali threw caution aside and scrambled on all fours.

Just as he darted behind the rocks, his moccasin slipped. A loose stone the size of his fist came free under his weight and went rolling.

He dove behind the stand and lay on his side, heart hammering against the sunbaked rock, and he could hear the stone tumbling down the slope and knew they heard it as well.

Get away—now.

He stayed low and crawled up through the cover of the rocks and made his way back into the woods.

* * *

Gouyen and Nantan dressed in a panic beside the warm spring, their passion turned at once to fear and fury.

It had finally happened. They'd been discovered after those long years of risking their pleasure so rarely, their secret laid bare at last. The springs had been Gouyen's idea. They hadn't touched each other since the last moon and she burned for him so that desire overthrew caution.

"An animal might have knocked it loose," Gouyen said. "Or maybe it just fell."

Nantan shook his head. "You don't believe that."

"No," she said, "I don't."

No one ventured far along that side of the ridge, the terrain too broken and steep. The warm springs should've been safe. Only one trail led to it. They'd posted guards out of sight down at the trailhead, Neiflint and Oblite, boys who performed their duty with honor. Nantan told them the pool was off-limits while he and Gouyen conducted a special cleansing ceremony, a ritual to ensure the People's well-being. Absolute privacy was necessary. If anyone came up the trail, the boys would sound the alarm and refuse them passage.

"What are we going to do?" Gouyen asked.

He stared up at the ridgeside. "What we've always done. Survive." Then he turned and started back down the trail.

The pool lay empty and still.

* * *

Denali raced down the mountain. His life was in danger if the medicine man discovered him missing from camp. There was no way he could beat them back to camp, the ridgeside was too high—but others would be gone as well, boys playing in the woods, warriors off hunting. Nantan couldn't be sure it was Denali on the slope. Yet even Nantan's passing suspicion was too great a danger. Denali felt a tentacle of fear coiling around his heart.

He considered telling Carnoviste what he'd seen, but it was impossible. Even if the chief believed him, what good was the word of a lone witness?

Nantan's power was too great.

Denali ran down the trail, ran till he thought his lungs would catch fire and his heart explode, but at last he reached the edge of camp. He paused there a moment to slow his breath and compose himself. Then he hid his bow and quiver in the brush and circled around and entered camp unseen. He went to Ishton where she sat working over a deerskin and lowered himself to the ground beside her. Several warriors lounged in the shade and he spotted Nantan napping under a pine as if without a single care. Most of the women were busy preparing for the night's feast, but Gouyen was nowhere to be seen among them.

"Are you all right?" Ishton asked. She was studying his face, the intense expression he wore.

He glanced at her belly swollen under the buckskin and he tried to smile. "Of course, I am."

She returned to her work. "I thought you went hunting. You didn't find anything?"

"Today was a bad day for hunting."

* * *

In the meadow Gouyen kneeled holding her rifle and examined the ground. Where the hunter had lain in wait. Where the dried spots of blood led away through the pines. She rose and followed the path of the hunter and the wounded deer. Across the broken country she came to the place where he'd lost the trail and he'd stumbled out onto the slope and seen what was never meant to be seen. Undone by an accident, simple twist of fate. Gouyen backtracked. She found the sign he'd missed and resumed trailing the prey.

Nearing sunset she found the doe in a thick tangle of briars where she had hidden waiting for the hunter to pass, waiting on death. The arrowshaft was stained darkly. Gouyen kneeled and drew her knife and cut into the doe's flesh and cut the arrow free with its sharp iron head still attached.

She turned it in her hands, studying the craftsmanship. Hawkfeather fletchings, the bloodgutter grooves.

Divining its maker.

* * *

That night at the feast amid the laughter and sacred songs Denali looked past the fire and circle of dancers and saw Gouyen staring his way. She turned and stepped back into shadows.

* * *

Bronze babies hung in shaded tsochs from the boughs of a pine. They slept in peace while a warm breeze touched their round cheeks and their mothers worked filling baskets with wildberries.

About the camp goldenrod and maidenhair fern colored the rolling hills green and yellow. Boys played at war with blunt arrows and a Spanish cap and ball pistol, rusted and long since without cap or ball. Ishton sat beside the widow Dahtese, helping her sew a sacred dress for her daughter Haozinne, preparing for the time when the girl would undergo her Sunrise Ceremony, the rite of womanhood. Jacali, the widow's older daughter, came and sat with them and she posed Ishton a string of questions about Denali, his favorite meals and songs, if he ever spoke of any maidens. Ishton answered her queries with an amused smile.

Carnoviste dipped a gourd cup in an olla of water. He raised it to his lips and stood drinking.

Neiflint and Oblite ran up to him and spat out the mouthfuls of sinew they'd been chewing for bowstrings. They held the sinew in their palms and showed their father.

"That's enough, isn't it?" Oblite asked.

"Keep chewing," he told them.

Carnoviste looked across camp and saw Denali sitting in the shade of a pine. The boy had been staying close to camp the last few days, refraining from his usual wanderings, but solemn and aloof. As if he'd found himself without purpose.

"Run to the top of the hill," Carnoviste told Neiflint and Oblite. "Get there fast or the Mexicans will catch you."

The boys placed the strings of wet sinew back in their mouths and ran toward the rise where the women were picking berries. When Denali saw them, he rose and started to run after them.

"Wait," Carnoviste called.

Denali stopped.

"Get your bow and catch up our horses," the chief told him.

"Are we going hunting?"

"Not for four-legs."

"Then for what?"

"I'll show you what we're looking for when we find it."

After Denali had gone for the horses Ishton looked over at her husband. "Are you sure he's ready?" she asked.

"It's time he had his vision. Whether he's ready for it or not."

* * *

They rode out in the heat of the afternoon. Great silver clouds passed overhead and the shadows of clouds sailed along the waving grass of the valley floor. Denali and

Carnoviste rode side by side and there was little talk between them.

Late that day they reached a rocky country and Carnoviste stopped and sat his horse looking over the terrain. Ocotillo and yucca. Scattered patches of grama under a line of red bluffs.

"Listen to the earth," Carnoviste said. "Wait for it to call out to you. We're here for a sacred plant that our People have harvested in this place since before I was born."

They got down and led their horses paralleling the bluffs, walking along the foot of the cliff. Denali scanned the ground but saw nothing save brush and bare stone. His eyes strayed to the cliff-face, an opening below the rim, a faint smokiness issuing forth. As though a secret furnace throbbed within.

When he glanced back down, he saw the little spineless cactus at his feet and a dozen more of them in plain sight edging the talus. Somehow he knew it was what they'd come for.

"I found it," he said.

Carnoviste handed Denali his reins. The chief kneeled and drew his knife and cut a cactus at its base, leaving the subterranean portion to regenerate new crowns. Denali took a leather sack from his saddlebag and held it open. Carnoviste dropped the disc-shaped peyote buttons inside, then rose and they moved on to the next plant and harvested it as well.

When they'd filled the sack, Carnoviste placed his hand on Denali's shoulder. "The world won't allow you to be under my protection forever. The time's come to find your direction and walk as a man."

"Why do I need the plant?"

"It will help you find your vision. But before you go in search of your vision, you must ask Nantan for a blessing."

Denali was silent at this news. Some part of him wanted in rising desperation to tell Carnoviste of all he'd seen, but he couldn't bring himself to speak. After all, why should the chief choose loyalty to a captive boy over the medicine man on whose Power the People depended?

He couldn't bring himself to trust Carnoviste. The chief had been good to him, but that day on the trail was impossible to forget, when Carnoviste had stood by while Gouyen cut his mother's throat, while the brave Matzus killed his father and collected his scalp.

Carnoviste took his reins and started to mount up, then paused, staring at the opening high on the cliff-face. "You see the bees?" he asked. "Streaming out like smoke? There's an old cave up there. My father used to steal honey from it when he was a boy."

"I bet Ishton would like some wild honey."

"She loves the sweetness."

"But that cliff can't be climbed," Denali said.

"A boy can reach it if he's brave. We'll come back tomorrow. Don't worry, my father said the sweet cures the sting."

* * *

The following day a group of them returned to gather honey. When Carnoviste sighted the cave, they left Bihido below and circled the bluffs and rode up from the other side through a scrubland of juniper and mesquite. The People rode along the curving rim of the cliff. Carnoviste led the remnant of that lost nation, the sun on their copper skin, riding like nature's elect such was their pride and bearing. Bronzen gods in a final golden age. Only the boy served as pale reminder of the eschaton. Bihido stood below the cave to mark its position for them on the sheer cliff-face. When Carnoviste came to the place on the rim where he could see Bihido directly opposite them on the ground below, he knew they stood above the cave.

Carnoviste dismounted, a rawhide rope coiled around his shoulder. He walked to the edge of the cliff and stood looking down.

He dropped one end of the rope to test the length. It spilled out and slapped the cliff-face. Bihido gave him a wave—the rope hung just beneath the opening.

A fine mist of bees streamed from the cave.

"It reaches," Carnoviste said. He pulled the rope back up.

Several women had accompanied the warriors, Ishton and Gouyen among them, bringing along pots and other containers. They stared at Denali as he stepped slowly to the edge.

He looked down on broken rocks, Bihido tiny below. There was a sinking feeling in his gut. He wasn't ready to do this.

Carnoviste tied a stout stick to the end of the rope, then Ishton handed him a buckskin bag and he tied it to the stick and lowered the rope just off the rim. "Are you ready?" he called.

Denali turned to face the chief. A line of three braves stood gripping the rope—they grinned at him.

"I'm ready," Denali said.

"Don't let go," Carnoviste said, "even if a swarm of them stings you all over. Understand?"

"I won't let go."

"Make your father proud," Ishton told him.

Nantan stepped forward and took his place on the rope with the others. He didn't look at Denali.

Carnoviste took a firm footing. He nodded at Denali and reached out, his hands gripping the boy's forearms. Denali stepped backward off the ledge, Carnoviste lowering him until he straddled the stick, then he let go of one arm and the boy gripped the rope and Carnoviste let go of his other arm.

Denali gripped the rope in both hands. He hung facing the red wall, a hundred feet above the base of the talus, his knees scraping rock. They started lowering him. He could hear chanting from above, Nantan's medicine song.

Someone whistled like a bird call. He looked up, saw Jacali and two other maidens peeking over the rim and smiling down at him. He tried to look heroic, but his mind was aswirl with fear.

When he struck a sharp outcrop, the rope twisted around, turning him so that he looked out across the rolling country toward the far ridgeline, then he was facing bare rock again. His knuckles whitened. The wall was pocked and cracked, whole sections broken off and fallen to the talus where boulders lay like pebbles. He descended toward the cave and the enjambre inside.

Now he could hear their dull hum. He glanced down at the alternating traffic of bees, those going out to harvest nectar, those returning to make their deposits.

The warriors lowered him until he swayed back and forth just to the side of the entrance.

"All right," he called out.

They stopped playing out the rope and Denali hung suspended. He hooked his moccasin in the opening and pulled himself closer and reached inside with one hand, the edge of the round entrance slick and smooth, and got a hold. Bees darted by his face. He ducked inside still gripping the rope.

Sunlight shone against the chamber's far wall and cast his shadow on white and gold comb. He untied the bag and let the rope swing free, within reach. He was wearing only a breechclout and belt with his moccasins. If the bees attacked, he'd have to grab the stick and dangle over the fall, accepting their stings while the warriors slowly pulled him up.

He went naked into the hive.

Workers danced lemniscate patterns, communicating with their fellows. The bloodbuzz pulsed in his ears. Living walls, writhing black and yellow. A world in perfect order. He crouched low, staring at the ripe walls, and he understood this was no simple enjambre.

The cave had housed the colony for a century or more. Much of the honey was aged blackly. Hexagonal cells, sealed with wax, cradled larvae and the hive's sweet treasure. The walls rose to curve inward and meet in a gentle arch and he stood on the geometric comb and felt himself the yolk of an enormous mystic egg.

Bees flew about the matrix, strange and charmed. They returned from the outer world with nectar and carried with it the dust and spores attracted by quantum electric charge. They went about their business and ignored him, myrmidon workers in service of their great mother.

He kneeled and started tearing off pieces of pure white comb and placing them in the bag. A bee landed on his back, crawled along his right shoulder blade. He expected a sting, but there was none.

Denali broke chunks of comb from the wall and ceiling until the bag was full. Then he leaned out the opening like a hatchling and took hold of the rope and tied the bag and called for them to pull it up. The bag rose out of sight. He ducked back inside the cave. While he waited, he dipped his fingers in honey and licked them. Nothing ever tasted so sweet.

When they dropped the rope back down, Denali untied the empty bag and began filling it again. The afternoon sun and the warmth of his body in those stone confines melted the wax seals. As he worked, honey dripped like golden ichor from the open veins of a god and clung to his long hair, each drop infused with life.

194

All told he filled the bag seven times and still the hive's wealth seemed no less. The warriors pulled him up to the top and everyone remarked that his Power must be strong—the bees hadn't stung him once.

BILDUNGSROMAN IV

Carrion Angels

1901, Philippines—1916, Cuba

Cain visited Aubrey at the military hospital in Manila. In the ward with blue walls mosquito netting hung over cots that held the crippled and maimed. The patients' heads were shaved to prevent infestation of lice.

Aubrey sat in a wheelchair. The amigo's shot had missed Aubrey's spine, but the army doctors who'd dug the bullet out were little more than white-smocked butchers. They'd nicked one of the nerve roots low on that column of thirty-three vertebrae. The mistake, grudgingly acknowledged as an "unexpected complication," was only of minimal damage, but after it was stitched up, the wound soon became infected. Surgeons were forced to open the wound once more and in their attempt to clean it out, Aubrey suffered greater injuries. In the end he was left paralyzed from the waist down.

Cain lowered himself to the empty cot and lit a pair of cigarettes. He passed one to Aubrey.

"They're getting ready to ship me out of here," Aubrey told him. "Home to Boston. You can imagine my mother's delight at getting to play caretaker. Finally a way to balance the scales, make her last amends."

His feet were crooked and unmoving on the footrests. His countenance appeared a living death, face drained of all color, his cheeks gaunt. It was the infection and fever that had almost snuffed him out.

"Might not be so bad," Cain said. "It's been a long time and people can change."

Aubrey laughed. "No, we can't. We follow the path nature laid for us. We enact our chemical destinies, then crumble into dust. We are who we are."

"You don't believe that."

"It doesn't matter if I believe it or not."

They were silent.

Cain opened the newspaper he'd brought with him. "You want me to read you some?"

"I'm paralyzed, not blind."

"Figured I'd read a while so you could lay back and close your eyes a spell. Nurse says you don't sleep much. You need rest."

"I'll pass. Reading isn't exactly your métier and my interest in current events has waned. You still got that goo-goo sword I gave you? The kalis."

"I got a pair of em—the one you give me and one that I found on patrol a week ago."

"You found one?"

"Took it off a dead Moro sharpshooter. Strange thing

is they look to be twins, them swords. Same design, same engravings. Had to be the same smith who forged em."

"Bring them both to me."

"What for?"

"Just bring them. After curfew, the garden in the courtyard. Don't let anyone see you. And I need something else."

Aubrey reached in his breastpocket. He took out an envelope and several folded bills and handed them to Cain. "Go to the market. Find the old woman who sells potions and those amulets the insurrectos wear. Give her the money and the note. She'll have what I need. Do this for me, Cain. Please."

* * *

Night. The garden.

"You out here, bud?" Cain asked the darkness.

"This way," Aubrey's voice answered.

He found him in the wheelchair, hidden in a shadowed corner. Vines grew up the stone walls.

"I got it," Cain said. He kneeled and opened a carpetbag. The pair of blades and a small package were inside. He handed Aubrey the package. "I don't know what the hell it is, but I got it."

"Nobody saw you here?"

"I made sure."

Aubrey tore open the package and removed a glass vial containing a pale fluid. He unscrewed the lid and drank.

"What was that stuff?" Cain asked.

"Witchery," Aubrey said. "To kill the pain. Now show me the blades."

Cain placed the twin swords in Aubrey's lap and Aubrey unsheathed them, each blade curving serpentine in three waves and carved with a snake head at the base.

Aubrey examined the swords. "You're right—the same smith forged them. There's no mistaking that craftsmanship. This one is yours." He held up the kalis Cain had taken from the dead Moro. "Its name is Wormwood. Carry it with you wherever you go and the spirit of the blade will serve you well."

Cain took Wormwood from him and sheathed it and placed it back in the carpetbag.

Aubrey gripped the other kalis. "This blade is named Leviathan and tonight it will taste my blood."

"You're worryin me, bud." Cain pulled Leviathan from Aubrey's weakened grasp and held it. "Maybe you shouldn't have this right now. What are you plannin on doin?"

"Nothing. It's what you're going to do, not me."

"What are you talkin about?"

"You promised," Aubrey said. "You didn't think I'd remember, but I do. You swore on the ring."

"I didn't mean that," Cain said. "You can't believe I really meant that."

While Aubrey lay in the delirium of his fever Cain had kneeled at his cot and reached to press the cool rag to his brow. Aubrey's hand had shot out and gripped Cain's wrist. He'd begged him, desperate. Cain told him no, over and over, and tried to break free of his hold. Weak though he was, Aubrey wouldn't let go. "Help me," Aubrey pleaded. His voice rose to a shout. "Don't let it go on. Promise me the honor. The samurai way." At last Cain muttered the promise, anxious to quiet him, calm him before he woke the entire ward, then Aubrey lay back down with a look of peace on his face and he'd slept at last.

Now Aubrey's eyes burned with a strange light.

"You promised," he said.

"I can't," Cain told him. "Don't ask me to do that. Anything else. Not that."

Aubrey closed his eyes. "Put on the ring."

"What?"

"It's all right. Go ahead, put it on your finger."

"But I ain't earned it. That wouldn't be right—you're the one who taught me."

"It came to you. When its master died, the ring sought you out in the world, swam a river to find you. Give me your hand."

Cain held his right hand out.

Aubrey took it. "Place your thumb between my second and third knuckles. Good. Now press down. You know what this grip is called?"

He shook his head.

Aubrey told him. Cain was silent, puzzled that the name should be so.

"I'll syllable it with you," Aubrey said. "Go ahead."

"I can't."

"Bal," Aubrey began.

"Tu," the initiate continued.

"Cain."

They spoke in unison: "Tubal-Cain."

Aubrey took his hand once more and showed him the grip called the Lion's Paw, then pronounced Cain a Master Mason.

"Now put it on," Aubrey said.

Cain hesitated. "It's still wrong. That ring is for a 33rd degree."

"Do as I say."

Cain broke the twine around his neck. He slipped the dead man's ring on the little finger of his right hand. "It fits," he said.

"I give you the honor," Aubrey said. "Now give me mine."

"I can't do that to you," Cain told him.

"All right. You don't have to. Just don't try to stop me. Give me Leviathan."

Cain hesitated. His hands were shaking.

"I don't want this for you," he told Aubrey.

"It's not your choice."

"There's got to be a better way at least. Somethin easier."

"Don't let me go like a cripple or coward. It has to be the warrior's way. Like a samurai. Let me be who I am, one last time."

Cain gave him the kalis. Aubrey turned the blade toward himself, struggling to raise it. Sweat glistened on his brow. He lowered the kalis, hesitated, then tried again and it fell from his grip.

Leviathan lay like a serpent in the grass.

Cain picked it up. "What's wrong?"

"It's already affecting my hands. The potion. My fingers are numb. I didn't think it would be so powerful." He was weeping, tears running down his stubble. "Help me, Cain."

"Don't ask me for that."

"You're the only one. Please."

"No, Aubrey…"

"I'm afraid," he whispered. "I'm so scared."

Now it was Cain weeping. "Of what, bud? I won't let nobody hurt you."

"I'm afraid if I wait, once I'm on that ship I won't have the courage. Don't let them take me back."

"Please, Aubrey."

"It has to be you, son."

Cain rose in a crouch. He gripped the kalis in his right hand and draped his left arm around Aubrey's shoulders. He touched the tip of the blade to Aubrey's stomach.

Looked him in the eye.

Broke down and wept.

He pressed his face against Aubrey's chest. "Ah, Aubrey," he said.

"Do it."

Cain thrust Leviathan in deep and drew it left to right, cutting the descending aorta. Blood spilled around his hand on the grip of the kalis. He stood in that strange embrace and looked Aubrey in the eyes as the life poured out of him.

"Is that all right, Aubrey?" Cain asked.

"The way of the warrior is death," he whispered.

Footsteps in the garden—or so Cain thought. He turned and peered into the dark, listening, waiting for movement, but there was none. When he looked back, Aubrey was dead.

Year later Cain would realize the light in Aubrey's eyes that night had been nothing but pure madness.

* * *

A nurse discovered the body after dawn. The news shocked Manilla, a wheelchair-bound hero of the war murdered at the hands of vicious insurrectos. At the hospital Filipino orderlies were questioned and subjected to the water cure.

* * *

In September 1901 the 4th Cavalry's tour of duty came to an end. Cain didn't accompany his fellows back stateside, instead arranging a transfer to a special unit of scouts selected from multiple regiments. The assignment owed to his proven talents as a tracker, fluency in Spanish, and working knowledge of Tagalog.

It provided an outlet for Cain's rage.

Guerilla attacks continued unabated. Insurrectos struck and fled, struck and fled. When General J. Franklin Bell took command of Laguna province late in the year, he implemented a scorched-earth solution.

The army established zones of protection. They issued identification papers and herded Filipino civilians into camps where families slept in tents behind barbed wire. Thousands would perish from dysentery, rampant in those crowded suburbs of hell. Anyone discovered outside the fence after curfew risked being shot on sight. By Christmas of that year almost the entire population of Laguna was interned.

Cain led patrols to isolated hamlets. Men were questioned and tortured, executed when their answers proved lacking. They marched in monsoon rains and crossed swollen rivers. Resting one day in the home of a barrio chief, Lieutenant Reynolds spied a beautiful mestizo woman returning from the market. He ordered her brought to him. The officer had first go before gifting her to the enlisted men. Rape held no appeal to Cain. He sat outside and sipped whiskey and waited for them to finish.

They killed and burned, whole villages put to the torch, and the more they killed and burned the better it pleased Cain. They destroyed crops and livestock in an effort to make of the interior a howling wilderness.

Death reigned across the archipelago. On Samar, General Jacob Smith, still carrying a Confederate Minié ball in his hip from the glory of Shiloh, was marching across the island. His men were under orders to slay every male ten years of age and older. They exterminated all those deemed capable of bearing arms against the United States.

* * *

After the army finished with the Christians in the north of the archipelago they turned to the Mohammedans in the southern islands. Cain was sent to Moroland as a scout under Captain Pershing. There he would see the bloodiest fighting yet. For centuries the Moros had refused to accept the rule of Spain and now they rejected their new American overlords.

"Why do you come here?" the Sultan of Sulu demanded. "For land? You have plenty at home. For money? You are rich and I am poor. Why are you here?"

The enemy had no fear of superior numbers. To die battling the infidel was the assurance of reward in the hereafter. The path to Paradise began when a juramentado swore an oath before the imam, his hand on the Quran. Then he would purify himself in a sacred pool and shave his head. He'd pluck his eyebrows to the shape of a sliver of moon. Finally he'd dress all in white and bind his penis erect with a cord and then he was ready. The martyr rushed weary soldiers in broad daylight, hacking with his blade, lobbing off a man's head in a single blow, child's play, before they could fire their Krags and send him to his glory.

At all times Cain stayed hypervigilant, prepared for a melee attack from juramentado or amok. He watched in suspicion even the small children and he was never without his Krag and Colt.

The army was tasked with ushering the Moros into the modern world. They strung telegraph lines and built schools. They fought to suppress the slave trade, piracy, and intertribal raids, insisting on rule of law. The Moros observed their own law, honoring the traditions of their fathers, the code that had held for a thousand years. Rebels cut the wires. The Moros taught their children as they saw fit. Pershing came down hard on them. He bombarded their great cotas, fortresses of bamboo and mud, and Cain led charges through the broken walls, overrunning defenders who died with blades in hand.

In early spring of 1903 a local datu murdered an ex-slave. Datu Suleiman claimed the man had touched one of his wives and so he'd been well within his rights to execute justice. Pershing disagreed. When the soldiers came to arrest him, the datu fled with his wives and sons deep into Moroland.

Cain was dispatched on the manhunt. He led the platoon into a remote valley, the jungle floor veiled in mist, and they marched until sundown. That night they made camp and posted sentries. By dawn they were on the move again, proceeding with rifles at the ready and bayonets fixed. The trail was soon overgrown and bamboo stalks rustled at their passage. Cain warned Lieutenant Baker of the danger, the bamboo telegraph alerting ambushers to their approach, but the lieutenant wouldn't be dissuaded.

"Keep your eyes open," Cain told the boys, "or it'll be your turn to say good mornin, Gabriel. Sure as hell, they know we're comin."

He topped off his Krag, five rounds in the magazine, one in the chamber, for a total of six shots.

In the forenoon they'd started up a slight rise, almost

imperceptible amid the undergrowth, when the Moros charged out of the mist. A dozen figures in turbans and shroudlike white robes. The ambushers took long bounding strides, bolos raised high, and rushed the platoon at once, ferocious, screaming no God but Allah.

The soldiers fell back, blood gone cold with horror.

Only Cain and Baker stood firm. "Hold steady," the lieutenant shouted. He drew his sidearm and took aim.

Cain fired his Krag and dropped the lead man and then they were among them. Rifleshots cracked, Moros fell. Cain worked the bolt and fired again. A warrior dashed straight at him before he could chamber another round. Cain looked into those eyes, black pupils like yawning voids, and he shoved his bayonet into the Moro's belly and stopped him in his tracks, impaled at the tip of the rifle barrel. Cain tried to pull free, but the Moro reached out and gripped the barrel. The Moro screamed and swung his blade in a wide sweeping arc. Cain ducked, felt it slice the air above his head, and they moved in a surreal dance, then he jerked the bolt back, the spent shell flying, and rammed it forward as the Moro took another swing. Cain pulled the trigger and blew his enemy's guts out.

A trio of warriors raced for the lieutenant. Cain shouldered the rifle and took one of them out. He aimed for the second man and squeezed off another round, but the bullet passed through the Moro's flowing robes. At his next shot the runner's legs gave way. Then the Krag was empty.

The third man wore a red plume in his turban and

by this sign Cain recognized Datu Suleiman. The datu charged as his sons fell dead beside him. Always by the book, Baker carried a service-issue .38 and he fired his pistol into Suleiman's chest, but Suleiman didn't so much as slow. The lieutenant emptied his cylinder. Still the datu kept coming.

Suleiman swung his bolo. Lieutenant Baker screamed, then his arm was dangling by a tendon.

Cain let his rifle hang by its shoulder-strap. He pulled his .45 and thumbed the hammer—

Suleiman readied the killing blow.

—and shot the datu centermass, watched him stagger back, then drop to his knees and collapse at Baker's feet.

The fighting was over in seconds, Baker the only man wounded. Private Montrose applied a tourniquet to the stub of Baker's right arm while Cain and the rest of the boys finished the dying Moros with their bayonets. A heavy rain began, soaking the foliage and the men instantly.

Montrose cut the lone tendon still connecting Baker's arm. He removed a flask of whiskey from his pack. "Drink up, sir," he said. Then he wrapped the lieutenant's severed arm in a blanket and got on his knees and started digging a hole with his knife-bayonet.

Baker held the flask. He rose and stepped off the trail and walked out to the edge of a glade where a single tree blossomed with small white flowers. Under the shelter of the tree Baker sat down and drank from the flask, staring into the mist.

Cain went among the bodies. A quarter of them were

women dressed in the same pale robes as the men. He drew his kalis and severed the men's genitals and stuffed their mouths, then he kneeled over the datu.

Cain went out to the lieutenant under the tree. He dropped the pair of bloody ears beside him.

"Suleiman's," he said.

Baker glanced at them, looked back up. A sickly pallor to his face. "What could I possibly want with those?"

"Put em in a jar. Show em to the next son of a bitch, let him know what happens if he won't listen."

"Get those things away from me. I didn't come here for this abomination."

"What did you come here for?"

"To bring freedom to the islands."

"They don't want it," Cain said. He bent and picked up the ears, pitched them aside. Water ran down his hat brim.

"I don't understand you," Baker told him. "Mutilating the dead like a savage. Why do you do it?"

He spat. "If you don't understand, sure as hell nobody can explain it to you."

Cain turned and started out farther into the glade, indifferent to the rain. He paused and glanced back at the one-armed officer. "Told you to get rid of that peashooter," he said, then walked on.

In the distance a great many birds were alighting. He walked out through the high grass and he could smell death before he saw it.

Under a swarm of flies, scales glistened in the rain, their pattern broken by a great wound. Brown fur was visible through the ruptured belly. Dried blood stained the tines of the heavy antlers.

The python had swallowed the buck whole and the buck's antlers pierced the underside of the python and gashed it open, protruding out its midsection in a bloody rift, and they lay dead in the glade, the deer and the great serpent. Cain watched a murder of crows, their feathers black and sleek. Carrion angels tore at the flesh of predator and prey.

* * *

Cain knew his time on the islands was finished. He waited out the remainder of his enlistment. He had no faith left in the righteousness or ultimate purpose of any of it and he came to see that such a faith had only been a false justification. He saw that in truth the warrior served a greater master than flag or country. That war needed no cause to hallow it because the purity of war hallowed any cause. He held no totem sacred save the kalis called Wormwood.

* * *

Cain boarded a steamer departing out of Manila and they followed the western coast north and crossed the sea to Formosa. There he hired a fishing vessel to take him over the strait and they docked at Zaiton in the Chinese province of Fujian, the harbor much silted up since the time of

Marco Polo, who'd once called that port the Alexandria of the East. Cain stepped onto the pier with a McClellan saddle slung over his shoulder and a Mauser in his hand. Two Colts were strapped to his hips. The saddlebags held his kalis, a purse of silver coins, and all the ammunition that would fit.

He rented a room in a boarding house. From his window he could see the pagoda rising over a temple where Taoists worshipped the long-dead general of an ancient warlord. Later he made his own pilgrimage and kneeled before that altar. The air heavy with burning incense. He lit a joss stick and placed it into the censor.

Cain inquired among the city's famed tattoo artists. When he showed them a crude sketch of the work he wanted done, they refused the commission and in a flurry of angry Hokkien they demanded he leave immediately.

At last he found a young apprentice willing to take his silver. The work required many sessions. Cain would remove his shirt and lie facedown on a cot in utter silence as the needle pricked his back.

When the apprentice was finished, the great all-seeing eye stretched fully across Cain's shoulder blades.

He bought a horse and rode out of the city. For months he wandered as ronin, masterless once more but this time not without a code. He traveled north, never remaining in a single place more than a few days, eventually crossing into Manchuria to find a war waiting for him. He cared nothing for the imperial ambitions of Russia or Japan. All he sought was an enemy to set himself against. For a time he considered offering his services to the Japanese thanks solely to the admiration Aubrey had held for them, but he deliberated too long.

In the end the decision was made for him. Russian soldiers arrested Cain under suspicion of espionage. He didn't speak a word of Russian—what explanation could he give? It was madness to think an American would venture to that place for any other purpose. A firing squad was his certain fate. They disarmed him and searched his person and removed the little derringer he carried in a custom holster under his shirt sleeve. When they led him before their commanding officer, Cain took the only chance he had left.

A flash of the ring, Cain raising his shackled hands so that the officer was sure to see it there on his finger.

The Russian officer stared. "Remove his shackles," he ordered. "Hold your rifles on him, but do not fire unless I order it."

The soldiers did as they were told.

Cain stood with a pair of rifles trained on him.

The Russian met his eyes and reached out. They clasped hands—the Lion's Paw.

"Welcome, Brother," the Russian said.

Despite the historic efforts of Catherine the Great to suppress Freemasonry, the Craft was alive and well in the Motherland. It went about its dark workings while the Tzar slept.

Cain was hired as a soldier of fortune fighting alongside Russian troops. Nights of drinking, keeping pace with the best of them. He picked up a smattering of Russian, enough to engage in an argument over horseflesh with a Cossack cavalryman. They came to blows. They rearranged each other's faces. The fight ended in a draw and the cavalryman's offer for Cain to cast his lot with their unit, mounted scouts composed of choice elements. That was how it was when a Russian recognized another man of valor.

He rode with the Cossacks and found them natural-born horsemen, the equal of any he'd known. Dauntless hearts. Wild-eyed and merciless. Reconnaissance missions took them along the flanks and rear of the Japanese, far beyond the command of military authority, beyond the reaches of the war. Perhaps beyond even the witness of God Himself, a few among them supposed. They made little distinction between the Chinese and the enemy, looting many of the same villages the Japanese would soon plunder as well, and they left violated girls and dead fathers in their wake. They lived off the country, sustaining themselves, but often in the bitter cold of that winter their horses were poorly fed.

By February 1905 the entire strength of the Japanese Imperial Army was concentrated at Mukden. The Russians had superior numbers, but the attacking Japanese were determined to prevail against General Kuropatkin's defensive strategy.

One night Cain rode back from the line where he'd carried a special message. He traversed a desolate stretch of ground the Japanese had bombarded days earlier.

Ahead in the faint moonlight he saw an ambulance wagon trundling across the broken land.

A howitzer roared.

Cain drew up, listening. His horse pricked his ears. By now the horse could anticipate where a shell would fall by its shriek through the dark sky, the mount's prediction more accurate than Cain's own.

The horse snorted. Cain realized the shriek was wrong, death arcing down upon them. The mount tossed his head, begging to run, and Cain gave him the spurs. When the shell exploded to their right, they galloped on, never slowing. Artillery fire rained all around them, a howling barrage. They passed the ambulance wagon, the driver whipping his mule and cursing in a fury as the wounded in the back screamed like madmen.

The earth stretched forth, then snapped back like an accordion. As though tortured under a sadic hand. The mule took flight, liberated from its traces, an iron shoe flinging off, whirling away. Cain's horse fell instantly at the explosion and they went splashing to the bottom of a flooded shellcrater.

When he came out of the daze, the first thing Cain noticed was silence. Gone the screams, gone the cry and thunder of shells.

Was he dead?

Too cold.

Freezing water came up to his chest and chilled him to the bone. The ground rumbled beneath him, the battle raging on, and he realized his eardrums had burst when the shell exploded.

He tried to move, then the pain hit him. It knifed up his leg and he let out a scream he couldn't hear. The weight of the dead horse pinned Cain's right leg in the mud.

Above the crater the Pleiades shone clear and bright.

He looked at the horse's head, bloody meat. The shrapnel had struck Cain as well—metal burned in his left biceps and in his side below the ribs.

Cain cursed. He drew his knife and started digging. When he'd moved enough mud, he strained to pull himself loose, teeth gritted in agony, then his leg slipped out and he was free. His boot was gone, still under the horse. When he felt down the length of his leg, there was no pain—until he reached the ankle. He let go immediately and sat back gasping.

By the time he crawled to the rim of the crater, the artillery barrage had ceased and a wave of Japanese were storming the Russian trench. The muzzle flash of rifles and machine guns. Grenades bursting, soldiers falling with terrible wounds. He saw brave men give their lives to take the stretch of ground, brave men give their lives to defend it. All in utter silence.

If the line held, they'd simply do it again, repeat the entire process another night. Grinding attrition. Slow death, trench to trench. He kneeled looking out on that strange and bitter new order flashing across the dark, then he turned and stared down at his horse in the crater. "I'm sorry," he told the horse.

In the following weeks his wounds kept him out of

the worst of the fighting. When Japanese Field Marshal Ōyama broke through their final defenses, Cain joined the Russian withdrawal, soon a chaotic rout as the enemy pursed them over the cold ground.

September of 1905 saw the Russians admitting defeat, the Japanese victory shocking the world.

A year later he was in Bali marching with the Dutch. Approaching the royal palace they saw smoke rising from behind its walls, heard drums beating wild and feverish. Cain sensed an inversion in the atmosphere. The air gone heavy, ozone-clogged.

When they reached the palace, a procession went forth through the gates, the Raja borne on his palanquin by four servants and following behind him court officials and guards and priests, the Raja's wives and children and royal retainers. All dressed in white cremation garments, flowers in their hair. The Raja raised his hand. His bearers drew to a stop one hundred yards from the invaders and lowered his litter.

Cain and the Dutch watched transfixed.

The Raja stepped down and gave the sign. A priest came forward and promptly buried a ceremonial dagger in the Raja's heart. At once the entire procession drew their own blades. They stabbed themselves and their families and anyone close at hand in a bloody pageant of death.

Puzzled and sickened at the sight, the Dutch opened fire on the crowd. A suicidal flood continued to pour from the royal gates as rifles and artillery cut them down. In a mad mockery of conquest the Raja's women flung jewels and coins at the soldiers' feet. The mound of bodies climbed higher. When it was finished, a thousand inhabitants of the island lay dead outside the gates of the burning palace and the old kingdom was vanquished from the earth.

Before Cain departed the island a gray Yogi instructed him in the art of meditation. The sage cautioned that so long as he continued to run from the secret he carried, he'd never find peace and his Atman would be steadily driven mad.

Cain fought in Syria on the side of the Druze. He fought for the French in the Wadai. Suffered wounds and illnesses that by rights should have spelled his end. Still he went on. He traveled west across Africa and upon reaching Morocco he secured employment with the French once more.

Another year and he crossed the Atlantic aboard a steamer bound for South America. Yanqui fruit companies provided work. He put down peasant rebellions, labor revolts on banana and sugar cane plantations, protecting the interests of American companies. By the time U.S. marines began their occupation of Nicaragua he'd had enough of the mercenary life. He'd been cut by knives, shot by rifle and pistol, his body a patchwork of pale scars. The funds in his bank account, almost untouched through the years, were not insignificant. He purchased a first-class ticket to Cuba on a steamer and started spending money as though it suited him.

The continent became embroiled in war, but he was unsure what to make of a clash between civilized European nations. The prospect of choosing a side held little appeal for him—and then there was a woman in his life like a sudden storm. Teresa, a singer and dancer in the cantinas of Havana. Two decades younger than Cain, she'd been widowed a year earlier when her husband's fishing boat capsized and he drowned, leaving her with a young son to care for. In time the boy knew Cain as Papa. The pair moved into Cain's suite with him, a fine hotel in the city. Cain pushed the limits of his imagination. He attempted another kind of life. It should've been impossible, but with her it was easy. With her everything fell into place. The days passed, each one a pleasure, and Cain was astonished at the change in himself.

Then one morning in March of 1916 the bellhop brought him the paper. The front page was all news of Villa's raid on Columbus, New Mexico. Twenty-three Americans killed, many others wounded. Cain read the report, then carefully folded the paper. He dressed and went out to visit his banker. He transferred the entirety of his funds into an account under Teresa's name. The banker asked again if he was sure. "I don't repeat myself," Cain said. "You heard me just fine the first time."

He put on his Stetson and stepped out into the harsh light and walked down to the harbor where he secured passage back to the United States.

CHAPTER ELEVEN

They dried out the peyote and shaped it round and then it was ready. Carnoviste placed half a dozen of the buttons in a pouch and gave them to Denali.

"A gift for Nantan," the chief said. "To keep him from anger. Go to him and ask his blessing on you."

"Why would Nantan be angered?" Denali asked.

"The medicine man deserves respect for his Power, but anyone who eats the sacred plant can get Power for himself. Don't let him think you'd dishonor him. If you made Nantan an enemy I couldn't even protect you. Understand?"

Too late, Denali wanted to say. The secret caught on his tongue and died.

He had to face this alone.

"I understand," Denali said. "When do I leave?"

"Tonight after he's blessed you. Don't take your firestick or rifle. A knife and canteen, nothing else. You must fast four days, then eat the button. It will prepare you for the burden of your vision."

"The plant gives me the vision?"

"It only disorders the senses. It will open your eyes

and guide you to a place of light. Remember, my son, a true vision is for the good of others, not a man alone. Our lives aren't for ourselves. Some men are given great visions only to lose their meaning in the darkness of their own hearts."

Carnoviste picked up a peyote button and slowly turned it between his fingers. "Be sure to tell Nantan it's a gift and not payment. To pay for such a thing would offend him and he'd have a right to anger."

* * *

In the evening cool Denali went to the medicine man's brush arbor. Nantan's wife sat outside mending a moccasin. She was a small quiet woman well past the age of child bearing. In earlier years she'd given Nantan sons, all save one gone to the House of Ghosts before they'd reached their tenth winter. The sole heir who survived to manhood, his father's pride, was cut down in a clash with Mexicans.

Denali wondered if the old woman ever suspected her husband's twisted bond with Gouyen.

"You looking for Nantan, boy?" she asked.

"I have a gift for the medicine man."

"He's waiting for you at the springs."

He hesitated. "Waiting for me?"

"Take your gift to Nantan. He's waiting to bless you with his Power."

Denali set out for the springs, but his walk was slow, reluctant. Bullfrogs croaked to usher the night. Shadows lay over the trail and every step he took led him farther into darkness. Fear bloomed in his mind like a malignant flower. Swallowing up resolve. He watched for glowing eyes in the pines, listened for the rush of a bear.

When Denali came in sight of the pool Nantan was sitting alone on a rock, smoking a pipe.

"Look who comes to visit," the medicine man said. "The boy who'd teach me the ways of Child of the Waters."

"The chief sent me with a gift," Denali said. He approached the medicine man and offered the pouch. "I came to ask your blessing."

Nantan opened the pouch and looked inside, then dropped it at his feet, disinterested. "What do you want with an old cripple's blessing?"

"Your foot might be lame, but your Power is stronger than any man's."

"True. What kind of blessing do you seek? Good beef in the winter, success on a raid? Maybe a certain match for you in marriage."

"I'm leaving tonight to search for my direction."

"A blessing for a vision then," Nantan said. "I hope you have better luck than your father when he sought his. It's no easy thing to act as chief with so weak a Power. I try to help him when I can."

"Carnoviste is honored to have your friendship."

"What will he give me for blessing his son? What is it worth to him?"

"I don't understand," Denali said.

"Will he give me a horse, a rifle? How should he pay

me?"

"With his thanks," Denali told him. "And I give you mine."

Silence. Then— "You speak well. Did Carnoviste teach you what to say? Never mind, the blessing is yours."

Nantan rose and stepped to the springs. "Drink with me," he said.

They kneeled at a slight depression in the rocks where the water collected before overflowing into the bathing pool. When Denali reached to disturb the water, Nantan grabbed his wrist.

"What are you doing?" the medicine man demanded.

"We have to stir it before we drink. So we won't see our reflections."

"You fear a face on the water? Why shouldn't I see my own reflection?"

"But it's a ghost thing."

"Who told you this? It certainly isn't. Your image can't hurt you, boy. Don't tell me you've come in search of a vision, but you're too afraid to see your own face."

"My face is for others to see."

"What vision could a coward like you ever hope for?"

Denali jerked his wrist out of Nantan's grip. He splashed the water and rose. "Bless me or not," he said. "I'll find my vision."

He turned and started walking away.

Nantan laughed. "You did well, boy. Very well."

Denali paused and looked back.

"I couldn't have answered as wisely or been half so bold

at your age," Nantan said. "Carnoviste should be proud. I'll sing a blessing over you tonight at the fire, then you'll go off alone on your search. Let the sacred plant be your guide and your eyes will be opened."

* * *

On his four-day quest Denali wandered the woods alone without food. He dug no roots, gathered no berries. Hunger gnawed. The peyote button rested in a deep pouch hanging from his belt. Solitude was his world. He'd never been apart from another living soul so long in his life and he found himself lonesome for Ishton and his little brothers.

He grew weak from lack of food. He carried only his knife and canteen, following the instructions of the elders and leaving behind all other weapons. If Nantan was going to come for him, this would be the time. Denali knew the danger, but even so he wasn't willing to lose his vision by picking wildberries or eating the inner bark of trees. Strength alone wouldn't be enough to defeat the witch. His only hope was the Power of a true vision.

During the day he hid in tangled bowers or high in a jumble of rocks and slept a fitful sleep. Awake instantly at the slightest sound, prepared for whatever came—or so he told himself.

Nights he sat awake listening to the calls of the darkworld. Expressions of lust and alarm, sorrow and yearning. The cries of screech-owls like dismal forebodings. He stayed perfectly still in the brush and watched the dwellers of the woods come and go, those who stalked flesh and prized blood, those who were timid eaters of grass and nuts. The hawk and hare. Lords of sky and burrowers of earth.

There were a scattering of springs and seeps below the ridge. Going down to refill his canteen, he made a point never to return to the same watering place twice, careful to follow no set pattern of movement. The second night of his quest he'd approached a spring through the pines when he smelled the familiar reek. Like rotting death.

The grizzly lurked nearby.

Denali went absolutely still. He waited a long time. Moonlight shone on the little pool of water and his mouth was dry, lips and throat parched. The wind shifted and he could no longer smell the predator. He told himself he'd imagined it, the figment of a beast waiting in shadows, but he knew the truth and a cold sweat chilled him.

Slowly Denali retreated, heading back the way he'd come. He spent that night without a drop to drink.

On the fourth day he wandered the ridgeline with a sharp ache in his belly. He craved meat and honey. For some time now he'd been feeling light-headed. A wave of dizziness swept over him and he paused to rest until it subsided and he sat looking out over the country.

To the west dark clouds, crimson filigrees. A burning aura over the mountains. A great rolling cloudbank was massing and coming his way and he hoped the storm would die out before it reached him.

At sunset Denali walked a high trail littered with the droppings of bighorn sheep. A single flower stood to the side of the trail and its bright red bloom swayed on the stem against the breeze. A pale spider balanced on those scarlet petals. Like a strange arachnid blossom.

Denali sat on a rock and stared at the spider. After a while he opened the pouch and rolled the peyote button onto his palm and studied it as though it were a living creature. Perhaps deadly, perhaps curative.

Evening of the last day—

If he intended to eat the peyote, tonight was the time.

If Nantan was coming to silence him, tonight was the time.

Denali reared his arm back and snapped it forward and pitched the button far down the slope. He didn't need the peyote—Carnoviste had told him it would open his eyes and disorder his senses, but the vision itself was a gift from the Other World.

Everything in his heart told him he'd find his vision alone or not at all.

Denali rose and walked on. Thunder boomed over the woods, the air electric. The storm was fast approaching and its fury felt as though it would shake the sierras from their foundation and topple the peaks to the valley below. Denali glanced down the slope and saw dead trees broken like matchsticks, felled in older storms. The wind came on and there was a rising hiss of pine-needles, falling to silky murmurs, then rising again.

He was aware he needed to seek out shelter, but something came over him, this sudden sense of euphoria, and he stood defiant on the ridgeline and saw the world washed in a strange clarity. Everything made hyperreal. Heart and mind and body at once awake to profound joy, all fear and grief vanished.

He ran along the spine of the ridge and the sky hurtled overhead. Stars dancing like a drunken swarm of fireflies. After a while he noticed the tears streaming down his face, then he was laughing and he felt himself without bounds, infinite as every living thing.

It occurred to him he'd felt something like this before. Long ago in the orchard of a boyhood afternoon, just before the seizure racked him, just before the fall, and he knew the ecstasy for a presentiment of the pain that was to come.

A filament of light twisted at the corner of his eye. The world accordioned before him. Compressing and elongating, some objects very close and others seemingly miles away, then everything was moving like a fractal in flux. Images atavistic, geometric flashed translucent.

Something descended upon him. A presence that was like a flood of grace filling him from the inside and flowing outward and he could sense the personal nature of it. No cold and indifferent force, the presence wished to know and be known. He felt himself enraptured by a superabundant outpouring of love.

This is pax oceania, adrift. A scent like burning flowers. Mirror shards of self speak to him. Now a taste like salt but not salt, something else, the spice of a forgotten word on the tip of his tongue. He would give his life entire for this moment, the quickening that has no counterpart in human experience. The rest of the world couldn't even suspect what joy that joy is which consumes him now. Open your eyes. Do you doubt the light in your gaze eternal? Everything shot through, illumined red and blue, this inextricable admixture of sight and sound, taste and touch, aswirl along every axis and dimension. Tolls of indigo, tangs of madder rose. I would be the one to unveil inner light, outer dark.

The agreed-upon set of facts that constituted his identity fell away—and he knew himself for who he'd been created to be, an echo of that shining presence, and created so that he might know Him.

He turned and darted into the trees and ran fast and light as a fawn.

When he burst into the clearing, everything shone in a pure white light, a circle of radiance so absolute he cast no shadow. Waves of love crashed over him. Denali raised his hand to shield his eyes and looked toward the source of the light.

A solitary tree stood at the center of the clearing. Brighter than a noonday sun. It bled forth a vast and shattered love—calling to him, drawing him close.

He saw the silver cords like strange umbilicals that ran from every tree of the forest, from every stone. From the robin perched on a high bough, the rabbit hidden in its hole. A luminescence rose from Denali's own chest and flowed bright and true to the midpoint of the circle, to the heart of the world where the four cardinal directions are one. Where every Godmade thing is bound together by threads of light.

Then he saw the figure on the tree. Arms out-stretched, head bowed. A thorny crown. Denali knew it was Jesus alone, battered and foul-treated, His perfect body stricken with every kind of sickness and deformity. A fearful thing to look upon and heavy under the weight of the world. This was courage beyond equal. The mission freely chosen, accepted before time was born. The Word made flesh made sacrifice.

When He raised His head, Denali saw His eyes were bright with sorrow that was all the sorrow there ever was. Something else in that gaze as well. It had the look of defeat but was ultimate victory. Unforsaken even now though He cried out. And the Son of the Father's love drank from the cup of death and reconciled unto Himself all creation, lost sons and daughters by blood ransom.

Denali thought if he were to encounter another person they would cry out and cover their eyes and ask him to look away for the intensity of the glow that surely radiated from his gaze. Who could bear to have him look upon them now?

The spirit of God was there and truth on the earth. He felt as though he were more than himself. As if the realization of all the potential of being itself were present within him at once, every weakness burned away, every strength mastered and made perfect in wisdom and love, his heart transfigured in the flow of the light.

He sensed that the spirit was making an offer. An invitation calling him to a new and living way, to be as he was now all the time, from that moment on, and it frightened him. He didn't know how he would live in the world, how to walk among men in that permanent elevated condition. The world would have no place for him anymore.

He was torn. His heart's cry was to receive that love and become it, but he didn't understand how he could function after that becoming.

"I don't know how," he whispered.

The spirit seemed to accept that as an answer, though with what felt like no small sorrowing, and it began to recede from him.

Then all at once the vision of light was gone and Denali stood in the pitchdark of the clearing. There was the smell of ozone. A sudden sense of dread. Lightning split the sky and in the ghostworld that manifested he saw a darker shape against the night's shadows, lurking at the edge of the trees.

The grizzly stood on its hindlegs.

Fear rooted Denali. A lightning bolt struck the ridge and blinded him a moment. The silver imprint burned on his retina and lingered and he could see its afterimage in the flash that followed.

The grizzly was gone. Vanished somewhere in the night.

An instant later another strobe. Denali caught a glimpse of the bear coming fast, rushing across the clearing, then lost him in the dark. Too late to run. He fumbled for his moccasin, the knife in its sheath, but his hands were numb and he struggled pulling the blade free. He was determined to at least draw blood.

There—he glimpsed the white star on the grizzly's chest.

He pulled the knife. Fought to keep his grip, something wrong with his body. A growl rose from deep within the beast's throat.

Lightning flashed—

The bear rose up before him.

Then something stole Denali's breath and everything was utter darkness as though he'd been dropped in a black void. He had a sensation as if he'd boarded a fast train. The bear slammed into him and they fell as one.

An involuntary scream escaped Denali's throat—the muscles around his vocal cords seizing up, forcing the air out. His body stiffened, contracting in on itself, and a terrible weight pressed down. Cold claws against his chest, warm spittle on his neck.

He was helpless against the predator as his limbs locked down in a series of tight convulsions. Muscles jerking, uncontrollable spasms. He lay contorted by the grand mal.

A towering gray thunderhead illuminated out of the night sky. As though the cloud were a colossal brain, sheet lightning like a synapse misfiring in that great hemisphere, the spark of chain reaction, electric chaos in a macrocosmic cerebrum. The heavens burned.

From unreckoned depths Denali summoned a final fleeting strength. He struck out blindly, desperate, thrusting the blade upward as he subvocalized a single word—

Die.

—and the jagged blue bolt flashed down from on high. Denali's blade pierced the beast's eye in the selfsame instant the lightning struck. There was a great roaring blast and the knife burned in his hand, the blade splitting down its length, and the bone grip shattered. Jolting pain shot down his arm to his chest, then blood was dripping from his ears. A white light surrounded Denali's body as though he were wrapped in an electric bubble. Flames lapped at the beast's fur.

Denali's eyes rolled back in their sockets.

* * *

When Denali woke in the cold wet grass, the rain had ceased, but it was still dark.

He was lying under Nantan, his cracked blade still buried in the medicine man's left eye. He didn't understand what had happened. Every muscle in his body ached and he was drained of strength. Denali felt as though he'd been punched in the back of the head.

He struggled to push the corpse off, but he was too weak. Finally he managed to slide out from under. He scrambled away and rose and stared down at the man he'd killed. Slowly the memory of it returned to him and his confusion fell away.

Nantan had come for him in the skin of a bear. He'd painted a white star on the fur at the breast and wrapped the disguise around him, the bear's head atop his own like a savage crown. A long knife rested in his right hand, his carved staff clutched in his left. Nantan was naked under the old bearskin save his Izze-kloth or medicine cord.

Fire from the lightning strike had burned the bearskin and burned Nantan's back beneath it.

Denali's right palm and fingers were burned raw and he couldn't close his hand. An intricate pattern of scars ran up his arm and chest, branching out like the limbs of a tree, tracing the path the lightning had taken as it burst his capillaries in the discharge. He bore the image of a great tree, inscribed with fire. His skin burned all along the branching scars.

A small leather pouch was tied about Nantan's waist beside his medicine bundle. Denali reached and opened it—a peyote button inside, half-eaten.

He'd killed the immortal medicine man.

Denali knew what it meant—the chief's son or not, he'd find no mercy for his transgression. Only death was fit punishment. Gouyen would demand his life and even the warriors loyal to Carnoviste would call for vengeance.

He'd seen his vision, but what good had it done? Now he was more lost than ever.

The world was silent all around him. He saw an owl light in a tree without a sound and the wind stirred the high branches, but there was only silence. Then his right ear canal opened with a pop. Blood ran down his neck and he heard the sound of the nightworld, sudden and painful. He pressed a hand to his ear and grimaced, head bowed.

He stood thinking what to do—run away, leave the mountains, go down to live among the valley people. He thought about it for a long time.

There's nothing left for you down there, he told himself. They're all dead.

But if you stay here, you're good as dead too.

When he finally made his decision, the sky was paling over the eastern escarpments. Denali gave the witch one last look, then turned and started down through the trees toward camp. The sierras were his home, the People the only family he had left in the world.

* * *

When they rose to sing their morning prayers, Denali was watching, hidden in the trees at the edge of camp. He watched and waited. He had to tell Carnoviste what happened, but he couldn't walk into their midst. Perhaps Ishton or one of his brothers would stray from camp and he could approach them to carry word to the chief.

The morning passed and luck wasn't on his side. They never came close.

Nantan's absence had yet to concern the camp. It was understood the medicine man's duties obligated him to wander alone in search of herbs and roots. Even so, time was running out. Denali himself was expected to return that very day—a vision quest was meant to last four days in accordance with the sacred number. If he was gone much longer, they'd grow worried and come looking for him. He had to get a message to Carnoviste soon, but who to trust?

He struggled to keep his eyes open. He was tired and sore all over and ravenous.

Sometime later he saw the maiden Jacali and her little sister Haozinne walk from camp. Each held a piece of the honeycomb he'd gathered, taking bites of the sweetness and chatting as they strolled into the trees. Jacali carried a spider-stick and she used it to tear down the dewy gossamer stretching across the path while the young girl followed after her. The older maiden was Denali's own age while her younger sister had yet to undergo her Sunrise Ceremony.

He watched the girls a moment, then rose and followed alongside through the woods, keeping out of sight. They were talking and laughing. It startled him to hear his own name.

"Denali will make a strong warrior," Jacali said. "If only he finds his vision."

"Gouyen says he's a coward," the little girl told her older sister.

"He's no coward. This honey proves it."

"But remember how he didn't want to punish the rock scratcher anymore?"

"Denali was wrong to show mercy to the enemy."

"You just like his red hair," Haozinne teased.

Jacali flashed a shy grin. "It is nice to look at, don't you think?"

Her sister laughed and agreed his hair was quite beautiful.

They walked on a ways, then lowered themselves side

by side under a large oak, their backs against the trunk. Denali crouched in the brush and watched them finish their comb.

He hesitated. Then stepped out and called to them.

The girls were immediately on their feet, turning as one to stare at him. Denali stood pale and haggard.

He'd wrapped his burned hand in a strip of bearskin he'd cut from Nantan's disguise. They stared at the strange scars on his arm and chest.

"What happened?" Jacali asked.

"Lightning struck me," he said.

"Are you all right?"

"I need to talk with you."

She began to step toward him, but Haozinne grabbed her arm and stopped her.

"You can't," Haozinne said. "It's not allowed."

Denali knew what the little girl said was true. It was forbidden for unmarried members of the opposite sex to converse freely. Should a boy wish to speak with a maiden, they could do so only with a tree or bush between them and standing back to back. The custom applied even to cousins and was kept between a man and his mother-in-law. Those who violated this rule of conduct risked shame and punishment.

It was a gamble whether Jacali would be willing to talk with him or not, but she was his last hope.

"It's all right," Jacali said. She shrugged free of her sister's grip.

"Uncle will cut your nose," Haozinne said.

"Not for talking to a boy."

Haozinne eyed Denali. "Sister, why does he want to talk to you?" she asked Jacali.

"Maybe I was in his vision. Go on back, I'll be right behind you. Go on, he's not going to steal me away."

Haozinne lingered. "Be careful," she said. Then turned and started through the trees, glancing backward once in suspicion.

Jacali approached him. Her eyes were calm.

"I didn't mean to scare you," he said.

"You didn't scare me. Did you find your vision?"

"Last night. But I don't know what it means."

"Maybe if you told someone. I could listen if you wanted to tell it."

"You'd hear my dream?"

"If that's what you want."

"Someday I'll tell you. But now I need your help. I'm sorry to ask you to do this. Will you go to Carnoviste and tell him where to find me, that I need to see him alone? No one else can know."

He was afraid she'd ask questions he couldn't answer, but the maiden surprised him, no hesitation in her decision.

"I'll do it, but I'll have to tell Haozinne something. So if she tells the secret, she'll think it's the truth."

"What will you tell her?" he asked.

"I'll say you had a vision you're to be a great warrior and that I was your wife and our children made the People strong again. That you wanted to tell me what you saw."

"Will she believe it?"

Jacali's eyes flashed. "Of course she will."

"All right. Thank you."

His belly growled.

She said, "I'll tell Carnoviste to bring something for you to eat."

He thanked her again. Jacali turned and hurried toward camp. She looked back once, the slightest trace of a smile, and ran on.

* * *

Carnoviste entered the woods alone. He came to the place the maiden had directed him and found Denali waiting.

Denali rose and faced him. Without a word of greeting he told the chief he'd done something that could never be made right again and he needed his help.

"My son," Carnoviste said, "I love you too well to refuse you anything you ask. What's this thing you've done? Maybe it's not so bad as you think."

"Gouyen's brother rides the ghost pony."

Denali told him all that had happened. How he and Chatto came to suspect Nantan of changing himself into the bear, what he'd witnessed at the pool, and the attack in the clearing when the lightning fell.

When he'd finished, there was a look on Carnoviste's face that was a mixture of deep worry and grim determination.

"We can't let anyone find him," the chief said. Relief washed over Denali and the tension in his body eased. Carnoviste believed him.

"We could bury him," Denali said. "Maybe in one of the canyons."

"It's not his body that's the true problem. There's no grave deep enough to hold back such a witch's spirit. It has to be a place where Power flows, a Power strong enough to keep his spirit confined. And somewhere no one would think to look. He has to be a secret even from the coyotes."

"Where then?"

Carnoviste hesitated. "I know the place," he said. He gave Denali a bundle of dried venison. "Stay here and eat. I'll go back and tell them I'm going to check on you. We'll need a mule and some rope. Don't worry, my son, no one can harm you while I'm alive."

* * *

The rain had destroyed whatever tracks there had been, man or beast. Carnoviste kneeled over Nantan's corpse. Lost in thought, wondering at the future of the People now their medicine man was gone. He reached and gripped Denali's broken knife and pulled it from the dead man's eye and wiped the blade on the bearskin and turned the blade and wiped it again. They loaded the body on the mule and set out afoot, choosing lonely trails where no one watched. Clouds were building once again.

"The rain will get rid of our tracks," Denali said. "We're lucky."

"Not luck," Carnoviste told him. "Power. Your Power is working to protect us. It brings the rain."

They led the mule up the hillside to the crest above the honey cave. Denali was exhausted, his head buzzing, and there was much still to do before he could hope to rest. He dumped the body off the saddle and Carnoviste readied the rope.

Denali peered over the cliff-edge.

"It made everyone proud when the bees didn't sting you," Carnoviste said. "Be careful. If you get stung this time, someone will notice."

"I can't stop them if they want to sting me."

"Of course you can. You've seen your vision. You're a man now, a man of Power."

"I can't feel Power. And I don't understand my vision."

Carnoviste waved his hand. "It makes no difference. When Gouyen's brother was young, I saw a Mexican shoot him from closer than we're standing now. I saw with my own eyes the bullet holes in his buckskins, but there were no wounds. He should've died, but his Power always kept him from harm—until he came against you. Nantan made himself a bear and came to rip you apart, but your Power was stronger. You called down the lightning to kill him."

"He wore a bearskin and I killed him with a knife. The lightning was just bad luck."

"You killed the bear with Power, then he changed back into a man. Don't doubt your Power. Tell the bees not to sting you and they'll obey your command. All right?"

"All right," Denali said.

"Good."

Carnoviste tied a long heavy stick to the reata. Taking

241

the reata's opposite end he stepped to the mule and looped the rawhide around the saddlehorn, then squatted and checked the latigo and backcinch. He walked the mule down the slope until the reata lay stretched on the ground almost its entire length. The mule stood flicking its long ears at a fly.

Denali sat on the cliff-edge. The stick at the end of the rope dangled several feet below the rim. He was exhausted, but there could be no rest until their task was finished. He gripped the rope with his good hand and swung his legs out over nothing and lowered himself to the stick. When he was ready, he called out and Carnoviste began backing the mule toward the edge.

Once again Denali hung between talus and rim.

When he reached the cave, he pulled himself inside. His footprints from the previous visit were visible in the broken comb on the cave floor. Bees streamed past, buzzing thinly.

"Ready," he called.

Carnoviste led the mule forward. When the end of the rope reached the top again, he halted the mule and picked up the rope. Carnoviste went to the medicine man. He secured the rope under the corpse's arms and around the bearskin, made sure there wasn't too much slack, then eased Nantan off the cliff. Carnoviste stepped to the mule and began leading it backward, slowly lowering Nantan down the cliff-face.

Denali crouched in the mouth of the cave and watched the dead witch hang over the void.

When the corpse came even with the opening, he reached and took hold of the legs and pulled him halfway inside. Beads and shells jingled from the Izze-kloth. Denali held him in an awkward embrace, strangely tender, and his fingers worked the knot loose.

Denali got him inside and yelled to Carnoviste. The rope went up out of sight. As he dragged Nantan to the far wall the bees grew agitated and flew about his head. He positioned the body upright, leaning against the wall, then stepped back. A bee lighted on the medicine man's single remaining eye, went crawling over that dark iris.

The reata descended again, Nantan's staff and knife tied in a bundle with Denali's own broken knife, and he unbound them and placed them at Nantan's side. Bees circled him, flying between his arms and legs. A loud collective hum. They reeled in the air, bounced off walls as if drunk, while others fell into his footprints and became trapped, honey adhering to their translucent wings. Chaos reigned in the hive as surely as though the queen were assassinated on her throne.

"Don't sting," he told the bees.

They swirled away.

Denali leaned out and grabbed the rope and called to his father that he was ready. He glanced down at the rocks broken on the talus, then held on while Carnoviste raised him up.

If they searched the honey cave, everything was lost.

CHAPTER TWELVE

New York, 1929—Detroit, 1930

Cain's opium dosage spiraled day by day. The hideous vision he'd suffered in the warehouse, old ghosts come calling, was too much to bear. He rode the hop train full-steam and didn't look back, though Mosby chided him over his escalating habit. Cain laughed and told him the issue was above his pay grade. They lapsed into the first of many bitter silences. Opium and yoga were Cain's only forms of relief and he owed all sleep, all forgetfulness to them.

He'd smoke, then sit up and begin a session of deep meditation, trailing the blue dot through chasms of time, and more than once Mosby had to shake him out of a trance. Sometimes on waking he'd find he had been gone so long he'd released his bladder unawares.

During nights of guard duty he held himself together through sheer force of will, the selfsame determination that had seen him through a thousand battles, diminished though it was.

Months rolled past.

One day in late October of that year. Cain opened the *Times* to news of the crash. The paper tried to reassure panicked investors, but the truth of it was plain to see. "Wall Street's gone belly-up," he told Mosby. "You watch and see—banks are goin to drop like flies." Black Tuesday stitched a caesura in the world economy. Billions were lost in the crash, entire fortunes wiped out in a matter of hours, and the despair that reigned on Wall Street rippled through the country.

On a December evening Cain and Mosby arrived for work and found the warehouse afire. Flames raging inside, smoke billowing from the loading dock. Already fire crews had abandoned any pretense of trying to save the building, satisfied with containing the blaze. The warehouse owner sat in his Essex Super Six parked across the street, watching the fire, and the foreman stood hunched at the open window, conferring with the man.

"Torched it for the insurance money," Cain said.

"You reckon?" Mosby asked.

"I'd bet my last dime."

After a while the foreman came over to them on the sidewalk. He produced a flask from his coatpocket and sipped, then offered it to Cain, who took it and swigged and handed the flask to Mosby. The black looked at the foreman and received a slight nod. Mosby drank. "Keep it," the foreman told Mosby when he tried to return the flask. The foreman wished them both luck and shook their hands, then turned and started down the sidewalk away from the blaze.

* * *

Cain spent the last of his meager savings at the Bloody
Angle. He took the long walk back to the flophouse with
the bundle pressed under his arm, the sidewalk slick with
ice and snow. A soup line stretched around the corner.
An old man lay sleeping on a subway grate. Wrapped
in yesterday's *Times*, headlines of despair. Cain passed a
circle of dispossessed men huddled around steam rising
from a manhole cover and they held their hands out to the
warmth like a congregation at worship.

He tightened his hold on the package.

* * *

Cain and Mosby cut expenses, began sharing a room at
the flophouse, but in time even the paltry rate for the
single room was too much for them and their rent was
soon overdue. Only one of them could leave the room
at a time for fear O'Mara would change the lock in their
absence. Cain had nothing left, no money or hope for
another day. He craved opium and dreamless sleep. The
thought of going without the hop, quitting cold turkey,
disturbed him far more than the prospect of living on the
street. He didn't speak a word of it to Mosby, but Cain
resolved that when he'd smoked the last dose he had left,
he'd do as the Voices bid him and end the struggle.

All too soon the final taste was gone.

Surrender always foreign to his nature, Cain fought through ravenous need. His hunger seemed impossible to deny—heart hammering, the shakes coming on. He couldn't suppress the tremor in his hands and Mosby saw the sickness taking hold.

When Mosby went out that morning, it was with no word of goodbye. Cain felt only relief at seeing him go. Alone in the little room, Cain opened the nightstand drawer and took out the .45 and racked the slide. He sat cross-legged on the floor. Surrender was no easy thing, not to a soldier. Pistol in hand, he tried to meditate. Always in the past he'd been ardent till the end, win or lose.

Now he struggled to clear his mind, but the silence was broken.

Put the barrel to your head, they whispered.

He didn't dare open his eyes.

Pull the trigger.

He concentrated on the blue dot. The Voices repeated the old secret, the shadow that had followed him all his life, and he fought them longer than he'd have believed himself capable. Sweat soaked through his clothes.

The son is the father's secret revealed.

Finally it was too much to bear.

Cain pressed the gun barrel to his head. The pistol trembled when he touched his finger to the trigger.

A key turned in the lock. Tumblers clicked—

The door creaked open.

Cain lowered the gun and opened his eyes.

Mosby stood in the doorway. He glanced at the gun in Cain's hand, then at the sergeant's face slick with sweat.

He tossed the package in Cain's lap. "It's a long walk to Chinatown," he said.

"Thank you, Mo." Cain almost sobbed.

"How you goin to use it?"

"To kick," Cain said and surprised himself that he meant it. The thought of what Mosby had done for him gave new strength to his will. He steeled himself for what he had to do.

"Then I'll help you," Mosby said. "But you can't do it here. The old lady's fixin to throw us out and that was the last of my money."

"I got nothin. No cash, no place. No friend but you."

"There's still one place you and me can count on," Mosby said. "Put that gun away, Sergeant. Let's go."

* * *

They turned to the kindness of brother Masons.

Years ago Cain had initiated Mosby into the Craft. Now in their time of trouble Mosby proposed they plead asylum with a lodge of Prince Hall Masonry. Cain agreed it was their best hope. He used enough of the opium to keep the shakes at bay and they set out on the long walk after sundown. They passed a bright automat where customers walked along a wall of glass-fronted compartments, selecting from the meals on display. A fat woman in a heavy coat fed nickels into the machine. She lifted a

249

hinged window and took out a slice of pie. Cain and Mosby walked on. Icicles hung from the naked branches of the oaks in Central Park. A bum begged Cain for a dime and when Cain shook his head, the bum spat and hurled curses after them. They left the park behind and journeyed through the Harlem night.

The Temple stood three stories high, just west of the Harlem River, and the pale stone façade bore the engraving *Prince Hall Masonic Temple*. When Cain and Mosby arrived out front, they saw light bleeding through the blue-curtained windows. A meeting was taking place that night.

"Go ahead," Cain said. "Give the knock."

Mosby gave the blue door two short raps followed by a heavy third. They stood waiting on the stoop.

The door swung open and the Tyler loomed over them gripping a broad sword. He was a hulking black in a pinstriped suit with a cauliflower ear. White gloves covered his massive hands.

Before the Tyler could challenge them, Mosby posed the question.

"Is there no help for the widow's son?" he asked.

The code indicated he was a brother Mason in distress. Upon such a signal, all brethren were required to render aid.

The Tyler looked from Mosby to Cain shivering in the cold. Then he set the claymore down and reached and clasped Mosby's hand and they exchanged the grip.

The Tyler motioned toward Cain. "Your friend also a

travelin man?"

"Travelin from the east to the west," Cain said.

The Tyler offered his hand. Cain gave him the grip.

"Welcome, brothers," the Tyler said.

* * *

Prince Hall Masonry was exclusively negro. Membership of the Harlem Temple included shopclerks and steelworkers, barbers and garbagemen, a few musicians who supplemented their income by trading in illicit spirits.

Three candles glowed upon the altar. The Masons of the lodge donned mystic aprons and took their stations on the black and white checkered floor. That evening a young acolyte was to be initiated into the First Degree.

Cain and Mosby watched from the shadows. While a pipe organ played softly, a deacon conducted the initiate into the Lodge-room, leading him by the cabletow, a blue cord tied about his neck. In the antechamber he'd been stripped to prove his manhood and they'd dressed him in the ritual garment, a strange kind of union suit, worn with the left arm slipped out of the sleeve, baring his chest, and a pantleg rolled up. On his right foot he wore a slipper. The hoodwink covered his eyes, a black satin mask, darkness all he knew.

The Senior Deacon took the compass from the altar. He approached the initiate and pricked his naked chest.

"A torture to your flesh," the deacon said. "Remember it should you attempt to reveal the secrets of Masonry

251

unlawfully."

He took the cabletow and led the youth in the circumambulation, passing each officer's station. Then from his seat in the east the Worshipful Master sounded the gavel. The initiate was made to kneel before the altar.

They put the questions to him, one after another, and he recited the Masonic catechism and made his oath. "Binding myself under no less penalty," the young negro repeated, "than having my throat cut from ear to ear, my tongue torn out by its roots, and my body buried in the sands of the sea."

When the ceremony was complete and his blindfold removed, a new brother found himself accepted into the lodge. He had surrendered his will to the lodge and now he was theirs to do with as they pleased. The lights came on and the Masons congratulated their fellow.

The Worshipful Master rose and went to the candles and extinguished each with a breath. He was a white-haired man in a top hat and black suit with pale gloves. He stood hunched like an old scholar. In the improved light Mosby recognized him as Enoch Lemont, owner of a Harlem bookshop and publisher of a small negro journal, a well-known eccentric in the neighborhood.

Lemont removed a glove and placed his fingers to his lips. He whistled, dispensing with the protocols of the formal ceremony, and everyone turned to him.

"There's another matter to discuss," he said. "I'm informed that our visitors wish to plead sanctuary."

They looked on the newcomers.

Cain stepped forward. The Tyler had furnished him with the rightful apron of a Master Mason and he wore it now. "My name's Cain," he said. "My friend here is Eustace Mosby. We've been soldiers together more years than I can remember and I owe him my life. He's the bravest man I know. Even now when the wise blood would say to cut and run, he won't desert me."

"Why should the wise blood offer such counsel?" Lemont asked.

"Because the hop's got a hold on me. I'm no good to anybody till I kick free from it."

"Why come here?"

"Nowhere else to turn. This is the one place we're never alone, beside our brothers."

Lemont paused. Then he said, "Tell me what you request."

"Shelter and time to heal. I'm askin on the level, for a widow's son."

The Worshipful Master looked from Cain to Mosby. He deliberated in silence for a time, then reached his decision. "Our brothers petition for sacred grith, the right of asylum. So mote it be."

"So mote it be," his fellow Masons echoed.

* * *

They set up cots in the Temple basement. It was dank and windowless, a far cry even from old Mother O'Mara's cheap rooms, but Cain was determined to take his stand there against the opium and the ghosts.

They had no money for food. The Prince Hall Masons took a collection and passed the coins to Mosby, enough to scrape by, with the understanding that Mosby might be called upon to aid them in certain tasks from time to time. He accepted the debt.

Cain went to ground. He'd made up his mind to kick and now he began tapering his intake, slow progress, cutting off only a grain a week at the start. Soon enough he discovered he'd have to pay back at a stark premium every millisecond of sleep the opium had given him. Insomnia returned full force.

He fought the opium's hold. Jailer and prisoner in one body. He believed there was no true cure other than a man wanting to quit and he had to keep wanting it.

During the day Mosby went out in search of work, but never any luck. The Tyler was an ex-heavyweight contender named Reginald Dubois. It was Dubois who informed Mosby that his debt to the lodge must be paid working security for poker games two nights a week. Mosby fulfilled his end of the bargain and the work earned him enough extra cash to keep himself and Cain supplied with food and bootleg whiskey.

Meditation and solitaire passed the time for Cain. He found a dusty copy of Cervantes in the basement and though he'd always thought fiction a waste of time, reading material better suited to women and children, he passed many an hour with the mad old don.

Twenty-three hours of each day passed in wait for

midnight and another dose. He wanted a last good jolt, to go down the pleasant river and forget the world and its haunted air, but the thought of Mosby's loyalty tipped the balance and lent him strength. He refused to act in a manner unworthy of such a friend as Mosby had proven to be.

The Voices kept a chorus of doom, but Cain refused to heed their calling.

Mosby brought him whiskey. In the long still hours when his nerves cried out for opium, Cain sipped from a bottle and drank till he collapsed on the cot in sweet oblivion.

At last he reached the point where he could skip a day's dosage and enjoy a couple hours of natural sleep. Then he tried skipping two days and got by, but on the third morning his stomach was tied in cruel knots. Muscles cramped, bones aching. Opium alone got him back on his feet.

He took to lying out on the flat roof of the Temple most afternoons, the sun's kindness on his face. After a while he could feel himself growing stronger, his appetite returning, and finally he got the dosage down to an eighth of a grain. Even the smallest particle, a dot on the tip of a toothpick, meant the difference between rest and a sleepless night.

A full three months passed before he brought the dose down to nothing. Still the need would rise out of nowhere, tearing his mind and will, making him half-crazy for hop, but he fought through it every time and every time it got easier.

* * *

One day after a long noon under the sun Cain returned to the basement, color and strength in his face.

He found Mosby waking from a nap on his cot.

"Mo, I didn't tell you before," he said. "But I'm grateful. I'd have said it sooner, just didn't know how. Thank you for all you done."

"Naw, Sergeant. It wasn't nothin."

"You're damn right. It was everything. I'd be a dead man if it hadn't been for you. So don't tell me it wasn't nothin. I know what it was."

* * *

Without the hop to regulate the hallucinations, Cain applied all his will, all the old power within him, to the practice of depth yoga. In large part he proved himself once more the master of his own mind. The dead whispered continually, Cain's truest companions, but he walked the line between reality and nightmare. Once he woke from a shallow sleep to find Aubrey at the foot of his bed and the little amigo silent in a dark corner. Cain closed his eyes and wished them a goodnight.

In time their appearances were less and less frequent.

* * *

Still insomnia tormented. All through the long unclocked hours of the night he lay awake. One evening while Mosby worked muscle at a gambling hall, Cain accepted that sleep wasn't coming. He rose from his cot and climbed the basement stairs in his stocking feet and went wandering the temple room by room. A meeting had been held earlier that night, but the Masons were since departed and the temple stood dark and silent.

The small theater on the first-floor was empty. On that stage the lodge would perform their mystery plays. A series of painted backdrops hung one in front of another, raised or lowered by a pully system. Beyond the stage now there was a deep green forest, a narrow path leading into darkened woods, faintly ominous, hinting at some presence lurking in the shadows.

He turned away from the stage and took the stairwell to the second-floor. Masonic aprons and other vestments hung in a series of haberdasher's cabinets. Quiet, dark.

He continued up the stairs, half of a mind to lay out on the rooftop and watch the constellations go wheeling, but when he reached the third floor, the great doors of the lodge room were open wide. He paused on the landing and stared.

Black candles burning on the checkered floor. A white-haired man kneeled facing the altar, his back to Cain, as a strange green liquid streamed down the altar steps and pooled at its base. Cain stared at the two glass jars resting on the altar. One sat empty, its lid lying beside it, but the other was sealed, full of bright green liquid, and floating in that emerald solution was a malformed foetus. A single eye in the center of its misshapen head. Cain had seen pickled punks before, on display at a carnival tentshow, stillborns preserved in formaldehyde, but none with a cyclopean eye.

Enoch Lemont turned and reached for the second jar. It was then Cain saw the dismembered form on the altar, the dagger in Lemont's hand. Lemont took the sealed jar and started unscrewing the lid, but he paused abruptly and glanced back toward the landing.

The worshipful master looked Cain in the eye, then slowly brought a finger to his lips. Cain saw that Lemont's mouth was stained with the green substance.

Without a word Cain turned and descended the stairs.

* * *

Cain didn't ask himself if what he'd witnessed upon that altar was another figment. All he knew was that he didn't wish to linger in the temple any longer.

But was he strong enough to face the world again?

Before they could depart the sanctuary of the temple they had to find work. Cain called in a marker. He reached out to a contact in Meyer Lansky's crew, a bookmaker who owed Cain a favor from his Continental Detective Agency days. Cain wanted a gig, but with one caveat—no trigger work. The bookmaker put the word out.

Word came back—the Purple Gang in Detroit was seeking out of town muscle to guard shipments against hijackers and the rare cop who wasn't on the take.

"Pack your bags," he told Mosby.

"Where we goin?"

"Whiskeytown," Cain said.

They shook hand with the worshipful master a final time, Cain promising to wire money as soon as they could, a contribution for the kindness they'd been shown.

"A brother Mason owes nothing except loyalty to the craft," Lemont said.

Dubois gave them a ride in the midnight rain and dropped them at the Greyhound station.

Mosby dozed on the bus while Cain stared out at the endless miles rolling by, the city behind them now and open country ahead. They skirted the southern edge of Lake Erie and turned north to Detroit.

Cain briefed Mosby on the Purple Gang. The young upstarts had managed to replace the old guard, the Moustache Petes, and now they controlled the bootleg funnel between Detroit and Windsor, Ontario. They kept Chicagoland and the local speaks supplied with Canadian whiskey. The gang was composed of Russian and Polish Jews. In the summer the Little Jewish Navy ran speed boats across the river and Lake St. Clair. Winter months they drove trucks over the ice. They had a history of hijacking loads from rival smugglers and they'd never hesitated to kill anyone who blocked their path to ascension. Even Capone took care not to cross them.

Through the summer of 1930 Cain and Mosby rode shotgun on booze shipments and guarded supply houses. They provided back-up muscle when Purple Gang lieutenants met with Capone envoys at the halfway mark, a quiet little town called Albion, for negotiations and exchanges.

They worked security at a gambling house frequented by negroes up from the south to work in the auto plants. The gambling operation was a partnership between a one-legged negro on the gang's payroll and Julius Horowitz, the son of the breweries' sugar supplier. It was a powder keg. When Cain realized how frequently the house used loaded dice, all subtlety out the window, he demanded reassignment for himself and Mosby. It was a mortal lock to end in blood. Time proved him correct. After the gamblers caught on to the scam, Horowitz barely escaped with his life and his negro partner wasn't so lucky.

Cain's demand for reassignment meant they pulled low tier duty. Now they guarded a cutting plant, an operation that watered-down shipments of Canadian liquor. The plant was housed in a mortuary outside the city limits, hidden in a secret basement and accessed via a false-bottomed casket on display in the showroom. Cain oversaw a pair of workers named Sol and Leon, who cut the liquor down and loaded out-going shipments into the mortician's fleet of long black hearses.

One evening in the basement Cain finished the latest edition of *The Detroit News* and tossed it in the wastebasket. Sitting opposite him at the metal desk Mosby was intent on a game of solitaire. Sol and Leon stood by the watertanks, busy cutting the latest shipment. Cain looked about their station for something else to read, another paper or magazine, only a stack of Mosby's pulps on the floor. Suspense tales held no interest for him, but he needed to distract his mind from ghostly whispers. He picked up a back issue of *True Cowboy Adventure*. On the cover a square-jawed cowpoke fanned a six-gun at marauding Indians while a buxom pioneer girl clutched his boots. He started flipping through it—

And stopped at a full-page advertisement, sudden recognition spiking his pulse.

"I'll be damned," Cain said.

For a moment all the whispers were silent.

"What is it, Sergeant?" Mosby looked up from his cards.

Cain stared at the page.

The ad read: *Last Apache Expedition—Sierra Madre, Mexico. Calling all fighting men! Hunt wild Apaches, save the kidnapped epileptic boy! No military experience required. Contact Douglas, Arizona Chamber of Commerce.*

"Mo, take a look at—"

A knock sounded on the steel door.

They paused listening, waiting for the second half. Knuckles rapped on steel, the secret rhythm. Mosby rose and picked up his shotgun and stepped to the door.

He slid back the strip of metal covering the Judas hole and peered through. Kessler stood at the bottom of the stairs leading down from the casket showroom. The mortician wasn't playing against type—he looked like Lon Chaney with a vitamin deficiency.

"They phoned," Kessler told him. "Said there's a problem with the last shipment we got, must've been tampered with. I need to check for poison."

"Poison?" Mosby said. He set down the shotgun, slid back the steel bolt on the door.

Cain lowered the pulp and picked up his own 12-gauge.

Mosby tugged the pull-handle and swung the heavy steel door open. "How come they think—"

Kessler jolted forward, falling to his knees. Three men charged after the mortician, a pair gripping Thompson submachine guns, the third man shoving a sawed-off 12-gauge in Mosby's belly.

"Don't twitch," he said.

Glass shattered by the watertanks, one of the startled workers dropping a whiskey bottle.

The third man wore a long dark trenchcoat. There was a pale starburst below his right eye, stubble on his jaw going gray. He spotted Cain. "Drop your gun, old man, or I'll paint the wall with your pet coon. Way I hear it, you're sweet on him."

"Don't you do it, Sergeant," Mosby said.

Cain studied them—

The older Thompson gunner's shirt strained against a bulging belly and he stood on a pair of stumpy legs. His young partner sported peach fuzz on his cheeks, not even old enough to shave. The kid's eyes were big and white and darting in his sweat-slick face. Not cops. Likely a rival gang, none of them professionals.

There was nothing Cain could do while the sawed-off was pressed against Mosby.

"I said drop it," the third man shouted. He jammed the twin barrels deeper into Mosby's stomach and the air went out of his lungs.

Cain dropped his shotgun on the desk and raised his

hands.

"Search the old guy," the third man ordered.

The fat gunner stepped up to Cain. "Turn around, hands on the wall."

Cain gave him a stare, then turned and pressed his palms to the cold concrete. The gunner patted him down one-handed, pulled the 1911 from Cain's shoulder holster, and tossed it aside.

Cain turned back around. The third man was patting Mosby down.

The gunners turned their attention to Sol and Leon by the tanks. Both workers had their hands up. "Don't fucking move!" the kid screamed at them.

"On the ground," the fat gunner shouted, contradicting his comrade.

Sol and Leon stood trembling, unsure whether to stay put or hit the desk.

"I said on the ground!" the fat man told them.

Sol dropped and went spread-eagle. Leon hesitated—there was broken glass on the concrete before him. He'd dropped the whiskey bottle, spooked when the gunmen burst into the room, and now he began to step away from the glass shards. His foot slipped in spilled whiskey and Leon fell toward the far wall and the rack of spare shotguns.

The young gunner spotted the racked weapons. He didn't hesitate. The spray of bullets cut through Leon's body and into the tank behind him, water and booze spilling out, and then Leon was dead on the floor. Ricochets whined off concrete walls and up through the ceiling, then abruptly the gunfire ceased.

The gunner stood cursing. His Thompson was jammed, a stovepiped casing, and he fumbled with the weapon, attempting to clear it.

"You dumb bastard," the third man shouted. "Are you trying to kill us all?"

"I didn't mean to," the gunner whined.

The watertank poured out its content onto Leon's body. Kessler lay trembling on the floor with his hands over his ears.

The third man kicked Kessler in the ribs. "On your feet," he said. He shoved Mosby aside and motioned with the shotgun toward the crates of whiskey. "You assholes start hauling it upstairs. Get moving."

Cain held up his empty hands. "All right. No call for more shootin."

The young gunner was still struggling to clear the jam. Then Cain saw Aubrey standing at the kid's shoulder, leaning down to whisper something in his ear. The gunner paused in his struggle with the weapon and cut his eyes to the side as though he'd heard something, hesitating with the stovepiped Thompson useless in his hands.

Aubrey looked across the room.

"Do it now, Cain," the dead man told him.

Cain knew he wouldn't get a better chance. He stepped toward the crates, lowering his hands, then in a flash he reached in his left shirt-sleeve. He pulled the single-shot derringer from its custom holster.

He pivoted on his heel.

Raised the derringer.

Shot the fat man in the face—

Point blank.

The gunner staggered back, blood pouring from a wound in his brow, and dropped the Thompson to clutch at his face.

Cain threw down the empty derringer. He dove across the metal desk and snatched up his 12-gauge, chambered and waiting.

The third man discharged one barrel of the sawed-off. Lead pellets hailed into the metal desktop just as Cain rolled onto the floor on the far side.

The young gunner cleared the jam and threw the bolt back. He shouldered the Thompson.

Cain's arm swept out across the concrete and he pointed the 12-gauge and fired one-handed. The shotgun blast cut through the gunner's ankles. His knees slammed down to the floor and he let loose a burst of automatic fire that went howling off concrete.

Cain rose and pumped a fresh shell into the chamber.

The fat man was crawling, a curtain of blood over his eyes, and he reached out blindly for the weapon he'd abandoned.

The third man pointed his sawed-off at Cain. Mosby's hand flashed out, sweeping aside the shotgun, and the last barrel fired into the wall. Mosby's ears rang and powder burns stung his arm.

Cain leveled his 12-gauge—

And shot the young gunner in the chest.

Pumped and swung.

He blew off the back of the fat man's head.

The third man wielded the empty sawed-off like a club and struck Mosby full in the face. Mosby heard a crunch, then blood gushed from his nose. The third man dropped his empty weapon and went for the .38 on his hip.

"Duck, Mo," Cain shouted.

Mosby hit his knees.

The third man brought the revolver up.

Cain racked the pump as he strode forward. He pulled the trigger. The blast caught the third man centermass and there was a clang like metal on metal and he staggered back on his heels.

Cain worked the pump and stepped up. He fired again, striking him in the chest once more, and the third man dropped his pistol. Then Cain's last shell exploded and the pellets sent the third man sprawling across the doorway.

Cain lowered the empty shotgun. "You all right, Mo?" he asked.

Mosby stood up and wiped his bloody nose on a shirtsleeve. "I'm all right, Sergeant."

Cain started to turn away from the steel door.

"Keep your eyes on him," Aubrey whispered. *"He's got a secret."*

The third man lay motionless.

Cain saw his fingers twitch.

Then the man was reaching out, going for the .38 on the floor beside him.

Cain dropped the shotgun. He spotted his 1911 on the concrete where the fat gunner had thrown it aside. He hit the deck. His hand closed around the grip just as the third man brought his revolver up. Cain intended to aim centermass again, but he remembered the metal-on-metal clang. Only a headshot would put him down. He was leveling the semi-auto, flicking off the safety, when the third man thumbed back the hammer, then they fired in the selfsame instant.

The bullets went supersonic—

The .38 darted by Cain's head, half a span to the right, and ricocheted off concrete before slamming into the watertank.

The .45 cut through the air. It caught the third man just above his left brow, then the back of his skull burst like shattered eggshell.

—and Cain's brass casing clinked to the floor.

Cain rose. He stepped to the third man and kneeled and tore open his trenchcoat. A steel plate hung from his neck, scarred with buckshot.

"When are you going to start listening to me, boy?" Aubrey asked, kneeling before him.

"I hear you," Cain said.

"What's that, Sergeant?" Mosby called.

"Wasn't talkin to you," Cain said and rose once more.

Sol was cowering in a corner. Kessler lay with his palms pressed tight to his ears and his eyes squeezed shut.

Cain released the tension in his body.

A flash of movement from the corner of his eye—

He brought up the pistol, finger on the trigger. The little amigo, the long-dead Filipino boy, stood watching by the tanks.

Cain lowered his gun and looked away from the old ghost.

"What is it, Sergeant?" Mosby asked.

"Not a damned thing," he told him.

Cain bent and picked up his derringer. He took the pulp magazine from where it had fallen on the floor. There was blood staining a corner of the cover and he wiped it with a handkerchief, then rolled up the magazine and stuck it in his jacket pocket.

* * *

Cain found the truck waiting outside in the driveway. Engine running, no driver. They'd come with only a three-man crew, likely acting on a tip-off, a leak somewhere in the ranks of the Purple Gang.

He brought Kessler back to his senses with a slap across the face. The mortician led them upstairs to the crematorium while Cain and Mosby carried the bodies wrapped in sheets. They searched the dead for identification and found driver's licenses for two of them. The shotgunner and the kid with the Thompson were both named Marciano, father and son from a closer look at their faces. Cain recognized the surname. They were a Detroit family who'd run a small bootleg operation until the Purple Gang started hijacking their shipments and finally assassinated the old man. So the Marcianos had decided to strike back and now they'd joined their patriarch in the hereafter.

They cremated the three gangsters and they cremated Leon's body as well. The house was far enough out in the country that Cain wasn't afraid the shots had been heard, but he worked fast to destroy evidence nonetheless.

He carried a five-gallon can of diesel from the garage and climbed behind the wheel of the idling truck. Mosby followed him in a hearse while he drove deep into the countryside. He took a fire road into the woods, then parked and got out and unscrewed the lid from the diesel can. He doused the truck's interior and exterior. Stepped back and struck a match, flicked it onto the front seat.

Flames enveloped the truck.

Cain slid into the passenger seat of the waiting hearse. Mosby turned them around and they headed back toward the blacktop. There was a powerful boom and they saw the truck in the rearview mirror burst into a fireball.

Cain took the rolled-up magazine from his coatpocket.

"What you got there, Sergeant?" Mosby asked.

"Our ticket out," Cain told him. "That's the last time I clean up for Jewboy gangsters." He read Mosby the headline of the ad.

"So them Apaches are still holdin the boy captive," Mosby said.

"There's a whole band of em up in the sierras. Just like Geronimo never surrendered, like we never civilized em at all. But they're dyin out and they need all the young bucks they can get. They took that McKenna boy for fresh

269

blood."

"What you mean they want his blood?"

"They plan on usin him to breed a whole new generation. A tribe of half-breeds, every one of em a killer and thief."

"You figurin on joinin up with the mercenaries for the reward?"

"Off this ad?" Cain laughed. "It's a damn joke. Every moron in the Tom Mix Fan Club will apply to be a real Indin fighter. McKenna don't need play-pretend soldiers. He needs the real thing. But the operation's got to have a backer, a money man to outfit us for the campaign and guarantee pay for the men I hand-pick to ride with us."

"I don't know nobody who could cut that kind of check."

Cain was silent. He took a flask from his coatpocket and unscrewed the lid.

"I know a man," he said. "An old man who lives on hate. The way regular people get their nourishment from food, he gets his from pure constant hate. I worked for him once. He hired the agency to ferret out a spy in his company, sellin trade secrets to the competition. This man's richer than the devil. Puts old Mammon himself to shame."

In the backseat Aubrey whistled the tune to *Stars and Stripes Forever.*

Cain didn't flinch. He kept his gaze locked straight ahead. He took a pull from the flask, felt the fire going down, burning away his craving for the hop.

"This old man I got in mind, he won't like the plans

the Apaches got for that boy. No sir. Not by a damn sight. And I'm bankin that he'll spend a king's ransom to put a stop to it, one way or the other."

CHAPTER THIRTEEN

December, 1930

Jubal rode alone in the backseat of the Pierce Arrow limousine. The luxury car was bloodred with black running boards and whitewall tires. His suitcase sat in the floorboard and a gray Stetson rested on his lap. His boots were freshly shined and he wore a new suit and tie and for the first time in a long while he didn't carry a pistol.

The negro chauffer drove him. Applegate's driver had picked up Jubal at the railroad depot in San Francisco and they'd driven north out of the city, heading to the financier's estate near the small town of Monte Rio deep in redwood country.

They turned off the main road and took an asphalt drive marked RESTRICTED. Treetops obscured the early stars of evening. Ancient trunks rose out of the groundmist like floating giants. Many of the old-growth redwoods had been saplings at the time of the First Crusades, now standing over three hundred feet, dwarfing the car and its occupants.

When the driver pulled up to the gatehouse and rolled down his window, an armed guard stepped out to meet them. An owl of Athena emblem was stitched to the breast of the guard's uniform jacket.

"Jubal McKenna to see Mr. Applegate," the driver said.

The guard bent down and shone a flashlight in the driver's face, then directed the beam into the backseat. Jubal blinked against the glare. The guard glanced from his face to a newspaper clipping he'd taken from his pocket. Jubal realized it was a photo of him the papers had carried in their reporting on the kidnapping. Applegate was a careful man, it seemed—and one with enemies.

"Sorry about that, Mr. McKenna," the guard told Jubal. "Can't be too careful these days."

"That's all right," Jubal said.

The guard straightened and nodded at the driver. "Okay, you're good to go."

The driver put it in gear and they motored through the redwoods. When they rounded a bend, Jubal could see the lights of the mansion on the hilltop, waiting above the fog.

* * *

"A fair wage for fair labor, sir—that's my policy," Horus Applegate told Jubal across the dining room table. "I support a national family wage. Not least of all because it will allow us to curtail the flood of undesirables rushing in from Europe, willing to work for a pittance. The price floor should also force the negro out of the low-wage economy of the southern states."

An electric chandelier hung from the high ceiling and illuminated the dining room. The old man smoked an amber-colored Meerschaum pipe. A painting by Goya hung in a golden frame—*Saturn Devouring His Son*. A serving girl appeared from the kitchen to carry away the empty plates in silence while a snowy owl watched from its perch in an iron cage. The owl's head twisted around and those yellow and black eyes stared at Jubal.

Throughout dinner Applegate had talked only of business and legislation, speaking in a high-pitched piercing voice, almost feminine, that Jubal found grating.

He'd been warned to keep a pokerface. Holloway, the old man's aide who'd arranged the meeting, had informed Jubal of what to expect days earlier. "Show no reaction to his shrill voice," Holloway said. After Applegate lost his hearing, his pitch had begun drifting higher and higher each year, no way for him to gauge it, until it was nearly a screech. Family and employees alike had been too timid to make the old man aware of the gradual change in his voice for fear he'd fly into one of his infamous rages. "If he's deaf," Jubal had asked, "how am I supposed to talk to him?"

"Another rule," Holloway said. "Never turn your head to the side when Mr. Applegate is in the room. He reads lips quite proficiently."

Now Jubal looked the man in the eye. "Thank you for the supper, sir. It was a fine meal, but I still don't understand what I'm here for."

"How'd you like that blank check?" Applegate asked.

Jubal reached in his breastpocket and withdrew the check that had arrived at the ranch weeks earlier, hand-delivered by special courier. It was signed and dated, only the amount had yet to be filled in. He placed the check on the table.

"Your man called it an invitation."

"I wanted to see the last Indian fighter in the flesh." Smoke escaped from Applegate's nostrils and curled and drifted toward the ceiling.

"It was a long trip just to satisfy your curiosity," Jubal said. "Tell me I came up here for more than that."

"Name the amount, Mr. McKenna. I want to bankroll your next expedition. Hire the best trackers and guides, outfit yourself with whatever weapons and supplies you need. In return all I ask is the opportunity to share your story with the world."

Applegate was ninety years old, hunched and gray. A wizened skeleton bundled in a heavy greatcoat. Once he'd cut a dashing figure in his youth, the envy of his fellow Princeton alumni and the subject of not a few young ladies' most indelicate journal entries. Time conquered flesh—he was frail under the burden of its passage, a shrunken thing. In his lifetime he'd strengthened the family fortune to such heights of power and prestige his mere presence on the floor of the New York Stock Exchange was sure to gorgonize all onlookers.

"The story's already been told," Jubal said. "All the big papers have done articles, one time or another."

"I wasn't thinking of a news item."

"What then?"

"My imagination has been enamored of late with financing a movie, free from the constraints and political persuasions of the Hollywood system. What would you say to your story up on the big screen?"

"I'd say it's my life, not a matinee."

"This won't be any cowboy serial. No sir. A factual account—dramatized, of course, but with stark realism. There won't be a single American family unaware of your son's name and the truth of what happened. Let me show them your struggle."

"Why are you so interested?" Jubal asked.

"I have my reasons."

"And what are those?"

The old man only smiled around his pipestem. "Rest assured money is the least of what I have to offer. I can provide something far more valuable. Do I capture your interest?"

"If it helps me find my son."

"You've been taking action from the standpoint of attempting a rescue. A critical misstep, sir. The solution isn't rescue but revenge."

"I don't see how revenge brings John Russell home."

"I'm told you had some trouble with your men on the last excursion. Discipline problems. Something about a lost mine turning them deserter."

Jubal started to reply, but Applegate cut him off with a wave of his hand.

"Don't worry, I have no interest in Tayopa or Cibola or whatever the hell. You didn't come all this way to talk buried treasure. I only bring it up to illustrate a point. You can't expect domesticated animals to hunt down a beast wild in all its generations. You understand me? Even if you did maintain perfect discipline over your men, what good would it do? Search those mountains till your eyes go blind and you'll never find the boy. The territory's too vast, too many places to hide."

"I don't give a damn how big it is. I won't stop till I find him."

"A strategy designed for failure."

"What exactly do you want me to do?"

Applegate leaned forward. "Bring them to their knees. Make the cost too great. Kill their bucks and fat-faced squaws and papooses, then I guarantee you they won't be holding onto that boy of yours like he's a good luck charm. They'll surrender him up when they see the cost. Won't have any other choice. You've got to take the scientific approach."

Applegate placed his pipe in a carved walnut holder. His bull's prick cane leaned against the table, a great cured and varnished phallus. He snatched the cane and gave the floor three hard taps.

A servant girl stepped into the room holding a tray with a decanter of brandy and a pair of snifters. On the hem of her skirt the insignia of a little owl with huge round eyes. She placed a glass in front of Applegate and poured from the decanter.

"Conditioning modifies behavior," Applegate said. "You ring a bell and give the bitch a biscuit often enough, pretty soon she starts licking her chops every time she hears a bell. Whether she's hungry for it or not. That's how it has to be done. Strike the savages hard and often and you'll break their will."

The girl filled Jubal's glass. He thanked her and she turned and retreated back into the kitchen.

"Assume you find the camp where they're holding your son," Applegate said. "What's your next course of action?"

"We ride in and hit them with everything we've got."

"Your boy could be injured in the battle. Hell, for as long as he's been with them? Likely gone native by now. You could end up staring down the barrel of his gun. But if you bleed their other camps long enough? They'll beg you to take him off their hands like he's death incarnate. That's a strategy that wins, sir."

"Maybe they won't ever give in," Jubal said.

"Is the boy of their blood? No man or woman loves the adopted child more than their own blood. I understand you have one of them living with you. An Apache girl."

"How's that any of your damn business?"

Applegate raised a hand. "I don't mean to touch a nerve, but you take my point. Would you trade her for your boy? Of course you would, I can see it in your eyes. You have to make them understand the price of keeping him captive. The Apaches will give him up without hurting a hair on John Russell's head when you employ my strategy. They'll do what it takes to save their own."

Applegate sipped his brandy. "It fell to men like us to keep this world turning," he went on. "That's our inheritance by birth. An honor and a duty. What can a culture that never saw the need to invent the wheel possibly comprehend about that kind of responsibility? Nature overlooked them in her selection. Better to do to them quickly what she herself would see to in time."

"I don't mean any disrespect," Jubal said, "but I'm nothin like you."

"Don't be so sure. We're both men who command, who bring order to our respective worlds. Allow me to elucidate my position—I may be old, Mr. McKenna, but my ideas are not. I'm proud to call myself a progressive in all things. My family has always kept an eye toward the future. We Applegates were abolitionists long before Lincoln ever ran for public office. My father believed it our duty to cleanse the land of slavery's abomination. Finally the Great Emancipator loosed the slaves from their chains, but he left the job half-finished. That play-actor killed Lincoln before he could carry out the final purification, before he could ship the negroes back to deepest darkest, where they belong. We see the consequences of his failure today. The most unfit among us outbreed our best by a disastrous ratio. The negro problem inspired me to devote my fortune toward research in the field of eugenics. You're familiar with the science?"

Jubal stared at the brandy snifter in his hands. Slowly turned it. He kept his voice flat. "I read about the rulin by Oliver Wendell Holmes a few years back. The sterilization case."

"Buck vs. Bell. Yes, sir, a landmark victory."

"Your movement doesn't seem too concerned with individual liberty."

"I take it you object to Justice Holmes's ruling?"

"I do," Jubal said. "Even if you don't respect the U.S. constitution, there's still such a thing as God-given rights."

"Ah, a stalwart defender of the laissez-faire." Applegate drained his snifter. "I'm pleased to know you, sir. You're wrong as hell. Superior blood outweighs individual rights. The well-born shall inherit the earth, provided we don't squander the germ plasm entrusted to us. Provided that we stop pursuing false forms of noblesse oblige to the downfall of our race. The great mass of negroes and the feeble-minded reproduce like rabbits and if it's allowed to continue, they'll outnumber us within a few short generations. Can you conceive of such calamity? Infanticide was practiced in Sparta with great success—it must be revived if we're to hope for survival. The negro is too low in impulse control to ever be trained in the use of contraception. We must grant them access to a practical method of terminating careless pregnancies. Abortion is the only reasonable path forward, the perfect compromise between the sterilization and elimination factions of the movement. As it stands now, we breed animals with greater care than our own citizens. We've got to raise up a race of thoroughbreds. Those who have fought, tooth and claw, to the top of the evolutionary pinnacle and planted their flag are deserving of the power they wield. As Plato said, the race of the guardians must be kept pure."

Jubal stared at him. "Are you finished?"

"I've only just begun. You don't appreciate my oratory?"

"Save it for the soapbox."

Applegate laughed. "On occasion I do get carried away."

"I think now I understand why you invited me here," Jubal said. "You want my son for a symbol. You want to make your little movie—"

"Nothing little about it, I assure you. A true epic."

"—and show the audience your ultimate nightmare. A white boy taken captive by wild Indians to keep their tribe alive."

"Young John Russell's situation mirrors the precarious state of our race as a whole. Captive and alone. In time, no doubt, forced to mix his bloodline with that of savages."

"What happened to my family," Jubal said, "that's not fodder for your propaganda. I'm not goin to let you use it to advance some crazy agenda."

"Imagine for a moment the final scene. The hero dispatches the last bloody warrior, then rides in and swoops up his long lost son. A grand homecoming, return to civilization. It could be the rallying cry for a nation on the brink."

Jubal swore.

Applegate screeched out his laughter. "No doubt you believe I'm a heartless old man. But I ask you, is it kindness to curse new generations with alcoholism, idiocy, syphilis, unrestrained gluttony? Real charity acts for the greater good. The Christian throws a coin in the beggar's

282

cup, but the truly charitable man sees to it that the beggar is never born. Do you think me a monster, Mr. McKenna?"

"No, I think you're Florence Nightingale."

A flash of anger in Applegate's eyes, there and gone. "You know how many men I'd tolerate speaking to me in that manner? Count yourself in rare company."

"Do you lecture all your supper guests to death, or is that also rare company? How do I get my name off the list?"

"I'm going to bore you with one last monologue." Applegate's stare was cold and unwavering. "You'd be well-advised to unstop your ears because I'm speaking of a mystery now. Our species holds a promise within. The promise of one day reaching a higher plane, if we submit to the wisdom of science and annihilate the defective protoplasm. We may yet storm the gates of Eden that never was. In short, Mr. McKenna, we must direct our own evolution."

"Evolution into what? A society of baby killers and tyrants?"

"Into God, of course. The greatest minds of the last century found Him lacking in our universe. If there is no God, then we must create him in our own best image. My organization, the Society for Applied Eugenics, is in the God-making business."

"Do you have any idea how insane you sound?"

"Genius and madness are two sides of the same coin, sir."

Jubal finished his brandy and rose. "I'm done here. You

can keep your blank check. My son isn't goin to be your damn mascot."

"Sit back down. Please—and that's a word precious few have heard from my tongue. Please, Mr. McKenna. There's something I'd like to show you."

Jubal stood hesitant over the table. After a moment he sat down again.

Applegate rose to his feet and went hobbling on the bull's prick cane. He stepped to a cabinet beside the owl cage and removed a key from his coatpocket and unlocked the heavy cabinet door. A hatbox inside on a shelf. He picked up the hatbox and carried it to the table and set it down in front of Jubal.

"Go ahead," he told Jubal. "Open it."

Jubal looked from Applegate to the hatbox. Then slowly raised the lid.

A skull resting on black velvet.

Jubal glanced up at Applegate, who was settling back into his chair. "What the hell is this?"

"A souvenir I purchased from a Yale fraternity. One of their boys was stationed in Oklahoma during the war. He dug up the grave and purloined the cranium, shipped it to New Haven. You know who's in that hatbox?"

"I don't have a clue."

"Geronimo, the old Apache himself. Go on, reach in there. He doesn't bite."

Jubal picked up the skull. The lightness of it surprised him. It seemed too macabre to weigh so little.

"Not much to them once they're hollowed out,"

Applegate said.

Jubal set the skull back in the hatbox and closed the lid. "I reckon there's a point to this."

"The point, my boy, is that no matter how many men the old warrior cut down in his bloody run, how many girls he raped to death, how many little tykes he killed, all he amounts to now is a hollowed-out paperweight. And he was the best their kind had to offer."

Applegate took his pipe from the holder and smoked. "There's a man I know. An old-time soldier. He sought me out to share your story with me because he believed I could help you. He was present at Geronimo's last surrender and he knows those mountains, knows how to track and how to kill. A man by the name of Cain. Compared to him? Old Geronimo was a shaking Quaker. You've got to bring them to their knees, sir, if you want your boy back, and Cain's the one to show you the way. Revenge, not rescue. Question is, do you have the stomach for it? I'm prepared to finance Cain and a squad of mercenaries he'll select to ride with you into the sierras. All you have to do is say the word, Mr. McKenna, and sign-off on my motion picture."

* * *

The wheels of the *Sunset Limited* clattered over the rails. The train slowed where the tracks curved along a steep grade, a broken hill in the Arizona desert, and Jubal looked out the passenger car window and saw the beam of the headlamp cutting through the night and the emptiness to come.

He tossed the file folder on the seat beside him. Applegate had called it Cain's curriculum vitae—military records, case reports, witness accounts. Confirmed and suspected biographical detail. After glancing over it, Jubal had no doubt regarding the mercenary's unique qualifications. The man was a killing machine.

Applegate had given Jubal the files along with a film contract. "Give it due consideration," he'd said. "You say no tonight, but in time you'll change your mind. I know you better than you think and I'm a patient man."

Jubal told him he'd think it over, relieved to escape the old man's ceaseless babble and his lonesome estate, but in truth it was out of the question.

Applegate was evil or insane—or both, Jubal decided. He wanted nothing to do with the man's dark philosophy. Killer Cain would have to find himself another war. Jubal wasn't in the market for a mercenary.

He lowered his hat down over his eyes and tried to sleep as the train carried him through the waste and void. In time he did sleep and all his dreams were of a world afire.

CHAPTER FOURTEEN

Summer, 1931

Bavispe Valley, Sonora

On the eve of the red moon Denali rode with the warriors down through summer hills deep green and thick with grama and into the valley. Their long hair was loose and greased with animal fat, war-charms dangling about their necks. During the last moon he'd served as attendant for a final time while the warriors stole a pair of mules from a small rancho. Now his apprenticeship was completed and it was his duty to join in the raid and claim his share of plunder.

Across the bow of Denali's saddle rested the .30-30, the rifle Carnoviste had presented him the night before they set out. A fine gift, better than many of the older warriors' weapons. Denali had thanked his father with a song bragging of the enemies he'd send to the House of Ghosts with the rifle.

He thought of Carnoviste now without reservation as

his father. Carnoviste had risked everything for him. There was nowhere he might lead that was so perilous Denali wouldn't follow.

After they'd secreted the body in the cave, Carnoviste had brought Denali back into camp, explaining to the People that he'd found him unconscious after lightning struck him. The branching scars on his arm and chest had vanished the next day, only their faintest trace remaining, and slowly he'd regained the strength the lightning had taken from him. It had been a long while before he recovered from the ordeal. Bouts of exhaustion and sudden bone-deep pains had battered him in the moons after the lightning struck. Now over a year had passed, his health restored, boyhood behind him, and he rode as a man, soon to be a warrior. The winter to come would be his sixteenth.

Nantan's disappearance caused an uproar in the camp, chaos and fear taking hold in the People's hearts. Gouyen led the search. They'd combed the woods and canyons and scoured the ridgeline, braving wildcat dens in small caves and checking the foot of cliffs, expecting to find his body broken on the rocks, but they discovered no sign. The rains had destroyed any tracks, obscured all evidence of Nantan's fate. Carnoviste suggested perhaps the medicine man had met with the grizzly on one of his walks gathering herbs. Gouyen was quick to dismiss the idea—Nantan possessed Bear Power, what danger was a grizzly to him? A darker fortune had befallen him, she insisted.

Nantan's widow cut her hair with a shard of flint and she cut her arms and breasts and bled herself of grief, her mourning cries filling the camp. As for Gouyen, she cut not a single lock nor did she shed a tear. The wise woman refused to accept Nantan's death.

Denali was certain Gouyen knew her brother had set out to kill him on that final night of the vision quest. She had to know as well that Nantan surely met the same fate he'd planned for Denali. For her the only mystery was what became of the body.

Gouyen held back any accusation against Denali. Not least of all because if he'd killed Nantan, it meant Denali's own Power was far more formidable than she'd supposed.

The wise woman bided her time.

Denali told his father that Gouyen would surely seek revenge. There was nothing they could do, Carnoviste said. They had no proof that Gouyen and Nantan defiled themselves with incest and turned their Power to witchcraft. No charge against Gouyen would stand. Yet neither could the wise woman accuse Denali of murdering the medicine man—who was an immortal, after all. The council of elders would reject any claim of Denali's guilt so long as Nantan's body was undiscovered.

There was nothing they could do but wait. Carnoviste warned him not to venture off alone and never to accept food or drink from Gouyen.

* * *

The raiders crossed into a country Denali remembered as though from a dream. Carnoviste led them in the dark along the curve of a wooded hillside. Deep among the live oaks he reined in his mount and swept back his right hand. As one they drew to a halt. Denali stepped his horse up beside his father's and they studied the terrain below, the river meandering along the valley floor.

"We cross the river, my son," Carnoviste said. "Then to where the trees stand in rows like enemy soldiers."

"What have we come to steal?" Denali asked. "Horses, mules?"

They'd ridden through pastures of cattle and left several modest ranchos unplundered, following Carnoviste deeper into the valley. Denali had no certain idea of their purpose there.

"The spoils are already taken," Carnoviste told him.

"I don't understand. What else are we here for?"

"Something that has to be done."

Carnoviste rode from the stand of oaks and the others set out after him. When they reached the river, the horses splashed into the water and swam across its gentle current, the night-cool Bavispe flowing around them, coming up to the necks of the mounts, and the warriors held their rifles with one arm raised above their heads. They rode up onto the far banks. Under the willows Carnoviste chambered a round in his rifle.

They went on some distance, keeping the horses to an easy walk, then Carnoviste dismounted. The others followed suit.

The chief turned and motioned to Bihido and Estoni. "Stay with the horses," he whispered.

Denali and Pericho handed over their reins to the warriors chosen to stay behind. Carnoviste did the same, then led them out afoot.

Soon they came to an open pasture where cattle stood grazing in the tall grass. The warriors lay on their bellies watching a long time before Carnoviste would risk crossing. A whippoorwill called. Beyond the grassland a tree-line jagged and black against the starry sky. After a while Carnoviste rose in a crouch and they went on. Denali could hear the wind through the branches before they reached the orchard.

The shadows between the ranks of apple trees welcomed them in. Denali's heart hammered—he knew this place well.

They reached the far edge of the orchard where the ground rose and the road running through the midst of the trees began its climb up the hillside. He could see a single light burning in the window of the house. Casting four illuminated squares on the slope below. Millers fluttered in the beam and knocked themselves softly against the glass.

Denali stared up at the glow. No longer home. The love that once had made it so lay cold in the ground. He tried to imagine the strangers who must occupy that place after its rightful owners and heirs all were slain that day on the trail.

Childhood's kingdom of days had seemed changeless, the surest promise. Now he felt a kind of hovering disposition, an unreal quality to a world that could alter so swiftly what had once been set in stone. He recognized a life he'd left behind, but everything appeared slightly out of focus, the faded memory of a dream. There was an ache within him like an unspoken prayer, groanings too deep to be uttered. It was as if he were a child who'd followed a faerie light through the woods and far into a netherworld beyond all return.

Carnoviste watched him closely.

Coyotes in the distance, sharp little barks and long quavering wails. On the hilltop a dog howled back at them.

An apple fell of its own weight, dropping from a high branch and striking the ground behind the warriors. It startled them. Like a footfall at their backs, something creeping up. They whirled around, fingers on their triggers, searching for a target, but there was none.

Denali kneeled watching the house a while longer. After a time a shadow passed before the window and the light went out and the house stood dark and silent on the hill.

Carnoviste placed a hand on his son's shoulder. Denali lingered a moment, then rose and turned and they departed the orchard.

* * *

After rejoining Bihido and Estoni they mounted back up and rode on through the valley. Just before sunrise they made camp in the overgrown brush of a deep arroyo. Pericho stood first watch while the others slept in the morning sun. All day they remained hidden in the arroyo. When night finally came and the full moon rose bloodred above the horizon, they headed out again.

Carnoviste spied the distant light of a campfire. It shone on a dark stretch of pasture below a windmill that turned slowly in the night breeze. They dismounted a long way back and Carnoviste sent Denali out alone to scout the camp.

The young warrior moved through the grass, making a slow and careful approach.

It was four ranch-hands driving a small herd of the jinete's green-broke horses, resting for the night on their way to a mining settlement in the foothills. They'd watered the herd at the stocktank, then turned them loose in a little horse trap, the last remnant of an old line camp. Their bedrolls lay spread around the fire and a rabbit was cooking on a spit beside a pot of beans. The men spoke Spanish, too quiet for Denali to make out what they said, and laughed as they filled their plates.

Denali withdrew back into the night. He returned to the warriors and told them what he'd seen.

"What do you think?" Carnoviste asked. "Should we take them?"

"They all had rifles," Denali said.

"Were they alert? Did one man sit with his back to the fire or were they all facing the light?"

"All facing it."

"They aren't keeping their eyes for the dark. They're not ready for trouble."

"I say we take what's ours," Pericho said.

"But the night…" Estoni began.

"What of it?" Carnoviste asked.

"You know what the elders say."

It was a belief common among them that who kills at night must wander blind the House of Ghosts, stumbling through eternal darkness with his enemies. Every man present doubted the truth of this, but Estoni was only a winter older than Denali and he'd never fought at night, unlike the others.

"I've already killed in the night," Carnoviste said. "So if the elders tell the truth, it's too late for me."

Pericho and Bihido spoke up—it was the same for them.

"You have to decide for yourself," Carnoviste told Estoni. "If it bothers you, we can go on and maybe find something else. No one will think you're a coward."

Estoni looked at Denali, so far as he knew the only other brave who'd never taken a life in the dark. "What do you think, my brother? Is it a smart gamble?"

Denali hesitated, recalling his secret, Nantan dead in the night. Too late for him as well.

"I trust your judgement," Denali said at last. "Whatever you decide is my choice too."

Estoni fell silent. Finally he said, "I'm for it so long as we cut out their eyes. That way if our enemies meet us in the House of Ghosts, they'll be blind too."

* * *

The warriors hobbled their horses with lengths of rope and left them in a stand of oaks, for they were a mountain people and would always choose to fight on foot when they could. They picked up their rifles and started through the tall grass toward the camp.

Three of the vaqueros now lay sleeping while the fourth man sat up with a Winchester beside him. The watchman was careless. He still faced the fire, its glow destroying his night vision.

After a while the watchman cocked his head. He turned and stared out into the pasture. The grass moved lightly where the breeze stirred it. He turned back to the fire and reached to take a cigarette from his pocket—

At the crack of a rifleshot the watchman's right temple exploded.

Instantly the other vaqueros were scrambling out of their blankets, grabbing their weapons.

Carnoviste chambered another round and rose up as the rest of the warriors fired all at once. "Ussen protects the brave," he shouted.

They rushed the camp.

The vaqueros raced for their horses and fired back at the warriors as they ran. Estoni dropped a heavyset vaquero with a shot to the hip. The man fell, his rifle spilling from his arms.

A tall young vaquero snapped off two quick shots from his pistol. Denali heard the bullets go whizzing past his ear. The vaquero was running beside a bald man with a thick moustache, then abruptly he broke away from his fellow, abandoning their bid for the horses and swerving off toward the cover of the windmill tower. He called for the bald man to follow him.

The old corral was close. The bald-headed man kept running for the horses. Within the horse trap the herd was stamping and snorting, whinnying their displeasure at the scent of gunsmoke and blood. He made it to the corral and grabbed a rough-hewn post in one hand and swung himself up over the side-rail.

Pericho and Bihido fired in the same instant. Both shots hit the bald vaquero and he tumbled down into the corral and the horses in their terror trampled over his corpse.

Denali followed the last man with his rifle barrel. He hesitated, finger on the trigger, surprised none of the others had already dropped the young vaquero. It was only later, looking back on what happened, playing it over in his mind, Denali realized the warriors had abruptly held their fire. As though they'd been instructed to make sure Denali accepted his share of the blood.

Just before he reached the tower the young vaquero twisted around, raising his pistol once more. Denali took his shot. The bullet hit the vaquero in his shoulder and the pistol slipped from his hand. The young vaquero turned to recover his pistol. Denali levered the .30-30 and pulled the trigger and shot him in the chest.

He collapsed facedown in the grass.

The fat man Estoni had shot was still alive. He crawled toward his rifle and reached out, his hand closing around the stock—

Estoni's moccasin stepped on the barrel. He drew his knife and kneeled over the fat vaquero.

"Por favor," the big man said. "Por el amor de Dios."

Tears shone in his eyes and his voice was like the voice of a child begging not to receive some harsh punishment.

Estoni buried the blade in his bulging stomach. Whatever reluctance the warrior had harbored for the night killings was utterly forgotten in victory's bloodrush. He stabbed over and over and the dying vaquero's pleas for mercy became gurgles and moans.

Carnoviste stepped up to Denali. He nodded at the man Denali had killed. "Your mother will be proud," he told Denali. "His weapons and saddle are yours."

Denali nodded but didn't speak.

"Don't forget to take his eyes," Carnoviste said. "We made a promise."

"I'll do it."

"You're a true warrior now, my son."

Carnoviste went to inspect the horses.

Denali found himself watching Estoni. He didn't want to see, but when Estoni went to work on the fat man's eyes, he couldn't look away, the horror of it transfixing his gaze. The fat vaquero drew sharp pained breaths. Estoni held the vaquero's head down and worked the tip of his knife into his right eye socket. Estoni pried. The vaquero's eyeball dangled out of the red-rimmed socket by its optic nerve. Then Estoni pried the left one loose. Denali felt sick to his stomach—the big vaquero was still alive, writhing on the ground. Estoni yanked the eyeballs free of their cords as though plucking ripe fruit from a tree. He rose and stepped to the fire and pitched them into the burning coals and there was a hiss, then a moment later a pair of soft pops, the eyeballs bursting in the heat.

Denali turned and rushed toward the windmill tower, fearing the others would see him vomit. He fought to keep his stomach down. His shoulders and chest were slick with sweat and the breeze chilled him so that he shivered in the warm summer night.

He walked out to the young vaquero's body and kneeled down and turned him over. Something about him faintly familiar, but Denali couldn't say what. His eyes stared up at him. Mouth hanging open, a look of dumb surprise on his face. Disbelieving even in the final moment.

Denali hated him for that expression.

He'd felt no anger, no hate when he pulled the trigger. They'd both just been doing what was expected of them and should the situation have been reversed, the vaquero would surely have been standing over Denali's body with no great remorse.

Yet staring down at the look on the dead man's face, something rose up in him like an accusation. Denali was suddenly furious. Why should he look so surprised? That was the way of things. Everything changes, but the earth remains the same. What right did he have to expect some other fate?

Denali drew his knife from his moccasin, ready to alter that expression forever, but he paused holding the blade over the man's lifeless eye. He couldn't do it.

He buried the blade in the ground. Let Estoni cut out the eyes of the one he'd killed. Denali didn't like to think of this man's people finding him that way. If the vaquero wished to seek him out in the House of Ghosts, then Denali would meet his gaze when that day came.

He removed the vaquero's gunbelt and cinched it around his own waist and found the pistol in the grass and holstered it. He went through the vaquero's pockets. A tobacco pouch and book of matches. A pocketknife with walnut grips. He emptied the wallet and threw the paper currency to the wind. A pocketwatch hung from the vaquero's vest on a silver chain and he picked up the timepiece and held it a moment. Soft ticking, moving against his palm like the pulse of a small animal. Then he opened the spring-hinged cover. Opposite the watchface a tiny black and white cameo, a dark-skinned girl in a pale dress, and well he knew that face.

His hands shook.

He tore the cameo out of the watchcase and threw the ghost image away, letting the wind take it, and snapped the watchcase shut and yanked the chain from the dead man's vest. Then he turned the corpse back facedown. He pulled the blade from the dirt and made a small cut to the heel of his own hand and let the blood drip onto the side of the blade so that it would appear he'd gone through with the gory work.

He stared a moment longer at the corpse.

No going back. Not now, not ever again.

When Denali returned to camp, Estoni was dancing about the fire with a bloody scalp. Carnoviste and the others had gone to retrieve their horses. The dead vaqueros lay naked and pale—empty sockets, members hacked off. Their bellies had been sliced open and their entrails uncoiled in the grass under the light of the moon.

Estoni ceased his dancing when he saw Denali. "We paid these shepherds for looking after our horses, didn't we? They got everything they earned." Estoni grinned. "How much better was it than hunting deer, my brother?"

"It's not the same at all," Denali answered, true enough. He still held the bloody knife.

Estoni nodded at the blade. "You cut his eyes, but where's his scalp? It was your kill—the scalp belongs to you."

"You're too eager, brother. You took your prize, but now you'll miss the feast." He was speaking of the rule that any warrior who took a scalp must thereafter undergo a four-day purification ritual in isolation. Estoni wouldn't be free to attend the celebration on their return.

"It's worth it," Estoni said and raised the scalp. "I can feel his Power in me. Go back and take your scalp, brother. Make yourself strong."

"I love the feast and dancing too much."

"Is that the reason?"

"What else would it be?"

"Maybe your knife's dull."

"I always keep my knife sharp."

"Then maybe it's your courage that's dull. Power belongs to the ones who take it, not to cowards."

"What if I take yours instead?" Denali asked. His voice was cold, flat.

They stared at each other. Estoni's hand went to his moccasin, the handle of his knife.

Carnoviste rode up leading a pair of horses. "Save your victory dances for later," he said. "Let's get the herd moving. We have to be in the hills before first light."

Denali looked away from Estoni. He bent to wipe his blade in the grass, then sheathed it and swung up into the saddle.

* * *

Dolores sat at the table eating supper with Jubal and Claudia when Hector strode into the dining room. The segundo held a pair of leather workgloves in one hand and his hat in the other. His face was grim.

He nodded at Jubal. "You need to come outside and take a look at something."

"What's wrong?" Jubal asked.

"Just come with me."

"Is someone hurt?" Dolores asked.

Hector wouldn't look at her.

Adela stepped out of the kitchen holding a pitcher of water. She noted Hector's expression and met his eyes. "What is it?"

"Keep the girls inside," Hector told his wife.

Jubal tugged his boots on and rose. The men stepped out the door. When Dolores started to follow them, Hector told her, "Stay here, Little Bird. You don't need to see. Not yet, not like this."

Cold fear ran up her spine. She knew something was bad wrong.

Hector slammed the door behind them.

"Sit down," Adela said. "Maybe it's nothing."

Dolores didn't move.

"Sit with me, Lola," Claudia told Dolores. The girl mopped her plate with a piece of tortilla, but her eyes were intent on the two women. The hacienda was quiet save the steady ticking of the grandfather clock in the hall.

Dolores jerked the door open.

"Hector said to stay," Adela called.

She ran out barefoot across the courtyard and into the road where the men gathered around a buckboard, covering their mouths and noses with bandanas. Jubal stood peering over the side of the wagon. When he stepped back down, she could see the rage on his face.

Angel and the others were late returning from the mining camp where they were driving the jinete's newly broken mesteños, the remnants of a herd of wild colts captured and culled on the ranch itself. They'd kept the best for their own remuda and arranged to sell the remainder to the camp foreman. The night before Angel departed she'd sat with him on the patio looking at a new pack of stereo-cards, taking turns with the viewer, and afterward they'd gone walking in the orchard. Dolores was seventeen, the young vaquero twenty. He said that when he came back it was his intention to ask Jubal for her hand. She'd been pleased.

Now she felt sure he was in the back of the wagon.

Jubal saw her coming. "Go back inside," he said.

"I want to see for myself."

"No, you don't."

"I have to."

"One of you take her to the house," Jubal ordered the vaqueros.

Wesley moved to stop her, but the old man was too slow. A ranch hand named Baca reached and took her arm. She jerked out of his grasp and glared hell itself at him. Baca stepped back.

She approached the rear of the wagon. Stiff and reeking forms were wrapped in blankets, their boots peeking out. Blood dried blackly on a spur tine.

"Was it them who did it?" Dolores asked. She didn't have to say the word Apaches.

Hector nodded.

"Tell me what happened," she said.

"Angel was shot. They mutilated the others, but they didn't touch his body. I don't know why."

"They didn't cut him up? Thank God. I need to see him."

Hector reached inside the wagon and pulled back a blanket. Dolores stared at Angel's ashen face.

A few moments later she said, "All right." Her voice was an empty thing.

Hector raised the blanket and covered the body.

"When did you find them?" Jubal asked.

"This morning," Hector said. "I stayed with them while Ruben went and got the buckboard from the line camp."

"How many Apaches?"

"Five by their tracks."

Jubal nodded toward the wagon. "You know if these men had family?"

"Caperon talked about a sister in Madera. Angel, I don't know. I think just his worthless outlaw cousin."

"I want to bury him by the orchard," Dolores said. "I don't care about a priest."

"We'll see that he gets a stone," Jubal told her.

"A cross would be good. Is that all right?"

"Of course it is. Whatever you want."

He reached and held her hand. She didn't cry, she never cried. She just said, "Oh, Papa," and Jubal put his arm around her.

One of the men asked if they should ride up into the foothills to trail the Apaches.

"We're done chasing ghosts," Jubal said. "I don't give a damn about searching the foothills. I'm going up there where they live and I'm taking a man called Cain with me."

TO BE CONTINUED…

The epic story concludes in *Sky Burial*, the final book of the Beloved Captive Trilogy.
Ride with Jubal and the soldiers of fortune high into the sierras…
Will Denali's heart remember his bloodfather, or will they meet in deadly conflict?

Read the first chapter of *Sky Burial* and get your copy now!

SKY BURIAL

MAX McNABB

BELOVED CAPTIVE TRILOGY BOOK 3

SKY BURIAL

MAX McNABB

Beloved Captive Trilogy Book 3

Late autumn, 1931

The Americans crossed into Sonora aboard a private Pullman coach. A pair of stockcars carried the horses and packmules they'd use on their journey into the sierras. Applegate had called in a favor and Phelps Dodge agreed to attach the stockcars and the Pullman behind their engine and hoppers. The mercenaries rode the El Paso and Southwestern toward the copper town of Nacozari de García, streamers of black smoke trailing in their wake and fading in the pale sky.

The men sat back in their seats, hats lowered over their eyes, long accustomed to catching sleep when and where it could be found. Most of them had only met for the first time at the El Paso station, but they shared a soldier's view of the world and their place in it. When you signed on for a job, you saw it through to the end.

Cain had spent the last part of the summer assembling his squad, each man chosen on the basis of his own particular expertise. They were veterans of the trenches in ravaged Europe, stripped of any polite myth regarding the truth of their inner nature, survivors of that storm of steel. They were ex-Foreign Legion and soldiers of fortune, a few of them bounty hunters, all experienced in guerilla tactics and wilderness survival. A trainload of professional killers.

Mosby woke from a brief slumber. He looked about the coach, then rose from his seat and walked to the rear door and opened it. Cain stood smoking a cigarette on the narrow platform and pressing the heel of his hand to his forehead. Mosby stepped up beside the sergeant, closing the door behind him, and leaned against the iron railing.

"Another headache, Sergeant?"

"It'll pass," Cain told him.

The Pullman clattered down the rails. It was the final car and they stood on the platform and watched the receding wasteland, the troubled country of their introduction years ago on Pershing's expedition. They'd ridden that hard land chasing Pancho Villa. In those days Cain was an ex-sergeant in the 4th Cavalry turned civilian scout, Mosby a green recruit in the negro 10th.

After a while Cain said, "Ever have one place in your life where you felt like you were really home?"

"I don't know, Sergeant."

"If you got to think about it, the answer's no."

"I reckon the closest I ever had was the outfit."

"That's a fair answer. No shame in it. I thought for a long time the 4th Cavalry was the only place I'd ever belong."

"But you found somewheres else?"

"I knew this woman in Havana. Teresa was her name. She lived with her boy in a little room about half the size of this train car. Why she took up with me, I'll never figure out. I had some money at the time, but if she was lookin for a man, she could've had richer and younger. Better too. One who would've stuck. I had a suite in a fine hotel in the city and I moved her and the boy in there with me. Those were good days. I liked to make that woman laugh."

"Sounds real nice, sergeant. I'm glad you got them good memories."

"Mo, you ever make a woman laugh? Not some polite little chuckle, I mean from the belly."

"Most the women I known, they was serious women."

"Serious women is all the women there is. That's the point."

"How'd you do it? Make that Havana woman laugh?"

"I remember one time we was layin in bed of a evenin and I kindly kicked at the covers with my feet and said, What's that under there? Like I felt somethin down at the edge of the bed. I raised up the sheet and Teresa stuck her head under to take a look. Well, that's when I let rip a big one."

"What'd she do?"

"Jumped out from under there like a cat with its tail on fire and stared at me so cool. Then both of us broke down laughin. She was a good woman. She'd have done anything to take care of that boy of hers."

"You mind me askin what happened? How come it ended between you and her?"

Cain smoked and stared out at the country. "I tried to look after em, Teresa and her son, but I couldn't always be who I was supposed to. Then Villa crossed the border. Maybe I figured I owed it to the outfit for the home they gave me when there wasn't no other. Or maybe I didn't think I deserved what I'd lucked into. So I left and went to scout for old Black Jack. Then I met up with your scrawny ass."

Mosby grinned. "You think I should try makin a woman laugh like you said?"

"By doin what, fartin in bed?"

"Yessir."

Cain looked at Mosby, his shirtcollar buttoned to the top, cheeks clean-shaven, standing straight and stiff with his shoulders back and eyes level. The toes of his boots shone. Everything in perfectly circumscribed order.

"I wouldn't advise it," Cain said. "But I won't say no either. Use your own judgement and maybe try it on a whore first."

Mosby took off his glasses. He pulled a handkerchief from his pocket and spat on the right lens and rubbed it with the cloth, then spat on the left and rubbed it as well.

"Polish them specs any harder," Cain said, "they're liable to catch the sun, burn the damn train to a cinder."

Mosby glanced at the man-shaped blur that was Cain.

"I like things to be clean."

"You don't allow a smudge on em, do you?"

"It's how I got to look out at the world." Mosby pocketed the kerchief and slipped his glasses back on.

"Well. You see clearer than any other man I know."

"Thank you, Sergeant."

"I need you to be my eyes for me, Mo. Watch those men in there and tell me what you see. I knew every man of em, one time or another, but the years can change you. I need to know who'll stick when it gets bad and who's gone soft enough to cut and run."

Mosby remained astounded that Cain had convinced the investment banker to fund the Sierra Madre operation. Cain had telegrammed Applegate's aide with a reminder of the work he'd done for the old man as a private operative, hinting at certain unpalatable secrets he'd discovered in the course of his work, corporate illegalities sure to be of interest to Applegate's many enemies. It was leverage to convince the aide to give Cain what he wanted—enough of Applegate's time for the old man to read a letter and the clipping from *True Cowboy Adventure*. Nothing more, nothing less.

The story of a white boy kidnapped by wild Apaches had been enough to hook Applegate—just as Cain knew it would.

"Maybe it won't be long," Mosby said. "We'll finish the mission, get that McKenna boy back to his family, then we can come home and start spendin Applegate's money."

Cain was silent. He took a long drag. "I'll bet you a silver dollar I can out-ride and out-gun any of you boys once we get in the mountains. But it's my last strength and I ain't goin to waste it. There's a place for them that die fightin and that's all I want. One last campaign."

It bothered Mosby when the sergeant talked that way. How Mosby looked at it, there were worse things than getting old—and being dead was at the top of the list.

"Come on now, Sergeant. Don't talk like that. Once them Apaches give up the boy, it'll be front page news. Just imagine all the papers callin you a hero. That's somethin to live for, right there."

Cain flicked the cigarette butt. It hit the steel rail in a little burst of glowing ash, then vanished behind them.

"Keep your eyes open, Mo. Help me see this thing clear."

"Yessir, Sergeant."

Get your copy of *Sky Burial* to see how the epic story ends!

Printed in Great Britain
by Amazon